OPERATION MIDNIGHT

SHARON C. COOPER

Operation Midnight (Reunited Series)
By: Sharon C. Cooper

ISBN: 978-0-9903505-7-6
Book Cover: Selestiele Designs
Editor: Melissa Ringsted, There for You Editing
Published by: Amaris Publishing LLC in the United States

Disclaimer
This story is a work of fiction. Names, characters, and incidents are either products of the author's imagination or are used fictitiously. Any resemblance to actual events, locales, organizations or persons, living or dead, is entirely coincidental.

PROLOGUE

"I want her dead."

Wiz paced the length of the small, musty cellar, his pulse pounding in his ears. He wished the steady drumming would drown out the anger seeping into his soul. Wound tighter than a man staring down the barrel of a semi-automatic gun, he took a few cleansing breaths to release the anxiety roaring through his veins. It wasn't working. Nothing was working.

He kept moving. Except for his combat boots stomping against the dusty concrete floor and the low hum of a nearby furnace, the space was quiet. Gagged and bound, flanked by his two best friends, the woman who had slithered into his life and almost destroyed everything he held dear, sat glaring at him. She wiggled in the hard wooden chair trying to free herself to no avail. Her eyes, cold and unyielding followed his every move, making him hate her that much more.

He stopped and stood before her, feeling nothing but disgust. Red, glassy eyes and the slight shakes confirmed she was high. Hell, considering her condition, she wouldn't even feel the torture he intended to inflict on her, but it would help him. It would help him try to piece his life back together. It would help him feel less guilt for not being on American soil to protect his wife. It would help him get retribution for the life this bitch had taken.

A life for a life.

"Wiz, think about what you're planning to do here," his friend Quinn said, his gloved hand propped against the closed door and the low rumble of his voice cutting through Wiz's thoughts. "Let me handle this. I can take care of everything and you can head back to the hospital. Your wife needs you. Besides, you have too much to lose."

"I've already lost almost everything and thanks to this woman, Olivia is fighting for her life."

Wiz had no doubt that his friend could make this woman disappear. Quinn, like Wiz, was a Navy SEAL. But unlike Wiz, Quinn had been on several special military teams participating in some of the most dangerous black ops. Q was good at what he did. Damn good. Legendary for his ability to disappear and make his enemies disappear.

"This is something I have to do," Wiz finally said, turning the ornamental handle of his tactical combat knife back and forth in his hand. "I want her to feel what I feel. I want her to know what it's like to have your heart jerked about and then ripped out of your chest."

"Well, if we're going to do this shit, let's get it done," Malik said.

The large flashlight Malik held trained on the woman didn't wobble despite the fact that he held a Glock 41 in his other hand, aimed at her head. As a weapons specialist, he was comfortable with any type of firearm and rarely hesitated to use one. He was a strike first and ask questions later kind of guy.

Neither of Wiz's friends thought twice when he requested their assistance in finding the person responsible for Olivia's abduction. Enduring Bud/s together, the Basic Underwater Demolition/SEAL training, they had vowed then to always have each other's back—no matter the situation.

"This isn't you," Quinn reiterated and stepped closer to Wiz.

No, it wasn't him. The navy might have trained them to be killers, but not this way. Wiz had never imagined that he would one day be driven to take a woman's life.

No women. No children.

He stared into unflinching eyes. Eyes so familiar, yet so different.

A whole new wave of rage pounded through his veins. No. This wasn't a woman. The female sitting before him was a monster. Only a monster could do the things she had done. But no more. Never would she be able to hurt Olivia again. Never would she get the opportunity to hurt another living soul.

"You know I'm with you all the way in whatever you decide to do, but think about this. There's no turning back," Quinn said. "This bitch isn't worth losing everything you've worked so hard for."

Q was right ... again. Olivia was lying in a hospital fighting for her life thanks to the piece of trash who was now glaring at him.

He ripped his gaze from hers. Bile rose to his throat remembering the condition his wife had been in when he left the hospital. No amount of military training could prepare him for the devastation of seeing the only woman he had ever loved battered, bruised, and barely holding on to her life.

Olivia's missing.

Thirty-six hours ago his father's words had almost

3

brought Wiz to his knees and they still played around in his head. A retired navy man, Sergeant Major Andrew Miller didn't rattle easily, but Wiz had heard the concern in his father's voice when he called. With connections Wiz could only dream of having, his dad had made arrangements for Wiz to head back to the U.S. immediately.

He and his SEAL team had just returned from a rough mission in Myanmar, and all Wiz wanted to do was leave the depressed country and head home. However, hearing his wife was missing wasn't what he had expected the moment they touched down in Germany on their way to the U.S. When Quinn and Malik were told what was going on, they hadn't hesitated to take leave.

Wiz's world had been thrown on its axis when he finally talked with his father. An icy fear had surged through his veins after being given more details regarding Olivia's disappearance.

Despite surviving in some of the world's most dangerous jungles and perilous waters, nothing was more terrifying than hearing the news that something had happened to his wife.

He, Quinn, and Malik had boarded the waiting plane. Eighteen hours later, they were in Chicago searching for Olivia. Quinn sought help from the underground world of gangs, and they found Olivia half dead in a drug house.

Wiz shivered at the memory. He had never experienced that type of fear in all of his life. Fear that he had lost the one woman who made his heart beat every day. The one woman whose smile alone could light up his world. And the one woman who he would lay down his life for.

He turned back to the person responsible. She should have been a person Olivia could count on, but instead she had been the one who left her sister to die.

The walls of the dark, damp cellar closed in around him. In the musty hellhole, rage gripped him, constricting the little air fighting to get to his lungs.

He had to do this. He had to end this. Because of her, he had nearly lost the one person he couldn't live without. And despite what his wife had endured, Wiz knew that if she ever found out what he was about to do to her twin sister, she would never forgive him.

I just have to make sure she never finds out.

CHAPTER ONE

Ten years later ...

"May I have this dance?"

Cameron "Wiz" Miller stared down at the woman who had captured his heart. His pulse still sped up whenever her big brown eyes zeroed in on him. Olivia Miller, his ex-wife, was the most beautiful woman inside and out. Twenty-two years since the first time he spotted her, his love for her was stronger than ever. And that smile. God, that smile had gotten him through some of his darkest days and still made him weak in the knees.

"Of course." She accepted his hand.

He led her to the middle of the dance floor. Their engagement party was winding down and he couldn't wait to take her upstairs. They were staying at the Four Seasons Hotel Chicago and had reserved a suite for the weekend. Though he was dog-tired, Wiz couldn't wait to get her alone. Between being stranded at Reagan Washington National Airport due to bad weather and his gut churning with trepidation for reasons he couldn't pinpoint, he needed to keep Olivia close. He wasn't sure if exhaustion was the only cause for the unease, but experience had taught him to never ignore his gut.

"I love having you in my arms," he whispered into her hair, placing a kiss against her temple and holding her tighter than he probably should. Her scent, a combination of baby powder and roses, wrapped around him like a warm embrace. He hadn't seen her in three days, but it felt more like a month.

The trip seemed even longer knowing that she had the flu. The last thing he had wanted to do was leave her behind in Chicago.

The unexpected one-day business trip to D.C. had sprawled into three. It had been risky leaving her only days before their engagement party, knowing that he could miss it, but the trip couldn't be helped.

Business was booming. Not only was he a private investigator, but he was the new Systems Security Director for Supreme Security Agency, a personal security company his best friend, Malik Lewis, had founded. Wiz's role required some travel since the agency was starting to expand outside of Chicago. After retiring from the Navy years earlier, they had both started their own businesses and had often helped each other on their individual cases. Becoming partners, officially, seemed to be the next logical step.

"I'm so glad you made it back in time." Olivia laid her head against his shoulder. "I've been looking forward to tonight for the last two months. Sometimes I can't believe we're at this point in our relationship." Her eyes met his. "I can't wait to be your wife again."

"I feel the same way."

His gaze took her in from her long dark hair falling in waves around her shoulders, to the strapless champagne-tone dress hugging her slim, shapely figure. After so many years, his body still responded to the sight of her. He had never stopped loving her even when she divorced him, vowing that one day she would be his again. When he said his wedding vows the first time, he meant every word. There wasn't another woman who made him feel the way she did. She tempted him in ways he never thought possible, and he would crave Olivia—and only Olivia—until the day he took his last breath.

"Are you feeling better? Have you eaten anything besides the soup I ordered for you?" He studied her face. Her voice still sounded a little throaty, but her eyes were clearer. Unlike the day before he left town, when she had been sneezing, coughing, and sleeping a lot.

"I feel better. Still haven't been able to stomach any heavy food since my throat is a little sore." She cupped his cheek and stared into his eyes. "I'm just glad you didn't catch my cold. Oh, and did I happen to mention that I'm so glad you made it back to Chicago in time?"

"Let me think." He squinted down at her. "I do seem to remember you saying something like that. As a matter of fact, I think you've said it at least ten times in the last couple of hours."

"Oh." A shy grin spread across her beautiful mouth.

He lowered his head and his mouth covered hers, devouring its softness. He'd had an aching need to kiss her the moment his plane touched down. It never ceased to amaze him how having her in his arms still did wicked things to his body. Granted, their relationship had been off and on thanks to his military days and their divorce, but he had never stopped loving her. Never stopped referring to her as his wife. And now that they were engaged to be remarried, there was no way he was ever letting her go again.

Lifting his mouth from hers, he gazed into her eyes, keeping his arm around her waist. She licked her lower lip and a small smile graced her mouth. He kissed her again, deeper this time, thinking it wasn't enough. He wanted to throw her onto his shoulder and carry her to their hotel suite.

"All right, break it up over here."

Wiz turned to find Tyler and Dallas Hollister standing behind him.

"Don't tell me you're leaving already," Wiz said.

"The night is still young," Olivia added, but then glanced at her watch. "Well sorta." They all laughed.

"Yeah, we have to go rescue the babysitter from the twins," Tyler explained.

"But we didn't want to leave without saying bye and congratulations again," Dallas said, pulling Olivia in for a hug. "We're so happy for you guys."

They had met the Hollisters when Dallas was being stalked and Wiz had been commissioned to investigate the situation. During his probing, Wiz had discovered that one of the partners of the firm Dallas worked for was the mastermind behind a huge Ponzi scheme. Since then, their relationship had grown into a friendship.

After saying their good-byes, Olivia stepped back

into Wiz's arms.

"They're taking the food away. Did you want anything else?"

"Nah, baby, just you." He nuzzled her neck until she giggled like a schoolgirl. Though he still felt a little uneasy, being near her did calm him some. Her sweet, tranquil disposition always brought him a level of peace he couldn't get from anyone else.

Wiz caught sight of Malik and his fiancée, Natasha, as they made their way toward them.

"We're going to head out. Great party." Malik gripped Wiz's shoulder. "You can fill me in about D.C. on Monday."

Wiz nodded.

"And, Ollie, we'll see you later." He kissed her cheek, but she swatted his arm.

"Malik, what did I tell you about calling me that? You know I hate that name," she chastised playfully. Wiz shook his head and Natasha rolled her eyes. Olivia and Malik went through the same ritual every time they saw each other. She claimed to hate the nickname Malik had given her, but Wiz thought she secretly liked it.

Wiz hugged Natasha, kissing her on the cheek. "Congrats again on the engagement. You have to be a helluva woman to bring this guy to his knees." An hour ago, Malik had popped the question on the dance floor. Wiz thought he would never see the day that his friend would propose marriage. Anyone who knew the giant of a man knew that the last thing on his list of things to do was to get tied down.

Natasha held her hand out in front of her, the large diamond on her finger sparkling under the lights. She looked up at Wiz and Olivia. "Thank you.

I'm still in shock. I hope Malik's surprised proposal didn't steal much of your spotlight."

"Oh please." Olivia waved her off. "We are so happy for you two. When you and I finish planning my wedding, we'll have to get started with yours."

"Deal!"

The women shared a long hug before Olivia said, "But when we start doing all of our running around for the wedding, you have to leave the big lug at home." She nodded toward Malik.

"Now you know he follows me everywhere I go." Natasha and Olivia laughed and fell into conversation as Wiz and Malik exchanged a look. Neither of them found it funny considering only months ago there was a brutal attempt on Natasha's life that sent Malik into a tailspin.

"All right, can I get you back into my arms so we can finish our dance?" Wiz asked Olivia after Malik and Natasha walked away.

"You can have anything you want from me," she replied saucily, flashing a smile that had him thinking to hell with the dance. He would rather have her flat on her back with her legs wrapped around his waist and him deep inside of her.

"Be careful, woman," he growled close to her ear. "I haven't seen you in days and I'm ready to have my way with you."

She laughed. "I know, but no way am I passing up an opportunity to dance the rest of the night with you."

Wiz pulled Olivia close and they swayed to the tune of Luther Vandross's "Still in Love" as if they danced all the time.

"I've missed you." She rested her head on his

chest.

Wiz placed a kiss on the top of her head, feeling her body mold into his.

"I know, but even a longer business trip than planned and a delayed flight couldn't keep me from getting to you. I'm glad we agreed that we would limit our traveling for work. I don't like leaving you here by yourself, nor do I like you traveling alone."

As a world-renowned artist, Olivia traveled around the world, her work featured in some of the most famous galleries as well as national art magazines. He was proud of her success and since reuniting, he traveled with her whenever he could.

"You're so overprotective. I was shocked you didn't sick one of Malik's bodyguards on me while you were away."

He had thought about it. That nagging sensation from earlier, which still lingered, had started days before he left Chicago. Normally when he got that churning in his gut, something bad happened soon after.

"Are you okay?" Olivia's voice broke into his thoughts.

He pulled back slightly. "I'm fine. Why do you ask?"

She gave a slight shrug. "It seems you've been distracted lately and like now, you're tense. Even our telephone conversations while you were away felt as if something was going on. *Is* there something going on? Is there something I should know?"

He wasn't sure how to respond. He didn't want to worry her, especially since he didn't know what his problem was. And he didn't want to lie since he never had before. The moment the thought popped into his head, a time in their past came to mind. A time when he hadn't been completely honest with her.

He shook the thought free, their bodies swaying in sync. "Everything is fine. Actually, better than fine. Do you realize that in one month, two weeks, and three days, you'll officially be my wife again?"

She leaned back and laughed, her eyes sparkling. "I can't believe you're actually counting down the days."

His brows drew together. "Aren't you?" He dipped her, causing her to squeal and burst into a fit of giggles before he pulled her back up. His number one goal in life was to keep her happy and her infectious laugh was music to his ears. "I was even thinking we should get married sooner."

"Cameron, I can't wait to marry you, too. However, January first is right around the corner. The day will be here before we know it. Besides, the last time we were married in a courthouse. This time I want a beautiful wedding with your family and our friends there."

They had originally planned to marry the month before, but had postponed due to their traveling schedules. They agreed then that they would make changes in their careers to where neither of them would have to travel as much. In addition, she had insisted that he not take on assignments that would put him in any unnecessary danger, which was partly why she had left him nine years ago. He had his reasons for not fighting the divorce at the time, but now he was playing for keeps.

A half an hour later, after everyone had left, Wiz wrapped his arm around Olivia's waist and guided her out of the banquet room.

"I'll be right back. I need to stop by the banquet

manager's office and sign off on the bill. Want to walk with me or meet me upstairs?" Earlier, she had complained about her feet hurting. Why she insisted on wearing four-inch heels was a mystery to him.

"It shouldn't take that long. I'll wait near the elevator."

"Sounds good. Be there in a few." He kissed her and walked in the opposite direction. When he arrived at the banquet manager's office, the door was locked. So he headed to the front desk.

Wiz slowed his steps when the unnerving feeling from earlier returned. He glanced around as his gaze quickly took in the lobby area. Two people stood at the hotel's check-in desk. Over to his left, the concierge spoke quietly to a couple near his booth and a small group of men congregated in a sitting area off to the side.

Nothing seemed out of place. So what was the problem? Something had the hairs on the back of his neck standing at attention. His years in the military had taught him to never ignore his gut feelings and his gut was telling him that something wasn't right.

After not seeing anything out of place, he shook the thought loose and ran his hand down the length of his paisley print tie. Tonight he needed to just focus on his wife.

He talked with the front desk clerk and made arrangements to meet with the banquet manager to square up the next morning. Anxious to get back to Olivia, Wiz agreed to stop by the office before they checked out the next day.

Heading toward the elevators, he took another glance around, feeling as if he were being watched, but still saw nothing out of the norm.

Man, you need to get a grip.

"I'm not interested," Wiz heard Olivia ground out just as he turned the corner. She shook out of a man's grasp and sidestepped him.

"Oh come on, baby. Don't be—"

Wiz snatched the guy by the back of his jacket and slammed him against the wall. He cringed at the amount of alcohol seeping through the man's pores.

"What part of *not interested* don't you understand, asshole?" Wiz growled close to the man's ear and jerked his arm behind his back.

"Ow!"

Wiz smashed the side of the drunk's head against the wall, trying like hell to rein in his anger as to not snap his neck.

"Th-that hu-hurts," he stuttered, his words slow and slurred.

"Cameron, please," Olivia said in a panic. Her hand wrapped around his bicep trying to pull him away. "He's drunk. He didn't mean any harm."

"He messed up when he put his hands on you." Wiz added more pressure to the guy's arm, lifting it higher up his back until he cried out again.

"Baby, please let him go. You're causing a scene and someone just went to get security."

"Good. I'll let his ass go when they get here. But in the meantime, there's a few things I need to say to this punk."

"What's going on here?" a hotel security guard thundered from behind Wiz as another approached from the side.

"What's going on is this sonofabitch put his hands on my wife."

"Okay. Okay, let's just calm down. Is that true,

sir?"" security asked the drunk.

"I-I didn't mean …" Wiz increased the grip on the guy's arm. "Ow! I-I'm sorry."

"Okay, sir, we can take it from here. We need you to release him," the second security guard said.

Wiz whispered into the drunk's ear, "You got lucky this time. If you even look at my wife or put your hands on another woman and I find out, your ass is mine." He released him, but not before giving his arm another upward tug for good measure.

Wiz stepped back and rubbed his hands down his face, adrenaline still soaring through his veins. With deep breaths in and out, he tried to slow his pounding heart as they took the man away. Seconds ticked by before he turned to Olivia, who was leaning against a wall with her arms folded in front of her and her eyes narrowed.

"Let's go," he said, a slight edge in his voice.

"What's going on with you?" she asked when he guided her over to the bank of elevators. "You've been uptight since you got back this morning. No, actually, since days before you left and I want to know what's wrong. That," she pointed her thumb to the area they'd just left, "wasn't you."

Olivia was right. Though he would admit to being the jealous type and definitely overprotective when it came to her, he rarely lost control or reacted before thinking. As a matter of fact, for the past week he hadn't quite felt like himself. Impatient, anxious, unfocused, and now quick to anger was definitely not him.

The elevator arrived and they stepped on. Wiz was glad they were alone. He moved to the back of the car and rubbed his eyes. It had been a long time since he'd felt a sense of foreboding, but tonight that uneasiness was stronger than ever.

Whatever was going on with him, he needed to get it under control so he could be ready for whatever was coming ... because something definitely was coming.

CHAPTER TWO

"I'm sorry."

"What are you sorry for?" Olivia asked, and pushed the button for the forty-second floor. "Sorry for manhandling the guy? Or for going all … all vigilante on the man? You almost snapped his neck." She stood in front of Wiz, her arms folded as she looked him over. Well over six feet tall with startling green eyes that were almost hazel and rarely missed anything, he stared right back at her. His blemish free café au lait skin tone had a slight reddish tint, probably because he was still a little riled.

What happened to her gentle giant? Sure he wasn't one to take crap from anyone, but for the past couple of weeks he'd been edgier than normal, and at times short tempered with people. He wasn't a big talker, but lately he had also been quieter than usual.

"I'm sorry if I embarrassed you." He sighed and cupped her cheek, caressing it with the pad of his thumb. Lowering her eyes, she leaned into his touch, feeling her defenses melting away. Damn her body for responding to the slightest touch from him. He dropped his hand and pulled her close, kissing the top of her head, something he did often. His large hand slid lower, cupping her butt. "We don't know what his intentions were or whether or not he was *defenseless* and, sweetheart, you know that. You've had enough self-defense training to know that you can never be too careful."

She nodded in agreement. She really didn't know what the man's intentions were, but she hadn't felt threatened, even when he touched her arm.

"Besides, there's no way in hell I'm going to let some man, *any* man, put his hands on you and not say something to him." He squeezed her butt and lowered his head until their mouths touched.

She moaned against his lips and he held her tighter. He was too irresistible for her to stay mad at him. With every touch, her body surrendered to his will and nothing else mattered.

God I love this man.

Slowly allowing her to come up for air, he stared into her eyes and said, "You're mine and you're very important to me."

Every now and then he spewed words of possession, and with the grasp he had on her ass, he clearly didn't want her to forget it. How could she? She felt the same as he and probably would have had a similar reaction if a woman had been coming on to him.

"Maybe I could have handled the situation differently, but," he shrugged, "I lost it there for a moment. His ass is lucky I didn't do more to him."

Olivia dropped her head to his chest. So much for

his apology.

The elevator opened onto their floor and Wiz wrapped his arm around her waist as they headed to their suite. She slid her arm around his back and leaned close. God she loved this man, even if he did get on her nerves sometimes. She couldn't wait until they were married. When she asked for a divorce, over nine years earlier, it wasn't because she didn't love him. No. Her feelings for her ex-husband had never waned.

She had never stopped loving him. Due to outside sources, they had gone through so much those first few years of marriage that she had lost herself. On top of that, as a SEAL, when Wiz received calls in the middle of the night saying they were going wheels up, leaving on a mission, after a while she couldn't handle it. She couldn't handle not knowing where. She couldn't handle being left behind for months on end. Most importantly, she couldn't handle not knowing if he would return.

Olivia didn't know why she thought putting distance between them would help her worry less or better deal with her own issues. If anything, her love for him and fear for his life had grown fiercer, at times crippling her from living her own life. During the years of their separation, she poured herself into her work, her art, while she continued her education to obtain her Master of Fine Arts degree. Now she could admit that back then she had been functionally depressed, unhappy and mentally in a dark place, but still able to do her day-to-day responsibilities.

She had also been afraid. Afraid of losing Wiz the way she had lost the rest of her family. For whatever reason she thought staying married to him would make her more vulnerable to hurt, to loss.

They arrived at their room and Wiz opened the door, allowing her to walk in first. Olivia was curious to see how the evening would end. The sweltering heat that had traveled between them on the dance floor less than an hour ago had cooled. And she had a feeling that things were going to get even chillier when she asked him to do something for her. Something she was sure he wouldn't want to do, but probably would since he rarely said no to her.

Olivia kicked off her shoes and left them near the "L" shaped sofa before moving to the large windows. She stared out into the night, not surprised to see fat snowflakes floating around. It was mid-November and the thirty-two degree weather was still better than minus five degrees they had experienced in Chicago days earlier. After one last glance at the city lights glittering from nearby buildings and traffic at a standstill below as if it were morning rush hour, she closed the curtains.

Turning to walk back the way she came, she stopped in her tracks.

Wiz had already tossed his jacket as well as his tie onto a nearby upholstered chair and had just pulled his shirttail out of his slacks. Their gazes connected and he knew what she wanted. She loved watching him undress. He took his time undoing the buttons on his dress shirt, and shrugged out of it, tossing it on the chair with the other items. Her mouth watered as his muscles contracted with each move. The intricate details of a tattoo, a massive eagle with its wings spread wide, covered his upper back.

When he slowly turned toward her, the tattoo on his left shoulder—bearing her name in bold, block letters—sent warmth to her heart. Then her gaze took in his chiseled chest.

Magnificent.

His broad shoulders, huge biceps, and an eight pack that a personal trainer would envy was on full display. The man's body didn't have a lick of fat and she couldn't wait to run her hands over every toned inch of his beautiful physique.

He dropped his pants, leaving on his black, boxer briefs, showing off powerful thighs, and long, toned legs. It was all she could do not to run across the room and leap into his arms.

Flawless.

Clearly the heat between them hadn't cooled as much as she first thought. His gaze caressed her body so intimately it was like she could feel his touch. Feel his large hands slide slowly down the length of her body. Feel every stroke of his fingers and the erotic heat that they transmitted.

It might have only been a few days since they'd been intimate, but in the past few weeks, she couldn't seem to get enough of him. If she wasn't thinking about kissing his full, luscious lips, she was imagining him being buried deep inside of her.

"I recognize that look." He adjusted himself and she squeezed her thighs together when the intense ache in her core intensified.

"And what look is that?"

"The one where you want to rip off all of my clothes and jump my bones."

Olivia laughed. "Oh, you know me so well." They moved forward at the same time, meeting in the middle. His briefs barely contained the erection that was now pressed against her belly. "And I see that you're ready for me," she purred.

"Sweetheart, I'm always ready for you." He captured her lips, kissing her with a hunger that rivaled hers. The velvet warmth of his mouth sent desire shooting throughout her body. Everything he did, he did with precision, and kissing was no different as his tongue tangled with hers and he explored her mouth. It felt so good to be in his arms, but she needed to ask him something. Something that couldn't wait. But his demanding lips didn't let up and she didn't want them to.

Maybe they could talk later … much later, after they got reacquainted.

With one last peck against her lips, he lifted his head and then touched his forehead to hers. "Why don't you tell me what's on your mind."

Unbelievable.

There had to be some type of vibe she gave off whenever she wanted to discuss something with him. Because it never ceased to amaze her how he could sense certain things.

"What are you thinking about?"

He moved behind her and lowered the zipper of her dress. Inching the silky material down her body, he placed feathery kisses on the side of her neck and goosebumps spread everywhere his lips touched. Her body trembled and her knees went weak, but he had an arm wrapped around her waist holding her steady.

He lifted her hair off her neck and his mouth worked its way down. "I see you're wearing one of my favorite bra and panty sets," he mumbled against her shoulder. She wondered if he realized that he said that about every set she wore.

Olivia leaned back against him, shutting her eyes

when his big, strong hands covered her breasts. She moaned as he tweaked her nipples until they were hard pebbles pushing against her lace bra.

This man knew how to make her hot and wet. His mouth went back to her neck, licking, nipping, and biting, sending erotic tingles to the tip of her toes.

Oh yeah, they could talk later.

"Tell me."

Okay so much for talking later.

But she couldn't think straight with his hard body grinding against hers and the heat from his hands shooting sparks to every nerve ending. And those lips… She groaned. She was defenseless when his lips touched her skin.

To her dismay, he stopped the mind-altering torture and wrapped his arms tight around her, his breathing as rapid as hers. Clearly he was trying to get himself under control. He turned her and his hands slid slowly down the sides of her body, stopping on her hips.

"Talk to me." He backed her out of the living room and into the bedroom, not stopping until the back of her knees bumped the edge of the bed.

Olivia sighed dramatically. "Well, if you must know, I was thinking about the wedding present I want you to give me."

A smile tilted the corner of his mouth before laughter rumbled inside his chest. Considering how distracted and uptight he had been most of the night, it was nice to hear him laugh.

"Isn't marrying me gift enough?" He gripped her bottom and lifted her onto the bed as if she weighed nothing and then laid down next to her. Lying on his side, he propped himself up on his elbow. "Why do I have to get you a wedding present?"

"I'll admit, marrying you is the best gift of all." She ran her hand over his hard chest, loving the way his muscles contracted under her touch. "But I know you've been trying to think of the perfect gift."

He pulled back slightly, drawing her attention to his eyes. "The only way you would know that is if Natasha said something."

"Well, she didn't actually come out and ask me what I wanted you to get me, but considering all the questions she's been asking, I figured you must have solicited her help."

"And here I thought I was the only P.I. in the family." He glided the tip of his index finger down between her breasts and didn't stop until he reached the top of her lace panties. "So ... if I were trying to think of the perfect wedding present for you, what would make you happy?"

Olivia folded her bottom lip between her teeth, suddenly hesitant in asking him for what she wanted. For the past couple of weeks, she'd toyed with how to present her request knowing that it wasn't going to go over well.

His hand covered her belly and shook her, regaining her attention. "What is it? What do you want?"

No. Now was not the right time for the argument that she knew would ensue. She rolled onto her back and slid under the cool sheet, pulling it up over her chest.

"You know there's nothing I wouldn't do for you." He stared into her eyes, concern on his face. The love she saw almost made her whimper. She knew he meant it, but knowing there was nothing he wouldn't do for her made it even harder to ask.

"Tell me."

She sat up and leaned her back against the headboard, bringing the sheet up with her. Seconds passed before she met his gaze again.

"I want you to find my sister."

He froze. Didn't move, didn't blink and though she was staring at him, she couldn't even tell if he was breathing. That love she saw brimming in his eyes only moments ago … vanished.

Wiz raised up slowly, his gaze never leaving hers. She could count on one hand the number of times he'd been angry with her, and sad to say, each time centered around her twin sister, Keisha.

Olivia watched his whole demeanor change before her eyes. His beautiful green eyes had darkened into narrow slits, his jaw tightened, and the bed covers fisted within his hand. She wasn't afraid of Wiz, but at the moment, this was a side of him she hadn't seen in years. Not since the last time she had seen Keisha.

"Cameron, please say something." She scooted to the far side of the bed and stood, wrapping her arms around herself.

"Say something?" The venom behind his words almost made her take a step back, but she stood her ground. She wanted to see Keisha and if anyone could find her, it was Cameron.

"I know how you feel about Kei—"

"No!" He stabbed the air with his index finger with such force, it was a wonder he hadn't wrenched his arm out of the socket. "You have no fucking idea how I feel about her, because if you did, you wouldn't ask this of me. You wouldn't even say her motherfuckin' name in my presence!"

Olivia's breath caught and she reared back, stunned by the fury bouncing off him like vicious waves crashing against the shore. Never had he raised his voice at her, nor had he ever cursed at her. She knew he wouldn't be happy with the request, but she had no idea he would freak out this way.

Olivia and her sister hadn't spoken since the last time Keisha had called crying, saying that she was in trouble and needed money. Alcohol and drugs had been her constant companion, so back then, Olivia hadn't been surprised to hear that Keisha was in trouble with her dealer. Problem was, each time Olivia bailed her out, Keisha's life went right back into a downward spiral, often times pulling Olivia into the whirlwind.

But being born three minutes before Keisha, Olivia had taken her role as the older sibling serious from the moment they started kindergarten. And now, looking back, she wondered if she'd done all she could do for her sister. Maybe if she had talked her into going to rehab sooner, she could have saved her.

Olivia stared across the bed at her hero, her protector, sure that he was remembering the number of messes Keisha had pulled her into. Wiz had always been protective of her. Though he never said, she was sure it had a lot to do with not only Keisha's shenanigans, but also the way his mother died. Killed by a man who lacked mercy all because he wanted her vehicle. His mother had resisted and the carjacker shot her in the head. Cameron was eight at the time and his sister, six.

It broke Olivia's heart to see him this mad, especially since she was the cause. The red tint to his light skin was proof that he was holding back the rage brewing inside. If that weren't a clue, the way his fists were balled at his sides were good signs that he was about ready to blow. But Olivia couldn't back down. She needed him to do this for her.

"Cameron."

He still didn't speak and she searched her mind for the right words to convince him, but her throat tightened. They continued to stand on opposite sides of the bed.

"I can't believe you're asking me to do this. Have you forgotten all the shit she put us through … put you through? Pick an incident that she dragged you into, any incident, and tell me you don't remember. What about the last time, Olivia? The last time when …" His face contorted in pain. "You will never know the fear I felt when I found y—" he choked, unable to finish his sentence.

Olivia hurried around the bed and reached out to him, but stopped when he took a step back. An ache lodged in her chest. He didn't even want her to touch him.

"No one remembers those times more than I do. But lately I can't stop thinking about her. Keisha and I will never be friends, I know that. All I want to do is see how she's doing, what she's up to, whether or not she ever got her life together. I can't do that without your help." Olivia also knew that her conversation with Natasha a couple of weeks ago played a part in Olivia's need to talk to Keisha. Natasha had recently spoken to her sister, Alandra, and talked about how well she and Quinn were doing in Bora Bora.

Considering all that Keisha had done to Olivia, she wasn't delusional enough to think that she could ever have the same type of relationship with her sister as

Natasha had with Alandra. Yet she did care about Keisha's well-being. After Olivia had first cut ties with her sister, she didn't want anything to do with her. Now that her life was back on track and she and Wiz had reunited, guilt for not trying to help Keisha more, rested in her chest.

"Cameron, I'm sorry to just spring the request on you, but I need to see her. It's been almost ten years and besides you, she's the only family I have left."

His expression clouded in anger as his chest rose up and down as if he'd just ran a marathon.

"Please say something."

"Say something? Okay, here's something." A quiver raked over her flesh as he eased up on her but stopped a foot away. "It will be a cold day in hell before I search for that bitch!"

Olivia's hand flew to her chest, her heart feeling as if it were being ripped out of her body. She stood rooted in place as he stormed out of the bedroom, slamming the door behind him. Wiz had always been there for her from the moment they first met when she was thirteen. Even while divorced, he had a presence in her life saying that he would always take care of her. And he had. Everything from making sure her lawn was maintained, to putting money in a bank account for her. Though she reminded him plenty of times that he didn't have to provide for her, he never backed off. He never left her alone … until now.

CHAPTER THREE

I want you to find my sister.

Wiz stormed into the living room and snatched his pants from one of the chairs. His heart thumped wildly at the words he thought he would never hear. He couldn't wrap his head around her request. Clearly she had forgotten about all the crap her sister had done.

"It's like suddenly I don't even know you." Olivia's voice broke into his thoughts when she silently entered the room.

Wiz shook his head and stepped into his slacks, keeping his back to her. "You know me. You know me well enough to understand that I would rather swallow a grenade than to have your sister in our lives."

She sighed loudly. "Cameron, I didn't say I want her in our lives. I'd like to connect with her for nothing more than a conversation."

Fastening his pants, he glanced over his shoulder

to find her standing near the bedroom door. The satiny red robe she wore stopped just above her knees, the color bringing out the warmth in her smooth, dark chocolate skin. His breath hitched as his gaze drifted slowly down her shapely body emphasized by the sash cinched tightly around her narrow waist. Damn if a certain part of his anatomy didn't spring to attention. He knew what lay beneath the thin material. He knew how soft every inch of her skin was to the touch. And he knew that if he stayed in that room much longer, he would tell her whatever the heck she wanted to hear. Everything but the truth that is.

His gaze moved back up to her face and his heart leapt into his throat. The love radiating in her eyes, even after the way he had spoken to her made the vice around his heart tighten even more. He felt like crap for denying her of her request.

Damn Keisha. Even when she wasn't around, she was still wreaking havoc. Just the thought of her made him want to rip something apart. But then there was Olivia. Staring at her now, the unyielding love he had for her made him want to take the three short steps it would take to reach her, and pull her into his arms. He wanted to come clean and tell her what happened to her sister all those years ago. But the bastard in him stayed rooted in place because he had vowed to take that one secret to his grave.

"I'm sorry," Olivia said.

He lifted the striped dress shirt that he had discarded earlier and slipped his arms through the sleeves. He didn't want her apology. He wanted to go back in time and wipe out the last fifteen minutes. Specifically erase the mere mention of her sister.

"I'm sorry I've ruined our evening."

He refastened the buttons on his shirt cuffs, trying like hell not to let her soft words and her intoxicating scent, which was uniquely hers, get to him. Why had he insisted that she tell him what was on her mind? This whole mess could have been avoided, at least for now.

He sat on the sofa and slipped into his dress shoes.

She moved closer. "Where are you going?" Despite the rash of emotions swirling inside of him, her nearness was doing wicked things to his senses. Everything about the woman from her sharp mind and her scent, to her graceful, lithe body was like his kryptonite. If she ever realized just how much power she had over him, he would be doomed. Hell, she probably already knew. He couldn't explain it. From day one, he lived to please and take care of her.

"I'm going downstairs to the bar."

For the first time in like forever, getting drunk, and numbing himself to his current reality seemed like a brilliant idea.

"I said I was sorry. You don't have to leave." The anguish in her voice made him slow his moves. But he knew if he stayed, she'd start the conversation all over again and it would definitely lead to an argument.

Anger swept through his body at the thought of Keisha Abernathy. To say he hated his sister-in-law would be an understatement. For years, he had felt guilty about discarding her from their lives, but for the first time in a long time, he felt no remorse for what happened all those years ago.

"At some point we're going to have to talk about this."

"Maybe. But it won't be tonight."

Olivia sat across from him. The opening of her robe revealed dark, shapely thighs. Thighs he thought he would be buried between by now. Blood shot straight to his groin and he sat up straighter, willing himself to divert his gaze, but failing. If he didn't know her better, he would think that she was intentionally trying to tempt him. But he knew better. She was the type of person who asked for what she wanted and gave whatever she wanted to give. She wasn't a game player.

He diverted his gaze, his eyes sweeping the room, taking in the large screen television, the mini bar, anything he could to slow his racing pulse and tamp down the desire swirling within him.

He wanted to be angry at her. Wanted to make her pay for even requesting such an impossibility. He couldn't. He had every right to be angry, yet, if he were honest with himself, he couldn't blame her for wanting to see her sister. Her twin. Of course she would think of her. It had been ten years and they had a birthday coming up.

"I don't ask for much and ... I want you to do this for me." Wiz saw the determination in her eyes. If he didn't at least pretend to consider her request, she'd figure out a way to find Keisha on her own. She wasn't one to let the word "no" stop her from getting what she wanted. "It would be nice to reconnect with the only family I have left."

"She's not the only family you have. You have me, my father, sister, and what about Malik and the gang? They are closer than any family we could have."

"That's different."

The annoyance from earlier seeped back into his

body and he narrowed his eyes at her.

"How can you act like nothing's happened?" He sprang up, his hands on his hips as he glared down at her. "As if nothing she did affected every aspect of our lives, of our marriage?"

"Forgiveness. I had to forgive her. Otherwise I would have gone crazy years ago." She stood slowly and reached out to touch him, but he stepped back. He'd be a goner if he let her touch him.

She glanced up at him with those dark, beautiful eyes that were filled with so much hope. If she was trying to make him feel guilty about his refusal, it was working. Almost. He couldn't help what he felt inside. He couldn't help the rage that flowed through his veins whenever he thought about all that her sister did to them.

"I haven't forgotten or forgiven."

It was too late in the day to be talking about forgiveness or anything else for that matter. He snatched the keycard for the room and headed for the door, Olivia hot on his trail.

"Please don't leave. Stay," she said to his retreating back.

"I can't."

It tore him up inside to leave this way, but he had to. Otherwise, he might do something stupid like tell her the real reason why he would never search for Keisha. Which was something he couldn't do. It would break her heart.

*

Wiz pulled his Land Rover into his assigned space in Supreme Security Agency's parking garage. He shut off his truck and laid his head back on the headrest, thoughts of Olivia running rampant through his mind. Dread had taken permanent residence in his stomach, heavy like a ship's anchor. It had been two days since he blew up at her and their fight tore him apart. Yet, even after they had returned home, he could barely look her in the eye. Searching for her sister wouldn't happen, couldn't happen.

Malik pounded on the roof of the car, making Wiz reach for the gun in his ankle holster.

"Man, what the fu— heck is wrong with you?"

Wiz would have laughed at his friend's slip up if his nerves weren't getting the best of him. He lowered his pants leg and released an exaggerated breath. Malik had always had a cursing problem, but over the last few months Natasha had surprisingly broke him from his excessive swearing.

Wiz grabbed his laptop from the passenger seat and climb out of the vehicle.

"What the hell is going on with you today?" his friend asked, walking toward the elevators that would take them to the top floor. "During that whole damn meeting you were in fucking la-la land. And don't get me started about Saturday, after you returned from D.C. I felt the tension bouncing off your ass from the moment you stepped into the ballroom, even Tasha noticed. So before we head into the office, you need to get yourself together. I don't want your shit jumping off on everybody else."

So much for having his cursing problem under control.

Malik stabbed at the up button. "Is there something going on that I should know about?"

Wiz hesitated. "Yeah, but nothing I want to talk about right now."

The elevator doors opened and they stepped on. Wiz swiped his ID card that would give them access to the top floor. Due to the cameras in the elevators, they rarely talked about anything of importance. Unlike in the garage where the cameras were for visual, these recorded visual and voices.

The moment they stepped off the elevator, Wiz said, "Meet me in my office when you get a chance."

Malik gave him a concerned look and then shrugged. "Will do, but first, I have to get some motherfucking lunch."

On that, Wiz laughed. "I thought you stopped cursing."

"I have … when Tasha's around."

Wiz shook his head and chuckled. *Some things never change.*

They entered the back hallway that serviced their two offices as well as the space Victoria used.

She was on the telephone and waved at Malik as he walked to his office, but stopped Wiz by touching his arm, asking him to give her a minute.

Victoria Bracero, their secret weapon. On paper, she was their executive assistant, but in reality, she was a fighting machine. With long blond hair curled at the ends and a body that could easily belong to a super model, no one would ever know by looking at her that she could take a man out, who was twice her size, without breaking a sweat. Wiz was glad she was on their team.

She ended the call. "Hey there. Sorry about that. I'm getting ready to head out for a couple of hours, but I wanted to let you know that Olivia called you a few times. She said she tried your cell phone with no luck. I told her you probably hadn't called back yet because of the meeting this morning." She pulled a large handbag from the bottom drawer of her desk.

"Call her. She didn't sound like herself."

"Will do. Thanks."

"I'm going to stop by the deli on the corner on my way back. Do you want anything?" She studied him as if sensing something wasn't right, but didn't say anything.

Wiz shook his head. "Nah, I'm good. I'll probably order in a little later."

When he walked into his office, he closed the door behind him and leaned against it. He couldn't keep avoiding Olivia, but he didn't know what to say to her. He had left the house early while she had been on her run, which was a first. Rarely did he leave before she returned home, always wanting to make sure she was okay before starting his day. Yet today, like a wimp, he made himself scarce.

Hours later, Malik knocked once and opened the door to Wiz's office. "Is this a good time?"

"Yep, come on in."

Wiz glanced at his watch, surprised that it was after four in the afternoon. It had taken him at least an hour to get focused on his work, but surprisingly he had gotten a lot done not realizing he had worked through lunch.

Malik unbuttoned his suit jacket and shook out of it. "I figured while we're meeting, we can talk about Greg's needs at the jewelry store."

Gregory Bates, a client and a friend, had recently hired their agency to look into a matter of missing diamonds. Diamonds being replaced with synthetic stones to be specific.

Malik sat at the small round conference table, his long legs stretched out and his thick arms folded across his chest. "I was thinking about something you said earlier. Does what you wanted to talk about have anything to do with Quinn? I know you told him that the *Los Hermanos* organization have been brought down. Did something change?"

Wiz shook his head and leaned on the back of one of the chairs. "Nah, my contacts say *Los Hermanos* have officially been disbanded in both Mexico and the U.S. And that situation with the CIA agent, Vance, not an issue anymore. Quinn and Lan can return to America whenever they want."

"Then if it isn't them, what's going on?"

Wiz straightened and shoved his hand into his pants pockets. "Olivia wants me to search for her sister."

Malik narrowed his eyes. "You have to be fuckin' kidding me."

Wiz told him about her request as well and how he responded. Minutes passed as Malik digested the information.

"Why now? Why the hell would she all of a sudden want you to find Midnight now?"

Wiz ran his hand over his head and down the back of his neck. *Operation Midnight.* Malik had dubbed their search for Keisha in connection with Olivia's disappearance all those years ago as a mini op. And had since referred to Keisha as Midnight.

"Why now?" Malik asked again.

Wiz had been asking himself the same question.

"Man, I don't know. Supposedly, Keisha's been on her mind and Olivia suddenly wants to reconnect with her." Wiz blew out a frustrated breath.

That same sick feeling that had been gnawing at him for the past couple of days rose to his throat. The things he had said to Olivia that night and the fear he'd seen on her face when he eased up on her, cursing her sister, would forever haunt him.

He had left their suite for a few hours to hang out in the hotel's bar. She had called his cell phone, leaving tons of messages for him to call her and for him to let her know that he was okay. By the time he returned to the room, she was asleep and barely said two words to him the next day.

Malik strolled over to the wall of windows, his hands stuffed into the front pockets of his dark suit pants. "What do I always say?" He glanced over his shoulder and Wiz knew what was coming. "Never leave loose ends. Never leave frickin' loose ends! First Quinn and that shit with *Los Hermanos* and now this. You should have told Olivia years ago that her sister is de—"

A knock sounded at the door, halting Malik's words.

"Come in," Wiz called out. He assumed it would be Raeanna, his tech assistant, who was working on a couple of projects for him.

The door swung open and Raeanna paused, her gaze going from Malik to Wiz. "Hey." She stepped in but stayed near the door. "Sorry to interrupt. Are you guys ready to discuss the Jefferson case? Oh, and Vicky wants to know if you want her to bring dinner back with her?"

"Yes and yes," Wiz answered as he and Malik reclaimed their seats.

Glad for the distraction, Wiz wanted to do anything but think more about the conversation he knew he had to have with Olivia. Since she taught night school on Mondays, he at least had the rest of the evening to come up with a way to avoid any mention of Keisha. But how was he going to tell Olivia that finding her sister was going to be impossible?

CHAPTER FOUR

Olivia rinsed her mouth and dabbed her lips with a paper towel. She thought for sure that she was over the flu, especially since she'd been feeling better the past couple of days, but her stomach was still queasy. If only she had known that before eating the turkey sandwich before class. Then again, if she had to eat another bowl of chicken noodle soup and crackers she was going to hurt someone.

Olivia took one last glance in the university's bathroom mirror, hung her hobo bag across her body, and headed to the door. Normally she couldn't wait to get home after class since Wiz made it a point to be there by the time she arrived. Yet tonight, she couldn't take more of the tension between them. Clearly discussing Keisha was going to be out of the question moving forward.

"Have a good night, Professor Miller," a student called out from across the hall.

"You too." She gave a small wave as he headed in

the opposite direction.

After receiving her Masters of Fine Arts degree, Olivia had entertained the idea of someday teaching at the college level. When her friend Valerie asked if she would be interested in filling in for her that semester, Olivia didn't hesitate. She had no idea she would enjoy teaching this much.

Olivia reached into her jacket pocket for her car keys. The moment she turned the corner, she bumped into someone.

"Oh I'm sorry. I didn't …" She smiled when she realized who it was.

"Hi, Professor Miller," one of her most enthusiastic students greeted.

"Hey, Amanda."

Olivia hadn't learned every student's name, but this one she knew. Happy, full of energy, and extremely talented, Amanda stood out from the others. They had talked after class about Olivia's work, which Amanda had taken a great interest in, as well as other more famous artists.

"Thanks again for helping me with the art project last week. Not too many instructors would have spent so much time with one student. I feel as if I should buy you lunch or dinner. Something to show you how much I appreciate all the extra help."

"It's my pleasure. I think you're more than ready for the national art competition."

"Yeah, thanks to you."

"Hey, you did all of the work. I was just there for guidance and support. By the way, the drawing you handed in yesterday was remarkable." They fell in step heading to the exit. "I'm very impressed with your talent. If you continue on this path, I wouldn't be surprised to see your work in an art gallery in the very near future."

The young woman beamed. "You really think so?"

"I have no doubt. You have a gift." They discussed some of Amanda's other projects as they went through the double doors that would lead out to Michigan Avenue.

"I'm sure I'm not the first person to tell..." Olivia stopped short, her hand flying to her chest when a black, tricked out Chevy Camaro came to a screeching halt in front of them. Rap music blared from the vehicle. She loved sports cars and this one had all the bells and whistles from the pristine paint job to seventeen-inch chrome wheels. What she didn't like is the way it had come out of nowhere and stopped right in front of them.

The dark tinted window on the passenger side eased down and anxiety coursed through Olivia's body.

"Come on, Amanda! I have to get going," the driver yelled. Olivia forced herself to relax. She wasn't all that comfortable leaving the university that time of night as it was, especially since she had to walk a couple of blocks to the parking garage. Normally she wasn't so jumpy.

Amanda groaned. "That's my brother. He has to be the most impatient person in the world." She had mentioned that he had raised her after their parents died in a car accident when she was ten. According to her, she owed him everything especially since he was paying her college tuition. "Hey, come meet him." She grabbed Olivia's arm and pulled her toward the car.

"I really should be ..." Olivia started but stopped

when they reached the vehicle.

"Corin, this is my professor I was telling you about. She's the famous artist."

His dark, cold eyes bore into Olivia and a tremor shook her body. She mustered the courage to hold his gaze and not cower away from the car.

She swallowed hard. "Nice meeting you. Amanda speaks of you often."

Not a word. Nothing. His eyes steady on hers as though he recognized her. Olivia was sure they hadn't met. She would remember his beady eyes, his nose that had clearly been broken a few times, and a strong jawline that made him appear hard, unfeeling. If that weren't enough, a tattoo that looked more like a vicious scar on his right hand made him unforgettable. Oh yeah, she would have remembered this brotha.

"Get in the car, Amanda," he growled, still not taking his eyes from Olivia.

Amanda grumbled something, but said her good-byes to Olivia and slid into the car. Her brother peeled away from the curb the moment she shut her door. Clearly he was showing off the car's ability to go from zero to sixty in five point nine seconds. It was almost as impressive as her Mustang.

Olivia shivered remembering how his gaze bore into her. She would hate to run into him in a dark alley, or anywhere for that matter. The guy was scary looking probably without even trying to be.

Olivia pulled her jacket closed and turned to head in the direction of the parking structure where she left her car, glad to see others walking in the same direction.

Good, I won't have to walk the whole two blocks alone.

Before she could take two steps, rain mixed with snow started falling from the sky.

"Oh no." She put her arms over her head, remembering that she had left her hat and umbrella in her office.

Hurrying back to the building, she trotted up the three concrete stairs and flung the door open. She took a step and "Boom!" The eardrum-busting sound cracked the air, sending her crashing into a nearby wall. She cried out when her head made contact and a blast of pain shot through her skull.

Throat tight, heart pounding she squeezed her eyes closed as she cradled her head, willing the room to stop spinning.

"Help me!" she screamed.

Breathe. Just breathe.

She slowly opened her eyes, blinking rapidly against the blurriness. Smoke filled much of the area and with her view from the floor, she could barely make out the bodies running past her. Her gaze darted around when she realized the only thing she could hear were muffled sounds.

Oh God. I can't hear.

Don't panic. Don't panic, she told herself over and over, tears pooling in her eyes. Her head spun and her eyes burned as people shoved past her hurrying toward the exit.

As the smoke slowly cleared, she saw one of the professors waving his arms and saying something. She tried reading his lips.

"Go! Go! Go!"

Panic roared through her body as her heart beat double time.

With her hands on the wall, she stood, but

crumbled to the floor when a shooting pain exploded through her ankle. Desperate to get out of there, she tried again, feeling along the wall, fear chilling her to the bone.

She flinched when strong hands grabbed hold of her arm.

"I have you, Olivia," the man said close to her ear. She almost sobbed with relief that she could hear him, barely, but at least she heard what he said.

She peeked over her shoulder. Adrian, one of the professors she shared an office with, guided her out the building.

The freezing sleet pelting against her added to her battered nerves. Dizzy, with her head throbbing and the ringing in her ears, she did everything she could to keep the nausea down.

With Adrian's arm around her waist, she hobbled alongside him, her ankle burning in pain. They kept moving toward a large group of people across the street and half way down the block.

"What happened?" Olivia asked, quickly realizing that talking made everything hurt even more. The November weather chilled her to the bone. She tried snuggling deeper into her coat, hating she didn't have anything on her head.

"I'm not sure, but I'll find out as soon as I get you somewhere safe." It sounded as if he were whispering. Maybe she was still having trouble with her hearing. She stumbled on a crack in the raised sidewalk and cried out. "I have you." Adrian held her tighter, practically carrying her. She didn't think her ankle was broken since she could put weight on it, but it throbbed enough to let her know she needed to get off of it.

Adrian helped her into one of the buildings that had a wide-open foyer. Though it was packed, he did find a place for her to sit near the window of a store that was closed.

His lips were moving, but she couldn't understand what he was saying. Pointing to her ears she started to shake her head, but stopped when the pain became too much.

"Can you hear me now?" he asked closer to her ear.

"Yes."

"You're not looking too good. I hear some sirens in the distance. I'll make sure we get you checked out. Someone should especially look at that cut on the side of your forehead. You might even need to take a trip to emergency."

She reached up with shaky hands to touch the spot, but Adrian stopped her.

"I'm sure I'll be okay," she said, not wanting to go to a hospital. Her vision wasn't as blurry, though the ringing in her ears was still prevalent. With her pulse pounding and her hands shaking, she tried to slow her hammering heart by breathing in and out. She had to pull herself together because no way was she letting them take her to a hospital.

Her mind tried to register what had just happened, but she wasn't sure. All she could remember was a loud boom and debris flying everywhere.

She lowered her head, cradling it between her hands. The throbbing wouldn't stop.

"Olivia?"

She jerked her head, quickly regretting the move when she slumped to the side, almost hitting the floor from dizziness.

"Whoa. I don't think you're okay." Adrian bent closer. Despite her eyes burning, she could make out the concern on his face. "I know it's cold outside, but not in here. Yet, you're shivering like crazy." He shook out of his jacket and put it around her shoulders right on top of her coat. "You might be going into shock."

"Hey! We need some help over here!" she heard Adrian say. "Olivia? Olivia, stay with me."

"Okay." Her one word was barely a whisper. The heavy pounding in her head and the constant ringing in her ears made it hard to keep her eyes open. "Please, no hospital. Just call ... call my husband."

*

"Anything else on our little impromptu meeting agenda?" Malik asked and yawned. "I'm ready to get the hell out of here."

"That should be it, except where are we with Gregory Bates, Raeanna?" Wiz asked. He glanced at his cell phone thinking that he would need to head home soon. He and Olivia might not be on the best of terms at the moment, but he still wanted to be there by the time she arrived.

"You told me to let you know when I received the security footage from Mr. Bates. I talked to him earlier today."

"Okay. Were you able to save the information to the E server?"

"Not exactly. He couldn't figure out how to copy and send it to me. One of us will need to go to the jewelry store and get the information. I can stop by there sometime tomorrow if you want."

Raeanna, one of their newest IT specialists, had recently graduated from college with mad IT skills.

She'd been shadowing Wiz for the last few weeks, proving that they'd made a good choice in hiring her.

"Actually, I have to go there to get Olivia's birthday present. I'll take care of it."

"Okay, just let me know if there's anything else I can do to help. Oh," she pulled a flash drive from her back pocket, "Carter asked me to give this to you regarding the Hollis case."

"Thanks." Wiz put the flash drive in the top drawer of his desk.

"You're welcome. Do you need anything before I head out for the day?" Wiz and Malik said no. "All right, then you guys have a good night. See you in the morning."

Once Raeanna had closed the door behind herself, Malik stood. "What are you going to do about Olivia?"

Wiz shook his head. "Not sure yet. I'm think—"

The door flew open, grabbing both their attention, and Victoria hurried in.

"I'm glad you're still here." The rush in her tone and the concern in her expression immediately put Wiz on alert.

"What going on?"

"It's Olivia. There was an explosion."

CHAPTER FIVE

Fifteen minutes later, Wiz rushed through the throngs of people crowding the sidewalk on Michigan Avenue, in search of Olivia. While Malik drove him downtown, Adrian, Olivia's coworker, had filled Wiz in on her condition and what he knew about the explosion which wasn't much. He also told him that Olivia had refused to go to the hospital which concerned Wiz, but wasn't a surprise.

Wiz kept moving, stretching his neck as he approached the location where Adrian said they would be. The area was sheer chaos with the number of people and cops blocking the streets.

He spotted Adrian standing on a curb looking around, probably for him. A few feet behind him, he caught sight of Olivia.

His heart constricted.

Wiz hadn't seen her so distraught since … He slowed and blew out a breath, not wanting to travel down that memory path that he wished he could keep buried. Instead, he focused on the fact that she was alive and apparently giving the paramedic hell based on the frustration written on his face.

"Adrian," Wiz said when he approached the man who had called him. They only met once during an open house early in the semester, but Wiz recognized him immediately.

"Oh good, you made it." Adrian stretched out his hand and they shook.

"Thanks again, man, for calling me."

"No problem. She's over there. Her hearing seems to be a little better, but she got banged up pretty good."

Wiz approached the ambulance where Olivia was sitting on the bumper with a blanket wrapped around her shoulders. From the short distance, it sounded as if the paramedic was telling her that she really needed to go to the hospital. She was sporting a large bandage on the right side of her head, so apparently she had let them do something.

Wiz made eye contact with the paramedic. "My wife." He nodded toward Olivia. The moment she saw him she stood, wincing in pain.

"Whoa, babe." He caught her before she fell.

She didn't speak; instead, she burst into tears. A vise tightened in his chest as her sobs grew and her body shook against him. Wiz had fought in some of the most dangerous countries in the world, stared down vicious terrorists, and could even handle having a gun pointed in his face, but this ... this he couldn't handle. Seeing his baby hurt and crying tugged at his heart.

"I'm sorry," she sobbed against his chest.

He kept a tight hold around her. "Why are you

sorry?"

"You were busy and—"

"Sweetheart, you're my number one priority. *Nothing* comes before you. You know that." He set her away from him, so that he could see her face. Her ashen skin and red eyes that were glossed over stood out more with the bandage on the side of her head. "We need to get you to a hospital and have you checked out."

"No. No hospital," she said barely above a whisper. The conviction in her voice told him that she was adamant.

He set her on the back of the ambulance, next to another woman.

"Olivia—"

"I just want to go home. Please just take me home. I'm fi— oh God, I think I'm going to be sick."

The paramedic shoved a barf bag into her hands just in time.

Damn.

Where the hell was her hat and scarf? She was just getting over the flu, now her hair and clothes were soaked. At this rate, she was never going to get back to one hundred percent.

"Sweetie, I need you to go to the hospital. I have to know for myself that you're okay."

"Call Natasha. She can meet us at the house." There wasn't much he could deny Olivia when she looked at him with those big brown eyes.

Natasha, Malik's fiancée, was the chief of staff at one of the largest hospitals in Chicago and a surgeon by trade. If he called her, she would come if she could.

"Please, Cameron."

Wiz sighed and pulled out his cell phone to call Malik.

An hour later, he paced the length of his family room. Natasha was upstairs with Olivia and Wiz prayed that he wouldn't regret not insisting that she go to the hospital.

"I have to tell you, I've had just about enough of the shit that's been happening to our women this past year and a half," Malik said from one of the leather recliners, flipping through the channels. He stopped when highlights of the Chicago Bears football game covered the large screen.

"I know, right? I think our little family has had enough excitement to last us a lifetime."

There was a moment in the evening that Wiz had wondered if Olivia had been the target. It wasn't until he contacted Chicago PD and talked with his detective friend, Sheldon, did he breathe a little easier. A couple of the students had created a dry ice bomb, placing it in a trashcan near the entrance Olivia had used. Thankfully, only a few people obtained minor injuries. After viewing security footage, the perpetrators had already been identified. Wiz had still been tempted to ask for a copy of the tape, just in case.

Wiz rushed to the stairs when he heard Natasha coming down.

"How is she?"

"Still a little dizzy from her headache and the ringing in her ears. If either of those is not better by morning, she'll need to get checked out at the hospital. It doesn't appear she has a torn eardrum from the blast, but a thorough exam is the only way to know for sure."

Wiz didn't even want to think about her having to go to the hospital, knowing Olivia would keep fighting him on the subject.

"What about her ankle? How bad is it?"

"It's not broken. The ice helped take down most of the swelling and I wrapped it. Make sure she keeps it elevated. You might have to ice it periodically for about twenty minutes at a time if it swells again. Now, I know it won't be easy, but try to keep her off her feet for a few days. She has already asked when she would be able to resume her daily runs. I told her no running this week. Even next week might be pushing it."

"Ha! Good luck in keeping her off her feet," Malik said to Wiz. "Although, if you need some ideas, I can give you a few." He wiggled his eyebrows and pulled Natasha against him, nuzzling her neck until she swatted at him.

Wiz chuckled. Out of all of his friends, Malik definitely won king of one-liners hands down. Wiz could think of plenty of times, even when traipsing through jungles, Malik's wit shined through, making them laugh even during serious times.

"My turn to ask a question." Natasha pulled away from Malik. "Why is she so terrified of going to the hospital?"

Wiz groaned and rubbed his forehead, backing away, but not going too far. This was something he and Olivia rarely talked about and very few people knew. She and Natasha had grown close, but apparently the subject hadn't come up.

"Ten years ago, Olivia miscarried. Though the doctors did everything they could to save the baby, considering the situation, she didn't think they did enough and hates hospitals."

Natasha nodded. "That explains why she wasn't there with you and Malik after I was attacked."

"Let's not talk about that," Malik growled and pulled Natasha back into his arms. That was a time that none of them would soon forget. Though Natasha had been the one attacked, Wiz felt it was hardest on Malik who still blamed himself.

"Trust me, Olivia wanted to be there for you," Wiz told Natasha. "She just couldn't seem to get past her ... hell, I don't know what to call it. Fear. Trepidation. Anger."

"No. No, I understand. She went through a traumatic experience. If the only thing Olivia is suffering from the experience is fear of hospitals, she's way better off than many women. Some never recover emotionally."

If Malik hadn't given Natasha the whole story about that time in Wiz's and Olivia's life, he wouldn't either. He, Malik, and Quinn had gone through serious shit with missions in some of the most horrific countries in the world, vowing to never tell a soul about half the things they had done or had experienced. What happened ten years ago ranked up there. It was the worst time in Wiz's life. A time he not only wanted to keep buried, but a time he wanted to forget. Unfortunately, with Olivia talking about Keisha, that was impossible.

Wiz locked up after seeing Malik and Natasha out. He set the house alarm, shut off all the lights on the first floor, and headed upstairs.

The last few days had been filled with so many different emotions. He couldn't wait to get a good night's sleep.

He shut off the hallway light and entered their bedroom, illuminated by the crystal lamp on Olivia's side of the bed and a sliver of moonlight shining through the skylight. As he stared down at her sleeping form, his heart swelled. He never knew he could love someone as much as he loved her.

Quiet for most of the ride home, she had only mentioned how scared she'd been when the bomb went off. Considering her proximity to the explosion, it was by the grace of God she hadn't been hurt worse.

Wiz pulled the sheet up to her chin, careful not to wake her, and then placed a kiss on her forehead. Turning off the light next to the bed, he headed to their sitting area. The cozy spot, dimly lit by a night light in a nearby outlet, had two overstuffed chairs and a small round table that faced the fireplace.

With the ordeal that evening, he had the mind not to let Olivia out of his sight despite how unrealistic that would be. He just never wanted to experience the type of fear that had ravished his body as they sped to the university. The invisible band that had wrapped tightly around his heart since receiving the call was finally starting to loosen.

Still too amped to fall asleep, he turned one of the upholstered chairs around to face the bed. Dropping down on the cushion, he stretched his legs out in front of him, his gaze on Olivia.

Wiz didn't know what he would have done if the situation had turned out different. He couldn't imagine his life without her. Incidents like tonight reminded him of how precious life was … and reminded him of his mother.

Like Olivia, she was one of the sweetest people he

had ever known. His father had often said, "Marjorie can sweet talk me into anything." Wiz smiled at the memory as he recalled other similarities that his mother and Olivia shared.

Though only eight when a carjacker shot and killed Marjorie, there were things about her Wiz hadn't forgotten. He remembered how she always smelled like flowers and how she never missed a night to read him and his younger sister a story at bedtime. Since his father was gone for long stretches of time while on active duty, his mother played many roles inside and outside of the home. She didn't have to work, but volunteered at a center for seniors, as well as Chicago Children's Hospital, while still taking care of home. Everyone loved her.

Wiz rested his head against the back of the chair and closed his eyes. He could almost hear the softness of her voice and her infectious laugh. She rarely sat still. His father often complained that she did too much and was too accommodating to people. He was afraid someone would take advantage of her or worse. Of course she waved him off, calling him a worry wart. But maybe he hadn't worried enough because someone still took a precious gift from them.

Wiz rubbed his forehead. He knew his overprotectiveness of Olivia had a lot to do with the way his mother had been taken from them. He didn't want to stifle Olivia from being who she was—a loving, understanding, generous woman willing to give her last to someone in need. And she was also the same person willing to forgive somebody who wasn't deserving of even licking the bottom of her shoe.

"Why are you sitting in the dark?"

Wiz startled at the sound of Olivia's voice. He straightened, surprised he hadn't seen her move or make a noise.

"Shouldn't you be asleep?" He strolled to the bed and sat on the edge. "Tasha mentioned she'd given you something to help you rest. I thought you would be out for hours."

"The medication wasn't that strong, but it helped relax me."

She scooted over, giving him more room. Stretched out next to her, he pulled her close, loving the way she molded against his body.

"Do you feel better?" He kissed the top of her head.

"I'm fine. My eyes have cleared and my headache is a mild throb. My ankle still hurts a little, but I tested it out earlier and I'm able to walk on it a bit."

Wiz glanced down to the foot of the bed realizing her leg was no longer elevated.

"Where're you going?" Olivia whined when he removed his arm from around her.

"Nowhere. I just want to readjust the pillows that Tasha placed under your foot. You need to keep your ankle elevated." He took care of the pillows and pulled her back into his arms. "As for you being able to walk on that ankle, don't. The more you stay off of it, the quicker it'll heal."

"Okay, but it's better. So you can stop worrying."

"I'm always going to worry about you, especially when you're not a hundred percent."

"Such a worry wart," she murmured.

She yawned and snuggled closer. Wiz knew she'd be back to sleep in no time.

Realizing he was still in his clothes, he thought

about undressing, but he didn't want to let her go. He had no intention of ever letting her go.

Now all he had to do was figure out how to handle the situation regarding her request for him to locate Keisha. He still couldn't wrap his brain around why she had such a need to reunite with a sister who treated her like shit and almost got her killed. As far as he was concerned, there wasn't enough love in the world for him to want to reconnect with someone like that. Yet he had to remember Olivia was different when it came to matters of the heart, whereas forgive and forget didn't come easy for him. Keisha had done some mess that not even the Pope would forgive and Wiz was glad she was out of their lives.

But he knew his wife well. There was no way the conversation was over. When she wanted something bad enough, she went after it, even if it meant digging up ghosts from the past.

In the meantime, he would just have to distract her until he came up with a way to tell her the truth about her sister.

Reunite my ass.

CHAPTER SIX

Two days later, Olivia glanced over the rim of her large coffee mug as Wiz tidied the kitchen. Sitting at the breakfast bar gave her a great view to his perfect body. She squeezed her legs together as a rhythmic pulse beat between her thighs while her gaze skimmed along the length of him. She tried tapping down the escalating need to get him naked. Yet the way the white fitted T-shirt stretched across his hard pecs, hugged his thick biceps and his flat abs made it almost impossible. His muscles rippled with every move he made, from loading the dishwasher to wiping down the stove and countertops.

Lately she'd been hornier than usual and it didn't help that this morning everything he did made her hotter by the minute.

Now, bent over, placing a skillet in the cabinet he gave her a nice view of his tight butt. For a man who only worked out a few times a week, he was in impeccable shape.

Wiz stood and caught her staring at him.

"What?"

"Hmm? Oh, nothing." She set down the coffee mug. "Just admiring the view."

"Well, if I knew you were going to be watching every move I made, I would have stripped down so you could see every inch of me." He leaned on the counter in front of her, his eyes sparkling with mischief.

"It's not too late." She grinned, always ready for one of his striptease shows.

He cracked a smile, shaking his head, and glanced at his watch. "Actually it is. I have to meet with a client this morning and I'm already running a little behind schedule."

Wiz had prepared a breakfast of her favorites. The blueberry pancakes, chicken sausage patties, hash browns, and everything else had been delicious. Though avoiding any conversation involving her sister, he had been catering to her needs since they arrived home the other night, not giving her a chance to do anything.

"I need to meet with a client this morning and I'm going to have Raeanna work from here until I get back."

"Cameron, I told you I was fine. I don't need a babysitter."

"I know, sweetheart, but I'm worried about you and I want you to stay off that ankle as much as possible. Raeanna will be here to help you if needed. Besides, you have to be mobile by next weekend for your birthday party."

That's right. The day is creeping up quick. She definitely didn't want to be limping around on that night. Since they planned to keep the event simple, and the food was being catered, there wasn't much she had to do as far as preparations.

Olivia took another sip of the steaming dark liquid that Wiz referred to as coffee and braced herself for the jolt it would illicit. Why he insisted on making coffee so strong was beyond her, but at the moment, an idea sparked. Raeanna being at the house might not be such a bad idea. The woman was almost as tech savvy as Cameron. She'd be perfect to help find Keisha.

"Okay," Olivia finally said.

Wiz narrowed his eyes. "Okay?" He folded his arms across his chest and stared at her. "That's it? You're not going to fight me more on this?"

"No."

He hesitated and Olivia almost laughed knowing she had caught him off guard.

"Why not? Minutes ago, I thought for sure you were getting ready to list all the reasons why you don't need anyone around. Why the sudden change?"

The note from Donna had her anxious to find Keisha. Their friend from the old neighborhood had called two weeks ago. Her family had purchased the house Olivia's grandmother once lived in and said some guy had recently stopped by looking for Keisha. Donna had told him that Keisha hadn't lived there in years, but that she might be able to get a message to her. Days later she had contacted Olivia.

Now, the only thing Olivia had to figure out was how to talk Raeanna into helping her, especially since she was so loyal to Wiz.

"I think you're right," she finally said to Wiz. "Somehow, I had forgotten about the dinner party and I want to be able to walk around with no aches or pains. If it means taking it easy for a couple of days, I'll do it. Besides, another professor is overseeing my classes for the rest of the week, but I do need to prepare some assignments for next week. "

Wiz studied her a while longer, not seeming too convinced, but he accepted her explanation.

He strolled around to her side of the bar and just stood there looking at her before bending lower, probably to kiss her.

Olivia grabbed the lapels of his shirt, pulling him within an inch of her lips.

"Whoa! Dang, woman." He braced his hand on the countertop to keep from toppling on top of her. "You're a lot stronger than you look."

"And I'm horny. Maybe you should reconsider being a little late for your meeting and I can show you how strong I really am."

He chuckled and covered her mouth with his, mumbling against her lips, "I'd like nothing more than for you to show me a few more things, but I'm going to have to take a rain check." He gave her a quick peck before pulling back slightly. "And you're still recuperating. But if you still want to have your way with me when I return, I'm all yours."

She yelped when he tweaked her nipple between his fingertips through the thin tank top, the sweet torture getting her even more excited.

"You can't do stuff like that if you're not going to go all the way."

He winked at her. "Later. But right now, let's get you into the family room." He lifted her and she laced her arms around his broad shoulders.

"You're going to spoil me if you keep carrying me

around like this."

"I live to spoil you."

The doorbell rang just as Wiz set her on the sofa.

"Are you sure you're cool with having Raeanna here?" Wiz asked as he backed slowly toward the door.

Olivia lifted an eyebrow. "Are you saying I have a choice?"

"You always have a choice, sweetie. I would just feel better knowing that someone was here with you."

The last thing she wanted was for him to spend his day worrying about her. "It's fine."

"Hey, Olivia." Raeanna waltzed into the room, a large bag hanging from her shoulder. "I hope you don't mind being stuck with me for a couple of hours."

"I should be saying that to you. I hate that you have to babysit."

"Oh please, I don't look at it as babysitting. I'm hoping some of your creative talent will rub off on me while I'm here. If so, maybe I'll be able to create something like that." She pointed to a large abstract painting hanging on the wall over the sofa. It was one of the first pieces Olivia had painted while in college. "If I had half your talent, I'd probably paint until my hands fell off."

Olivia liked Raeanna from the moment they met. Young, with a geeky like quality, she was like a burst of sunshine on a cloudy day. Her easy smile and gentle spirit could make the grouchiest person feel good. What Olivia liked most was her style of dress. Tar black hair, spiked at the top and tapered on the side with a streak of pink, went flawlessly with her all black attire and four-inch platform shoes. Such a contradiction to her bubbly personality.

Wiz walked back into the room. "What else can I do for you before I head out?"

"Nothing, baby. You've done more than enough."

He bent down and kissed her. "Don't forget our plans for later," he whispered close to her ear.

She smiled. "I won't."

An hour later, Olivia finished a sketch she had started days ago, something that had been playing around in her mind. The abstract wasn't like anything she'd done of late, but she had to admit, it was good.

"Are you okay, Olivia?" Raeanna asked from her perch at the kitchen counter. "Do you need anything?"

Olivia had gone back and forth on whether or not to solicit Raeanna's help in locating Keisha. Wiz would go ballistic if he had any idea of her plan, but finding Keisha was something Olivia felt she needed to do. Not just because of the note, but because it was time. It was time to reconnect with her sister and try to put the past behind them.

"As a matter of fact, I do need something," Olivia finally said to Raeanna. "If I wanted to search for a family member, where would I start?"

Raeanna tilted her head, her brows slanted in confusion. "Um, Wiz is the best at finding people. Why not ask him? Besides, he's a licensed P.I. He has access to informational databases that others can't touch."

That was one of the reasons Olivia was disappointed that Wiz wouldn't even consider her request. It wasn't like he would have to interact with Keisha. Olivia wanted to pass the note along and see how her sister was doing. That's it.

"Cameron has been so busy lately. I was hoping to do this on my own, but I don't even know where to start."

Raeanna still didn't seem convinced. "I hope I'm not overstepping here, but everyone who works with Wiz knows that he would walk on water for you—busy or not. I only hope that when my Mr. Right comes along he is half as attentive to me as Wiz is to you. Ask him. I bet he would search for your sister."

Olivia sighed and sat back. "He hates my sister," she stated simply.

Raeanna's eyes grew as large as saucers. "Wiz? He's like the nicest guy at the office. I can't imagine him hating anyone." Olivia gave her a look and Raeanna started back peddling. "But, I guess you would know him better than anyone."

She debated on how much to tell Raeanna without actually coming out and telling her that her sister deserved to be on Wiz's shit list.

"Cameron has every right to be against the idea of finding her. Keisha ..." Olivia stopped, searching for the right words to describe her sister. "When we were young, Keisha stayed in trouble. She has done some things to us that ... let's just say she has left some permanent scars on us."

Raeanna grabbed the note pad she'd been writing on earlier and strolled over to the family room. She sat in one of the chairs across from Olivia.

"Then why do you want to find her? If you don't mind me asking."

Olivia gave a half shrug knowing it was crazy that she wanted anything to do with her sister. If only Keisha hadn't been on her mind so much lately and if only that note didn't exist.

"I know we will never be as close as we were when we were kids, but I want to know what she's been up to. I want to know where she is, if she's okay, and whether or not she's changed."

Raeanna nodded but didn't speak for the longest time. "I can understand that. My sister and I aren't as close as we used to be, but that doesn't stop me from worrying about her."

Somehow, Olivia didn't think Raeanna and her sister's relationship could remotely be compared to hers and Keisha's. After their parents died, Keisha's behavior grew reckless. The drug use, the drinking, and the people she hung with back then were bad news. There were times when Olivia wondered if Keisha was even still alive.

Olivia shook the thought free. She would know. She knew in her heart that she would know if Keisha was dead.

"Okay, I'll see if I can help, but I won't be able to do it on company time."

"Whatever you can do or find would be helpful and appreciated. I'll gladly pay for your time."

Raeanna waved her off. "That won't be necessary, but I'm going to need some information in order to get started."

"Anything."

"I need her full name and her last place of residence, if you know. And if you have her social security number that would help."

Olivia answered the questions she knew the answers to and promised to get the information that she didn't have on hand.

"Oh, and when is her birthday?" Raeanna asked.

"November twenty-third."

Raeanna's brow lifted. "Wow. Isn't your birthday around that time? Wiz invited me to your birthday celebration next weekend."

"Actually, my birthday is on the twenty-third, too. We're twins. Identical twins."

The young woman's mouth dropped open. "You have a twin? That's so cool. I always wanted a twin. So did you guys dress alike as kids? Finish each other sentences?"

"Yeah, we did."

A smile found its way to Olivia's mouth. There was a time when she and Keisha were inseparable. Their mother always dressed them alike and back then, their parents were the only ones who could tell them apart. Happy memories of when they would try to confuse their teachers and pretend that they were the "other" twin came rushing back. They had a perfect life until—

"Olivia. Olivia?" Raeanna waved her hand in front of Olivia's face. "Are you okay?"

Olivia blinked several times and turned her head, trying to keep the tears at bay. It was hard for her to think of Keisha without thinking about all the bad that was her sister.

Olivia blew out a breath and swiped at the lone tear that made its way down her cheek.

"I'm fine. How about I make us some lunch?"

Raeanna stared at her for a moment before speaking. "Wiz told me to make sure you stay off your feet."

That man. Olivia loved him like crazy, but sometimes he was just too much.

"He mentioned that there was lasagna in the refrigerator. Or would you like something different?"

"That's fine. Thanks."

Raeanna stood and started to walk away, but stopped. Turning back to Olivia, she said, "I'll do everything I can to find your sister."

"Thank you and ... can we keep this between us?"

She nodded and headed to the kitchen.

Part of Olivia hoped they were able to find Keisha, but there was a part of her that wasn't so sure. Maybe Wiz had been right in saying that she should forget the idea of searching for her. But how could she? This was her sister. No they didn't have a telepathic connection like their friends used to ask them about years ago, but there were times when thoughts of her were stronger than other times. Like lately. Since last seeing Keisha, Olivia hadn't thought much about seeking her out. Until now. She just hoped she didn't live to regret it in the end.

*

Wiz pulled open the heavy glass door of the jewelry store and a bell chimed. Several people glanced his way. He was surprised by the number of customers considering it was Tuesday.

"Good afternoon, welcome to Diamonds and Gems," a perky redhead with heavy makeup greeted. "May I help you?"

Wiz gave a head nod to two staff members he recognized before approaching her as she stood behind one of the glass counters that held silver jewelry.

He removed his shades and tucked them into the inside pocket of his heavy leather jacket. "Hi, is Greg here?"

"Wow. You have beautiful ey—" she started. Her gaze darted around checking to see if anyone had heard her. "I'm sorry, I mean ..."

Wiz smiled and waved the comment off. "Thank you." He was used to the reaction, especially from women. It wasn't that often you saw a black man with green-hazel eyes. He had inherited them from his father, who had the same eyes as his mixed-race mother.

"Hold on a second. I'll get Mr. B."

While she was gone, Wiz glanced around the space, only spotting a few cameras. The store's security system had been installed five years earlier and at the time, Greg had been on a tight budget. The agency now had systems that were light years ahead in technology, compared to Greg's current equipment.

"What's going on, man?" Greg's voice boomed. He gave Wiz a one-arm hug, pounding him on the back.

Greg, a big man the same height as Wiz, carried around at least forty extra pounds. Dark complexion with thinning hair, he looked a little older than his fifty years. "It's good seeing you. Come on back."

"Remind me not to leave here without Olivia's watch." He had ordered her a new platinum one for her birthday.

"Actually, I have it right here." Greg unlocked the top drawer of his huge mahogany desk and pulled a square, gray velvet box out. "How is that gorgeous woman of yours anyway?"

Wiz opened the box and glanced at the timepiece.

"She's doing okay. Busy as ever, but good nonetheless." He hadn't told many people about the mess at the university the other night, trying not to think about it no more than he had to. Every time he thought about how the situation could have turned out, his blood pressure spiked.

"I'm glad to hear that. Let her know she'll be hearing from me in the near future. Deloris and I want to commission her to do another painting for us. We're always getting compliments off the two she's already done."

Wiz smiled. Olivia was very talented, and though he was glad she wasn't traveling as much, he hoped she kept painting.

"I'm sure she would be more than happy to hear from you." Wiz glanced down at the watch.

"If it looks okay, I'll print the final invoice."

"Looks good." Wiz closed the lid. "Was there an additional charge for the heavy duty fastener?"

Greg shook his head. "Nah, man. You're all set. I hope she likes it."

"I'm sure she will. So let's talk diamonds," Wiz said now that they had the small talk out of the way. "You really think Clayton is the one switching them out, huh?"

Greg nodded, his mouth devoid of the smile he usually wore. "I don't have any proof, but when I review the tapes, it really looks like he's up to no good. I figured I'd get you or Malik to check out the video surveillance footage before I get the authorities involved. I hope I'm wrong. He's a good guy who has been with me for years. But someone is stealing from me. In the past two weeks, there's been about ten thousand dollars' worth of diamonds that have been switched out."

Wiz whistled. "Okay, well I'll start with the video footage you have and we'll see what's going on." Wiz moved his chair around to Greg's computer. "Malik told me which system you have and I should be able to tap into it and send the information to the office. You really should consider upgrading and having the agency monitor your systems."

"After this, that's what I'm planning to do. I'm just going to have to talk Malik into giving me the family discount."

Wiz grinned. "I'll put in a good word for you." He began typing in codes. "Does anyone here have access to the cameras? And does everyone have the alarm code for getting in and out of the building?"

"No one has access to this computer, which is the only way to monitor the cameras in the building. My three managers have the code for getting into the building."

For the next hour Wiz asked questions to gauge which new security system would be best suited for Greg's needs. He also watched some of the videos. He had to agree, Clayton was up to something. The way he positioned himself when handling the diamonds, he clearly knew where all the cameras were located.

A knock sounded on Greg's office door.

"Sorry to bother you," the redhead said to Greg. "There's a woman out here who says she ordered a broach last week, but I can't find any paperwork on it. She said you were the person who helped her."

"Wiz, I'll be right back."

"Okay."

Wiz moved through more frames showing different parts of the store. He stopped and watched a few minutes of footage of the sales floor and then froze.

What the ...

He zoomed in on the woman who walked into the

store and approached Clayton. Her large sunglasses shielded a portion of her face, while the short, reddish wig added to her attempt at a disguise.

Ice crept through his veins as he rewound the footage, freezing it. Noting the date and time.

A week ago.

He scooted to the edge of his seat as his pulse hammered double time.

This can't be.

He continued to stare at the woman who—despite the disguise—looked just like Olivia, but he knew it wasn't her. That would mean ...

He slammed back in his seat. "No way. There's no way in hell that can be her," he mumbled.

Wiz rewound and started watching that part of the footage again, wishing the video had sound. The heated conversation the woman was having with Clayton definitely piqued Wiz's interest. But he couldn't get over how familiar she looked.

He paused the tape, his gaze steady on the woman, studying every inch of what he could see of her.

It can't be.

There's no way that can be Keisha Abernathy.

Olivia's sister.

CHAPTER SEVEN

"Daddy!" Olivia screamed, her heart thumping wildly. "The smoke is coming from our house! Hurry!"

Her father floored the gas pedal, then skidded the car to a stop and leapt out. Flames shot out of the basement and first floor windows as he ran toward the house.

Sirens blared nearby and Olivia struggled out of her seatbelt. The moment she opened the car door, she heard her mother's screams from a second story window.

"Mama!" Olivia cried, running across the grass to the house. Her foot touched the bottom step of the concrete stoop, but someone grabbed her around the waist, lifting her off the ground. "Noooo! Let me go!" Blinded by tears, she kicked and yanked against the person holding her. "I have to help her!" she cried, coughing from the smoke coming from the opened front door.

"You can't go in there. It's too dangerous," a young male voice said close to her ear, his body like a wall behind her. Still she fought. She had to keep moving. She had to help her family. "I can't let you go in there."

It was no use. He was too strong.

A firetruck pulled up to the house and firefighters jumped out of the vehicle. A small crowd had gathered and one of the firefighters directed everyone back.

"Please. Please. Help! My parents ..." Her throat tightened and tears fell faster. *She continued pulling against the person holding her. "I have to help them. I have to help!"*

"Olivia. Olivia."

She continued to struggle against the grip on her shoulder. Her arms flailed and legs kicked despite a pain in her ankle.

"Olivia. Sweetheart, wake up. It's just a dream. Come on, wake up."

She just barely heard Wiz's voice over the pounding of her heart.

"It's okay. You're okay."

All the fight seeped out of her like a slow leak in a bicycle tire. She fought to think past the fog clogging her mind and slowly opened her eyes. Wiz leaned over her, his hand cupping her cheek and concern marring his face. He wiped at her tears, but more fell just as fast.

"You know I can't handle tears." He sat back on the sofa and pulled her onto his lap, cradling her as if she were a small child. His chin rested on top of her head as he whispered comforting words.

It had been years since she'd had the dream. *Why now?* Why after all of these years had she dreamt about the fire that took her parents' life? The fire that started because her rebellious sister had left a cigarette burning in the basement thinking that she had put it out?

"Do you want to talk about it?" Wiz's voice rumbled against her ear.

"It was the same dream. The fire." She ran her hands down her face. "It seemed so real. My mother's screams, the smell of smoke, the firefighters yelling for everyone to get back. It was as if I was right there again. Living that nightmare. Feeling that nightmare." She shivered, wrapping her arms around Wiz's midsection.

The only thing that kept Olivia from running into the burning building to go after her father that day had been Cameron. He had come out of nowhere.

They had first met months earlier when she and her family had moved to the neighborhood. Cameron lived five houses down. One morning when she had been outside raking the leaves, he was riding his bike and had stopped in front of their house. She smiled remembering how he had asked if she needed help with the leaves. Since that day, he'd been her hero.

"This is all the more reason why I can't search for your sister." Wiz's words cut into her thoughts. "You haven't had nightmares in years. Now that you want to find her, they're starting again."

Over the last couple of months, she'd had dreams about Keisha though they hadn't been all bad. Today's dream, though, she figured was sparked by her conversation with Raeanna.

Raeanna. Olivia straightened and glanced around.

"If you're looking for Raeanna, she left about an hour ago."

How long have I been out? It seemed like she had just closed her eyes.

She climbed off Wiz's lap and sat on the sofa next to him, her thoughts on the conversation with Raeanna. Hopefully she could trust the young woman, but if Wiz happened to find out what she had planned, so be it. This wouldn't be the first time they didn't agree on a subject regarding her sister. However, she really didn't want to argue with him.

"What are you thinking about?" He turned slightly, his arm behind her on the back of the sofa and his fingers sifting through her shoulder-length hair. She leaned into him.

"I know you don't think searching for Keisha is a good idea, but shouldn't it be my decision? She's my sister. I don't know if she's dead or alive."

"What if she's dead? Do you think you'd be able to handle that?"

"She's not."

Wiz fingers halted and his body tensed against hers. "How do you know?" he asked quietly, still not moving. Olivia, baffled by his reaction, leaned back and glanced at him. She didn't know what she was looking for, but his facial expression was unreadable. Rarely did his eyes give anything away, except for when he was turned on or angry. Right now, his expression was blank.

"I would know if she were dead. I would feel it here." She pointed to her heart. "If there's a chance for me to see her again and find out how she's doing, I want that chance. I know the risks, and I'm willing to take them."

"Well, I'm not!" He stood suddenly. Rubbing the back of his head, he paced near the sofa. "I'm not willing to take *any* risk when it comes to your life, especially where she's concerned!"

Olivia's heart went out to him. He always worried about her and if she were honest with herself, she should be worried, too. For years, Olivia had tried to be there for her sister, helping her when needed and trying to encourage her to change her ways, but it never seemed to be enough. To this day, she still felt guilty about not being able to protect her sister from falling in with the wrong crowd.

"Cameron," she started but stopped when she saw him shaking his head. He must have seen the pleading in her eyes. Granted, Raeanna had said she would try to help, but Olivia knew that Wiz definitely could.

"I can't do it, sweetheart." The unmistakable sound of regret in his voice made her feel bad for even asking him again. He walked back over to the sofa and sat next to her, keeping a small amount of distance between them. "I love you more ... more than I can ever express. You mean everything to me. I never, ever, want to deny you anything, but this ... this I can't do. I can't allow Keisha back into our lives. Too much has happened. We lost our baby because ..." His voice hitched and she reached for his hand and squeezed. "I know you fault the doctors or hospital for not doing more to save our child, but I blame your sister. And the last time she was in our life, you almost died. I can't go through that again."

She knew he had taken the loss of their unborn child as hard as she had. She hadn't found out that she was pregnant until a few days after he and his team had gone on one of their secret missions. Wiz missed out on the first three months of doctor visits, ultrasound pictures, and he didn't get a chance to feel their baby move inside her womb.

Olivia eased closer to him and squeezed his hand tighter, feeling his pain. From the moment they got married, they'd been trying to have a baby. After a year, she assumed she couldn't get pregnant. They went on with their lives, her attending college, and pursuing a painting career.

After seven years of marriage, they had entertained the thought of adopting, but then out of nowhere, they were pregnant. Olivia still remembered how excited Wiz had been when she told him over the telephone. Everyone within a mile radius probably heard his excitement.

Their lives changed drastically after losing the baby. The pain was so great she shut down, pushing Wiz away in the process. At the time, she could only think of herself and all that she had lost over the years, not thinking that he was suffering as well. He poured himself into his career, staying away for months at a time and barely calling. It was his way of coping.

So she asked for a divorce, which was the hardest decision she ever made. Between losing their child and fearing for his life each time he went on a mission, she couldn't handle it. He hadn't wanted the divorce, but he didn't fight it. He had told her that she was the only woman for him and that he loved her more than life, but if she wanted a divorce, he would let her go.

"I'm sorry," she said to him now. "I don't want anything, especially my sister to come between us."

"I'm sorry, too. I hate not being able to do this for you, but …"

Seems they both had been saying sorry a lot.

"I know. I know you would if you could."

He lifted her chin with the tip of his finger and lowered his head. His kiss, soft and sweet, almost brought tears to her eyes. She loved everything about this man from his brilliant mind to his unselfish nature. Add the fact that he was built like a sexy linebacker, loved her completely, and treated her like a precious jewel, and she couldn't imagine her world without him. Yet, with all of that, the desire to seek out her sister didn't diminish.

Olivia and Wiz had always promised to be honest with each other, but this was one of those times when she had to do what she needed to do. She had to find Keisha. She would just make sure Wiz never found out.

*

"Is your team able to do an audit on Terry's security system between now and next Thursday?" Malik asked when he followed Wiz into his office. "I kind of promised him that we would get someone right on it."

Wiz dropped down in his desk chair and pulled up his calendar. For the past week, they had been busier than usual considering it was closing in on the end of the year.

"That shouldn't be a problem. But you might want to stop promising stuff until after you check with us. Remember, we're in the middle of upgrading the agency's firewall and revamping the disaster recovery plan."

Malik sat at the round table, a smirk on his face. "So what you're saying is your team can't keep up with the demands."

"What I'm saying is, get the hell out of my office so I can get some work done and go home."

Malik laughed and didn't move.

Most of the day had been full of meetings and at five in the evening, Wiz should be heading out, but instead he had more work to do before leaving.

"Speaking of home, how's Olivia doing?"

"She's actually doing well. Tonight will be her first day back to class since the bombing."

Just saying the word sent a cold chill down Wiz's spine. It took everything he had not to offer to drive her or put a detail on her, but he knew she wouldn't go for it.

"What about the other situation? Has she mentioned her sister again?"

"Surprisingly, no. But I haven't really given her an opportunity to. This past week, I've been swamped. When I leave here, I hang out with her for a minute, and then spend the rest of the time in my office."

"So you've been avoiding her in order to keep the conversation from coming up again."

Damn right. He had already been on edge when Olivia first mentioned her sister. Then he freaked when he saw someone on the jewelry store's video feed who looked just like Olivia and Keisha. So yeah, he'd been avoiding Olivia. The last thing he wanted to do was discuss Keisha Abernathy.

He had asked Gary about the woman, but he said he didn't know her. When he didn't say anything about how the woman favored Olivia, Wiz wondered if he were the only one who saw the resemblance. Malik thought he was crazy, saying it couldn't be Keisha. Wiz had also made a special trip to the store to see if Clayton knew the woman. He claimed he didn't and said that the woman wanted to sell some jewelry, and she got mad when he told her she needed go to a pawn shop.

"I guess I'm right." Malik's words interrupted Wiz's thoughts. "Your punk ass is scared of little ol' Olivia."

"Don't you have something else to do?" Wiz

logged into his computer.

Malik laughed. "Actually, I should probably get ready to head out." He stood and someone knocked on the door just as he reached it.

"Hey, Malik," Raeanna said, "Hank was just looking for you. He told me that if I saw you, to tell you that he took care of what you two were talking about earlier."

"Good to know. Thanks."

"Oh and, Wiz, we're all set with Shaw Industries. The meeting is Thursday and I put it on your calendar."

"That's good, Raeanna. Thanks for taking care of that."

"No problem. You guys have a good night."

"You too."

"Oh and one more thing," Malik said to Wiz and closed the door. "Regarding the ..." His cell phone rang. "Damn. Give me a second, its Stan."

Wiz wiped his hands down his face and sighed as exhaustion settled in. The restless nights were starting to catch up to him and the anxiety swirling in his gut wasn't helping. Maybe a trip to the gun range was in order. At least there he could take out his frustrations without anyone getting hurt.

Malik shoved his phone into his pocket. "I'll be right back. I need to check on something."

"All right."

Malik once again had his hand on the doorknob just as someone knocked.

"Hey, Ollie? I was just asking about you."

Wiz glanced at his watch, surprised she was there since she had to teach a class in a couple of hours. He stood and started around his desk, unable to see her since Malik blocked the doorway.

"Hello, Malik."

Wiz froze.

Malik stepped back.

They noticed at the same time that something wasn't right. Olivia never let him get away with calling her Ollie.

Unease crept through Wiz, twisting and tugging inside his gut. He didn't have to see the woman's face to know who the low, throaty voice with a twinge of attitude belonged to.

Midnight.

CHAPTER EIGHT

Olivia armed the house alarm and climbed into her car, debating on what she would say to Cameron. They had their share of disagreements, but she thought that once she stopped asking him to search for Keisha, their life would go back to normal. Apparently not. He'd been treating her with kid gloves since the accident, claiming she was still recuperating. They weren't arguing, but she didn't like living in a house with so much ... silence.

She reached above the rearview mirror and pushed the button on the garage door opener before sticking the key into the ignition. Instead of starting the car, she rubbed her hands down the steering wheel of her new Ford Mustang GT, an early birthday present from Cameron.

She was trying not to take his silence personal, since it probably bothered him to have to say no to her. He was the toughest man she had ever met. Rarely did anything shake him. Occasionally he would get quiet on her when he was working a case out in his head, but his behavior lately made her think that something else was going on.

Her cell phone chirped and she dug it out of her bag hoping it was Wiz. Seeing Natasha's number, she answered.

"Hello."

"Hey. Where you been?" Natasha's voice boomed. "I called you yesterday."

"Tasha, I am so sorry. I totally forgot to call you back."

"No problem. I was just calling because I forgot to ask you how it went when you asked Wiz to search for your sister."

"He went ballistic."

"Wiz?" The surprise in her voice was expected. Wiz was the epitome of cool, calm, and in control. "I find that hard to believe. Are you sure you're not exaggerating?"

"Dead serious. Tasha, I have never seen him like that and trust me, I have seen him at his worst, especially after some of his missions overseas, but he was livid. I brought it up once more since then, but he made it clear that it wasn't going to happen. That's why I'm on my way to the agency right now. I can't stand the silence in the house. I want my man back."

Natasha chuckled softly. "Okay, girl. Go get your man."

Olivia smiled for the first time in days. She had originally planned to drop dinner off, but maybe, if he wasn't too busy, they could make up properly. She had to teach a fine arts class that night at the university, but she could make time for a little office fun.

*

"*Midnight*," Malik seethed, his large body still blocking the doorway.

"My name is Keisha!" She squeezed around him and stopped short when her gaze collided with Wiz's.

A heavy silence filled the space. So many questions skittered inside Wiz's brain as he stared at Olivia's twin, but the shock of seeing her strangled his vocal cords.

"Hello Cameron."

His blood ran cold. Seconds ticked by before he put one foot in front of the other and approached her. With a slow stroll around her, he took in her appearance from her bone straight, shoulder-length hair, to the loose fitting Bohemian pants that were so much like what Olivia would wear. She had gone to great lengths to look like her sister, dropping her seductive, almost ho-like style for a classy, chic appearance ... like Olivia.

She fidgeted under his scrutiny.

His gaze moved back to her face. There was one noticeable difference. Her eyes. Cold. Challenging. Calculating. Their eyes. That's how he'd always been able to tell them apart.

When he remained speechless, she asked, "Can we talk?"

"Hell-the-fuck nah you can't talk to him!" Malik growled, standing in front of her again. "As a matter of fact, I'm wondering how the hell you got into my building!"

That was the one thing Wiz wasn't wondering. She was Olivia's identical twin. No doubt the receptionist thought she was his wife and let her in. With the new security system, that was the only way she could have gotten to the back offices.

"I wasn't talking to you. I was talking to Cameron!"

Keisha's voice shook Wiz out of his trance. He still couldn't get his words to work and gave a slight nod to Malik who stepped aside. Instead of leaving, Malik closed the door and leaned against it. They had an understanding. They never met with a woman behind closed doors if at all possible. And considering Wiz's history with this woman, there was no way Malik would leave.

Keisha turned back to Malik. "Do you mind? This is private."

"He stays." Wiz walked around to the other side of his desk, putting as much space between them as possible.

Her gaze raked over him with the hunger of a tiger sizing up its prey. Rarely did much rattle him, but the way her eyes took him in, he wanted to reach for his spare weapon, snug against his ankle and shoot her between the eyes. That's how much he despised her. Outside of some of the terrorists he and his SEAL team came face-to-face with, he had never hated anyone as much as he did Keisha Abernathy.

"You're looking good, Cameron." She licked her ruby red lips. Her deep, seductive voice felt like a knife slicing through his body.

"Get out." His words were spoken low, but had a lethal edge to them. Anybody else would have felt the anger behind each syllable and hightailed it out of there. Not Keisha. "I ... said ... get the hell out of my office!"

She jerked as if slapped across her cheek.

Malik opened the office door. "You heard the

man."

Her panic-stricken eyes pleaded with Wiz. "What? No. Wait! I need your help. Please, just hear me out."

Malik's humorless laugh bounced off the walls. "Damn, girl, you have some big cojones. I can't believe your ass was bold enough to ever show your face in Chicago again, but to ask for his help? Your brain must be fried from that shit you're probably still snorting."

"Again, I'm not talking to you," she growled at Malik. "I'm talking to——"

"It doesn't matter who you're talking to. You are out of your mind if you think you can ask me for anything." Wiz's voice was steady, despite the cluster of emotions roaring inside of him and the barely controlled anger seeping through his pores. "I spared your life once. That was it. As a matter of fact, you've gone back on our agreement." He reached for the phone on his desk with the intentions of calling his detective friend, Sheldon Baker. Wiz knew he should have turned her in years ago and he had a feeling he would regret the decision not to for the rest of his life.

"Please, Cameron. I've changed. Just give me a chance to explain why I'm here."

He set the phone down and sat in his chair, not trusting his legs to continue holding him up. Seeing her standing in the middle of his office sickened him, but curiosity was getting the best of him. The phrase keep your friends close and your enemies closer immediately came to mind.

"Cameron, I swear I've changed." She crept closer, her eyes pleading when his gaze met hers. He wasn't sure what she saw in his eyes, but she had sense enough to stop before she reached his desk.

His mind took him back to the time when she had tried seducing him. Had come into his home, into his bedroom, butt naked, pretending to be Olivia.

He shook his head, trying to clear the thought but failing. He had realized who she was the moment she stepped closer to him. Her eyes, her scent, and then the small mole on her collarbone gave her away. If that weren't enough, the moment she spoke his name, he put distance between them. And of course Olivia had picked that moment to walk in.

Wiz returned his attention to Keisha, saw her lips moving, but had tuned out to what she was saying. He still couldn't believe she was standing in his office and the fact that she looked so much like Olivia was screwing with his brain.

"I've been clean for over seven years and have stayed out of trouble."

"How did you find me?" Wiz asked, not missing the panic that showed in her eyes. "Speak or get out."

"I googled you. I saw that you were a P.I. and this address was listed. I took a chance and decided to stop by. The lady at the front desk thought I was Olivia."

That was probably the only honest thing Keisha had said since walking through the door. What he didn't like was that she'd sought him out. He also didn't like that she was at his place of business pretending to be his wife.

"We had an agreement. I agreed not to turn your ass into the authorities for attempted murder that probably would have led to a host of other charges. *And* I let you live if you agreed to stay the hell away from my wife ... forever."

"Olivia is not your wife!" she snarled, but must have remembered that she was there for his help. "I'm sorry. I didn't mean …"

Keisha's jealousy of her sister was one of her problems. She wanted the life Olivia had.

Wiz stood slowly, gripping the edge of his desk tightly instead of reaching out and wrapping his hands around her scrawny little neck. It appeared this woman had really done her homework if she knew that he and Olivia weren't officially married.

Instead of addressing how she knew, he said, "Olivia will *always* be my wife and you need to understand that. You also need to understand that if you go anywhere near *my wife*, you'll regret the day you every met me."

"I'm sorry." Keisha lifted her hands out in front of her. "I didn't come here to cause any trouble. I just need your help. If you help me get out of the country, I swear you will never see me again."

Wiz rolled his eyes. Memories of that night, the last time he'd seen Keisha, exploded through his mind. His fingers wrenched tighter around the edge of his desk. That was the night he had almost taken a knife to her throat. Olivia was the only reason he had spared her. Wiz knew he wouldn't have been able to live with himself if Olivia found out that he had killed her sister. As it was, he didn't want her to find out that he'd orchestrated Keisha's disappearance. The agreement was that she would never step foot on American soil again. Yet, here she was, standing in the middle of his office.

"You're already supposed to be out of the country!" Malik snapped, as if reading Wiz's mind. "Why are you here? Why are you back in Chicago?"

"I moved back a year ago … to New York to get married."

Wiz didn't know why he bothered asking her anything seeing that he didn't believe anything that came out of her mouth. But one thing he did know was that whatever mess she was involved in was more threatening to her than his wrath.

"I've been living there and had no intention of coming to Chicago. Cameron, I promise, I didn't come here to start any trouble. I just need your help."

"How long have you been in Chicago?" Wiz asked.

"A few days." She fidgeted and dropped her gaze.

Wiz glanced at Malik. That might have been her at the jewelry store. Which means she'd been in town for a couple of weeks.

"What do you want from me?"

"I told you, I need you to help me get out of the country. I want to start a new life. I … I just don't have enough money."

"If you came back to get married, why leave now? What about this fiancé of yours?"

"I saw … I witnessed something."

"Witnessed what?"

"A murder. I saw my fiancé kill a man and … and I ran. I left New York and didn't know where else to go so I came here."

Unease ran through Wiz's veins. He knew the type of people Keisha hung with. They were bad news. She might be clean. She wasn't shaking and didn't look to be having any withdrawals. Still, he didn't trust her.

He turned and stared out the window behind his desk. All he could think about was Olivia. Whenever Keisha was around, Olivia got hurt, either emotionally or physically. He couldn't let that happen again. He couldn't risk almost losing her again. On the other hand, Olivia didn't ask him for much and she wanted to see her sister. Maybe he could arrange it and then make Keisha disappear for good.

He needed to think about all of this. He turned and lifted the telephone receiver to his ear, hoping Victoria was back at her desk from a dentist appointment.

"What's up, Wiz?" she answered on the first ring.

"Can you come into my office for a minute?"

"Sure. Is Boss Man with you?" she asked of Malik.

"Yeah, he's here."

"I'll be right there."

Seconds later the door swung open and all eyes went to Victoria. Seeming to ignore their stares, she said nothing as she eased farther into the office, her gaze taking in Keisha.

"I didn't know Olivia was a twin."

"How the hell…" Malik started but stopped.

Wiz was shocked, too. As far as he knew, there were only two people who could tell the twins apart at first glance—him and Quinn. Now Wiz could add Victoria to the short list.

"Yeah, this is the evil twin," Malik grumbled and leaned against a far wall.

"Fuck you," Keisha said under her breath.

"Never going to happen," Malik added.

"Vicky, can you take Keisha to conference room D? I'll be there in a few."

He couldn't stand to look at Keisha and wanted to ensure that no one else in the building saw her. They had lucked out that it was the end of the day, and most of the people on that floor should've be gone by now.

"No problem." Victoria must have sensed the tension in the room. She didn't crack a smile, nor did she try to engage Keisha in conversation, which was something she normally would have done.

"And don't let her out of your sight," Malik added just before Victoria closed the door. Then he turned to Wiz. "Like I said before, never leave fuckin' loose ends! Do you see what type of shit happens when you fail to tie loose ends? This is what happens! Dammit, I knew we should have taken care of her back then."

His words were spoken vacant of emotion. More often than not, Wiz didn't agree with his long-time friend who was more like a brother. But now he had to agree. The decision to let Keisha live hadn't been an easy one to make, but he couldn't do that to Olivia. He couldn't take her sister's life and had decided on the next best thing. He made her disappear. Or so he thought.

"At least if she were dead," Malik continued, "you could pretend to search for her. Ollie knows that you're the best. If you can't find someone, no one can."

"I can't lie to Olivia. I never have and I never will."

"Omitting the truth is the same as lying."

"Not in my book," Wiz countered.

Wiz sat in his desk chair and closed his eyes. He didn't believe in coincidences and Keisha making an appearance out of the blue after ten years, days after Olivia's request, was too much of a coincidence. He'd heard that twins had some type of connection, but this was too much.

His heart rate kicked up a notch. Who knew what

Keisha was involved in, and the thought that she might have been watching Olivia from a distance scared Wiz to death. And worse, whatever she was involved in might have followed her to Chicago.

"I might need to put someone on Olivia." She would fight him if she knew, so he would have to do it without her knowing.

"Hell, we need to put someone on Midnight. There's no telling what she's involved in. We have to get rid of her once and for all."

"I know, but—"

"No buts. Her ass has to go. That shit she pulled the last time we saw her … that can't happen again. Olivia is like a sister to me. If you're—"

"I know, Tree. I know." His friend's nickname slipped out without much thought. The conversation felt similar to one they would have during their military days.

"Tell me you don't believe that crap about her changing. People like her don't change."

"I agree. I need to ask her some more questions and do some digging, but right now, I have to wrap my brain around her being here."

"So how do you want to handle this?"

"I want us to keep an eye on her until I get more facts about her story." Wiz stood and shoved his hands into his front pockets. "Then I need to decide if I'm going to tell Olivia that her sister is here."

CHAPTER NINE

Olivia stepped off the elevator and slowed once she was in the reception area. When Malik had first purchased the building, he commissioned her to do the artwork for the top two floors. It gave her pride to walk into a space knowing that all of the pieces displayed, paintings and photographs, she created.

"Hi Olivia. You're back," the receptionist greeted. "I'm surprised to see you here so late."

"Hey, Cynthia. Yeah, I figured I'd bring Cameron some dinner otherwise he'd probably forget to eat."

"I wish I could forget to eat sometime, but I'm too greedy for that." She patted her flat stomach.

"Please. You look great. Oh, and welcome back. How was your trip?"

Cynthia had been with the company for a year. Her warm personality and beautiful smile made her perfect for her position. One of the requirements of any position at the company was that you had to either be military, former military, or had some type of security background. Cynthia was army reserve and had just returned from her annual training.

"Rigorous, long, and exhausting. Other than that, it was great." They both laughed and talked for a few minutes longer.

"Here, I can buzz you through."

"That's okay, I'll use my code." Cameron had recently told her that it was best to use her code. It helped them keep a better handle on who was in the building and their arrival time, as well as the time they left.

Olivia strolled down the hall to where Cameron and Malik's offices were located. She slowed when she arrived in their area, surprised Victoria wasn't at her desk. Like Malik and Cameron, she often stayed later on Mondays.

Noticing the door to Cameron's office was partially open, she knocked before pushing it farther open.

He stood behind his desk, his head lowered as if in deep thought. So focused on the documents in front of him he hadn't noticed her appearance which was unusual. His senses were as sharp as a butcher knife and his lack of awareness would definitely go down as another first.

Olivia silently took in his appearance. The way the sage colored cashmere sweater stretched across his wide chest emphasizing his muscular biceps. The sleeves pushed up showed off his powerful forearms and no one filled a pair of jeans like he could. The way they emphasized his powerful thighs sent a shot of desire shooting to her core.

A slight shudder forced her gaze back up his body and guilt speared Olivia in the chest. He seemed to have the weight of the world on his shoulders and it was her fault. If only she hadn't asked him to search for Keisha.

"Cameron?"

His head snapped up. His reading glasses hung on the edge of his nose, giving him a nerdy, hunk-like appearance. He definitely had that Clark Kent thing going on that she absolutely loved and that always got her juices flowing.

She gave him an easy smile, but it slipped from her lips when she really looked at him. His gaze swept over her body, a haunted look in his tired eyes. Those green, laser-like beams bore into her and she quivered under his penetrating stare.

Maybe things were worse between them than she originally thought. He continued to stare wordlessly at her.

"May I come in?"

He removed his glasses and shook his head as if knocking away cobwebs. Lust-filled tingles skittered along her arms when his eyes softened and the love she always felt with him shone in them.

"Of course. I'm sorry, sweetheart. C'mere. It's been … it's been a strange evening and I guess I'm more tired than I realized."

She barely had time to place her purse and the dinner bag in a nearby chair before he pulled her into a tight embrace.

She wrapped her arms around him, closing her eyes, and breathing him in. His fresh scent, a mixture of soap and citrusy aftershave, relaxed her. The comfort of his hug made her feel like all was well. She never wanted him to let her go.

"I love you so damn much," he growled into her

hair, tightening his hold.

She almost told him the feelings were mutual, but he knew. Just like she knew their disagreement was troubling him. He wasn't the arguing type. Of his close friends, he was the peacemaker, the go-to guy. He took such good care of the people he loved, especially her.

"I hate when there's tension between us," she said.

He pulled back and cupped her chin, forcing her to meet his gaze. "Me too. I'm so sorry about what I said at the hotel. Making you uncomfortable ... I never want you to be afraid to ask me for anything. I know I messed that up, but I want you to know that you mean everything to me. Your happiness and safety is my top priority." He kissed her sweetly. Had he not been holding her, she would have easily puddled to the floor at his heart felt words and the tenderness of his kiss.

Olivia wasn't quite sure what to make of his declaration. After the incident at the university, he had apologized for his behavior at the hotel and she thought they had moved on, but maybe not.

He loosened his grip and closed his office door. His hand rested at the small of her back as he guided her farther into the office, sending a sweet thrill along her spine. She loved that after so many years, his touch still sent tingles through her body.

"So what are you doing here?"

"I've missed you. I wanted to see you since we haven't seen much of each other in the last few days. Also, I brought you a peace offering. Dinner." She handed him the bag of food and watched as he set it on the table and dug through it, pulling containers out.

"Thank you." He drew her in for another kiss. "I know we still need to talk about your sister, but right now—"

"Wiz do ..." Malik started when the door swung open, his words trailing off as he stared at Olivia.

What the heck is going on?

"Hey, Olivia. I'm surprised to see you."

Now she knew something was wrong. She couldn't remember the last time Malik called her by her given name. She didn't actually hate the nickname he'd given her, she just liked giving him a hard time when he used it, and now it was weird not hearing him say Ollie. And he claimed she was like a little sister he never had from the moment Cameron had introduced them, always greeting her with a hug. Yet, he hadn't moved from the door and looked as if he were seeing a ghost.

Studying them both, the tension was so thick she immediately went on alert.

"What's wrong? You guys are scaring me. Did something happen?"

"I'm sorry, baby. It's been a fu— messed up day." Malik wrapped her in a hug and then told Cameron, "Come see me when you're done here." Placing a kiss on her cheek, Malik told her he would catch her later and left them standing in the same spot.

"Please tell me if something's wrong. You and Malik are acting strange."

"Everything is fine." Wiz rubbed his hand over his head, something he did when he was tired or frustrated. "We just have a situation we have to take care of."

She searched his eyes for ... for what she wasn't sure. As far as she knew, he'd never lied to her, but she also knew that he never wanted her to worry. He would keep things from her if he felt she couldn't handle it.

"Does that mean you're going to be home late tonight?"

Wiz shook his head. "No. I should be there by the time you get home."

She studied him for a while longer. "Are we okay?"

"We will be." When he pulled her back into his arms, she could have sworn she felt him shudder. She wrapped her arms tightly around his waist, trying to help ease the tension ricocheting off his body. A hug might not have been much, but she hoped he felt the love she had for him.

Olivia placed a kiss on him just below his jaw, the light scruff on his face tickling her lips.

"I don't know what I'd do without you," he whispered near her ear, his voice full of emotion.

"Well, good thing you'll never have to find out."

She placed her hand at the nape of his neck, just below his hairline, and stared into his amazing eyes. She loved the way they turned colors depending on his mood, and right now they were a deep green, radiating with desire. Seems they had the same thing on their mind.

"I ..." she started, but stopped and gazed at his luscious mouth. Instead of saying more, she pulled him in for a kiss, putting everything she had in the lip-lock. She needed him to know how much she loved him, how much she needed him, and how much she wanted him.

After a brief hesitation on his part, he kissed her with a hunger that sent the pit of her stomach spiraling into a wild ride, leaving no doubt they wanted the same thing. He kissed and nipped at her neck causing goosebumps to raise up on her skin.

"God I want you," he growled and backed her to the door. Locking it. She gasped when he scooped her into his arms. Her legs went automatically around his narrow waist and her arms around his neck. "How much time do you have?" he asked—his voice a low rumble filled with longing—as he carried her to a nearby wall.

"Forty-five minutes before I have to be standing in front of my class," she mumbled against his lips, her inner core throbbing in anticipation.

"More than enough time." He propped her against the wall, lifting her skirt as he cradled her bottom. He ravished her mouth, her tongue tangling with his. The deep and thorough kiss along with the bumping and grinding was almost her undoing. They never had a problem in the bedroom, or against a wall for that matter. And she had to admit that she loved it when he got all hot, bothered, and out of control like he was now.

Normally everything he did in life was precise and methodical, even when it came to making love. He was always thorough, making sure her needs came first, but this ... This was different. The animalistic sounds coming from him, and the urgency of his moves lit a spark inside of her that sent heat through her body as he devoured her mouth.

He lifted her a little higher and his lips worked their way down her cheek, to her neck, stopping at the top of her V-neck sweater. Groaning, he kneaded her butt cheeks as he sucked the top of her breast. Her heart rate spiked when she felt a little sting where he bit her, marking what was his.

"I need you," he mumbled when he went back to her mouth. Capturing her lower lip, he gently pulled it between his teeth before teasing her upper one. He pushed her skirt a little higher and settled more between her thighs.

"You're so wet," he rasped as he palmed her lace-covered sex. The thin material did nothing to deflect the heat from his touch, scorching every single nerve ending within her body and sending her into a tizzy. When he edged her panties to the side and slipped two fingers into her heat, she moaned with pleasure wanting so much more.

Her hands gripped each side of his face as his tongue slipped between her lips, moving in sync with the fingers that were doing wicked things to the lower region of her body. Their kiss was urgent and demanding. He growled into her mouth as her hips moved to the rhythm he had set.

"Wiz," she breathed, breaking the kiss, her hands now on his shoulders, gripping them as his skilled fingers continued to slide in and out of her with more speed. Unsure of what she intended to say, if anything, she held on tighter and moved frantically against his hands. She had no idea how he could maintain the hold on her especially since she couldn't control her own movements. The sweet torture short-circuited her brain as she grew closer to her release.

She whimpered, her eyes tightly closed as she jerked and bucked in his arms. She gasped when he drove deeper and faster inside of her sending her mind into a tailspin.

"Come for me, sweetheart."

As if his words had the power to make her let

loose, an orgasm ripped through her body with such force, a scream rose to her throat.

Wiz's mouth quickly covered hers, stifling her erotic sounds as her body convulsed against him. Hot, molten lava coursed through her like a volcano during an eruption, sending her tumbling over the edge of a cliff.

"Hold on," he said as if she had the strength to do anything but. Her body, depleted of energy, sagged against him.

He lowered her until her feet touched the floor. Despite having the skirt bunched around her waist, he quickly slid her damp panties over her hips. Still trying to catch her breath, Olivia was no help as he tugged them down her thighs, along her legs, and past her knee-high boots before they landed on the floor.

With one hand, he made fast work of unfastening his pants, letting them and his boxer briefs pool around his ankle.

Hot. Hard. Sexy. Were the words floating around her head as she glanced down between their bodies. She would prefer if they were both completely naked, but a quickie when he was hot and bothered, she wouldn't pass up.

"I need you."

He lifted her before she could form her next thought and adjusted his grip on her bare ass before staring into her eyes, his orbs boring into her like a laser beam. She groaned when the blunt head of his cock grazed her slick folds, teasing, stroking and reigniting that flame he'd started moments ago. Her legs trembled around him and her stomach did a flip-flop when he continued to tease at her opening. The sweet torture pushed her back to the edge of her control. When he slid inside her, heat shot to the tips of her toes and her eyes slammed shut. The power he exuded, the way he held her as he lifted her body up and down his shaft, was just as much of a turn on as feeling him grow thicker and longer inside of her.

"Damn, baby," he said between gritted teeth. "You're wet for me."

His mouth suddenly covered hers with an urgency that sent prickles of heat down to her core. She squeezed her thighs together, wanting to feel even more of him.

Wiz cursed against her mouth when she tightened her legs around him. Her sex gripped him with force. He knew this was supposed to be a quickie, but the control she had over her body was sure to be his undoing if she kept this up.

He moved his hands to the bottom of her thighs to help regain some traction. Her eyes were barely open. The left side of her sweet lips tilted slightly, knowing she was pushing him to a point of no return.

Unable to get enough of her sweetness, Wiz captured her lips again, his lower body moving on its own accord. Her whimpering sounds of pleasure were driving him crazy, making him go faster, deeper, harder.

A groan rumbled from the back of his throat as her moves became more frantic, her muscles contracting around his throbbing length. The sensation of being buried deep inside of her, in this position was like no other.

Her head swiped back and forth against the wall. She was close to losing it as she rotated her hips, her moves more jerky. At this rate, he'd be right behind her.

Her body stiffened and she exploded around him. His fingers dug into her thighs as she shook violently, his grip tightened, and with one last thrust, he held on tight no longer able to control his own powerful release.

He dropped his forehead against the wall, unable to move, as their heavy breathing filled the office space.

Damn that was intense.

Seconds ticked by before he was finally able to lift his head. Still buried inside of her, he couldn't remember the last time he had been so out of control. He knew she liked it rough, but he didn't like taking her against a damn wall like some madman. In the military, keeping his head was key to staying alive. But when he was with Olivia, inside of her, he couldn't think straight.

"I didn't hurt you, did I?" he finally asked, still panting.

An exhausted, yet seductive smile graced her lips. "No. That was amazing." She slumped against him as he continued holding her against the wall.

"You're amazing." He kissed her cheek. Once their breathing was under control, he eased her down his body until her feet touched the floor, keeping a hand on her, making sure she was steady. He touched her chin, forcing her to meet his gaze. "You sure you're okay?"

She gnawed her bottom lip and nodded, suddenly looking a little shy. He smiled. Apparently the reality of what they had just done had finally hit her. Sure they'd had sex in his home office, in the garage, in their walk-in closet, but never here. He had to admit, that it was hot watching her come apart against a wall in his office, not knowing if any employees were within earshot.

After they cleaned up in the attached bathroom, Wiz walked her to the door.

"Maybe we can picked this up later," he said, and pulled her into his arms.

"I'm counting on it." She placed a kiss against his neck.

He loved it when her arms were around him. The way she held him, squeezed him had often made him forget. Forget how his mother had been killed. Forget the crap he had seen during missions, and almost made him forget how much he hated her sister.

The sudden thought reminded him that she was still in the building, assuming Malik hadn't tossed her into the trash compactor. He couldn't believe that he'd forgotten that he still had to deal with her. But he had to admit he enjoyed the beautiful distraction in his arms.

Wiz didn't know how long they stood there, near his office door, holding each other. He loved that Olivia never allowed him to stew for more than a day or two, always finding a way to pull him out of his funk. And tonight he was glad she had taken the initiative to check on him.

"Okay, I'd better get going so that I'm not too late for class."

"All right."

Instead of walking Olivia to the elevator, he rode down to the parking garage with her. The last thing he needed was for her to run into Keisha.

"I can't wait to see you later," she said when he opened the car door for her.

"Me too, sweetie. Drive safe." He kissed her soft

lips and waited until she pulled away before he headed back to the elevator. Now, to decide what to do about Keisha.

*

"Let me make sure I have this right." Wiz stood in the small conference room, his arms folded across his chest as he listened to Keisha's story. After the quick tryst with Olivia, he had walked into the room energized and feeling better than he had in days. Now, after going back and forth with his sister-in-law, he needed a stiff drink. "You met your fiancé, this Dwight Watson guy, while you were living in Argentina and he was vacationing there."

"Exactly what does he do for a living?" Malik asked, standing across the room appearing just as frustrated as Wiz.

"I told you. He's a business man. He invests in real estate and he's a diamond dealer."

"A diamond dealer?" Wiz and Malik said at the same time.

"How the hell did you hook a damn diamond dealer?" Malik asked, and Wiz's mind drifted back to the jewelry store's security footage.

"I guess I have it like that." She crossed her leg, her black wedge heel shoe dangling from her foot. "We hung out and one thing led to another," she shrugged, "and we clicked."

"How did you end up in New York?" Part of Wiz didn't want to know, or at least didn't want to know her version. What he really wanted was to send her on her way in hopes of never seeing her again. He had never met a woman as arrogant, and irritating with a penchant for trouble as her.

"That's where he lives. He sent me a ticket and

told me he wanted me to visit him. I told him I couldn't, that I didn't want to ever step foot in the country, but he was persistent. I gave in and everything was going great. He treated me like a queen."

"So you risked going to jail, or worse," Malik glanced at Wiz before returning his attention to her, "in order to be with this guy? I guess you conveniently forgot about the agreement you had with Wiz."

She glanced down and picked some invisible lint from her black sweater. Wiz had no doubt she was trying to form a good lie.

"I didn't forget," she mumbled. "I just … it was lonely in South America. He offered to fill that void in my life and we fell in love. Being with him was worth the risk. You know what that's like, Cameron. To love someone so much that you don't see reason. That nothing else matters."

"I know what it's like to love someone so much that I'd give my life to protect her from anyone who means her harm," Wiz said pointedly, his gaze never leaving Keisha. Surely this woman wasn't trying to compare what she had with some random guy with what he and Olivia shared. "Which means that since you forfeited our agreement, I should just turn you over to the authorities and give them everything I've collected on you."

"Isn't there some type of statute of limitations?" The smirk on her face showed she knew the statute of limitations for her crimes had passed.

Wiz didn't care. He knew her well enough to know that whatever really brought her to Chicago had to do with something shady.

"But none of that matters. I told you, I've changed." Keisha sat forward in her seat. "I've gotten my life back on track, but I just need your help this one last time."

Wiz pushed away from the wall and leaned on the table close to where she sat. "Cut the bullshit. Why are you trying to get out of the country?"

"I told you. I saw my fiancé kill a man, one of his friends. I don't want anything like that linked to me."

"You know what I think?" Wiz said. "I think you told your boyfriend that his friend came on to you. Knowing how you operate, I wouldn't be surprised if you told him that this guy assaulted you in some way, knowing that he'd get angry enough to kill someone."

"That's not what happened!" she spat angrily. Wiz didn't believe her. Even if that wasn't how things played out, he had no doubt that Keisha had more to do with the killing than she was making it out to be, assuming someone had been killed. "You weren't there. It was awful."

"What else? Because I'm sure there's more to this story. Where were you when all of this supposedly took place?" Malik questioned, leaning on the back of the chair next to hers.

"I was in the hallway. I wasn't trying to hear what they were saying, I was on my way to the kitchen, heard arguing and stopped near the door. Then he shot him … point blank. I was shocked. I ran to our bedroom, grabbed what I could carry, and got out of there as fast as I could. The first couple of days after I left, he kept calling me so I ditched the phone and haven't heard from him since."

Wiz had no intention of helping her get anywhere unless she was involved in something that would somehow affect Olivia.

"Give me a couple of days and I'll see what I can do. Where are you staying?"

She gave him the name of a seedy motel on the south side of Chicago as well as her cell number. Had she been anyone else, he would have found her better accommodations. But as it was, he didn't even want her in the same country as Olivia, let alone the same city.

"I'll be in touch." He opened the door for her to leave.

She stood and adjusted her clothes, paying extra attention to her small bosom. "Before I leave town, I'd like to see my sister."

Annoyance tightened in his chest. "That's not going to happen."

Though Wiz had considered letting Olivia know that Keisha was in town, after hearing her story, he knew it would be best to keep them apart.

"I've changed, Cameron. Besides, shouldn't that be Olivia's call, to see me … or not? She can make her own decisions and take care of herself. You're not her keeper or her daddy."

"You're right, I'm not her daddy. As a matter of fact, she doesn't have a daddy thanks to you. Or have you forgotten about the house fire that you started, killing your parents?"

"That was an accident," she replied quietly, having the nerve to look distraught. Wiz wasn't buying it. She hadn't shown much remorse then and he doubted she cared now.

"You just stay the hell away from my wife."

"And if I don't?"

"Try me and find out."

Without another word, Wiz escorted Keisha out of the building and to guest parking. He took note of her license plate number as she pulled away. It was time to dig into the life of Keisha Abernathy.

CHAPTER TEN

"Hey! Come on in you guys." Wiz opened the door to Victoria and her date.

The house was filling up with friends there to celebrate Olivia's thirty-fifth birthday. After the last two weeks she'd had, he was glad that tonight she would be surrounded by people who loved her.

"Hey, Wiz." Victoria accepted the kiss he placed on her cheek and then turned to her date. "This is Tim, Tim this is Cameron. He's one of the partners at the agency."

"Nice to meet you." Tim shook Wiz's hand, his grip solid, which said a lot in Wiz's opinion. Victoria dated periodically, mostly military guys, but rarely did she bring them around him and Malik. Mainly Malik. He scrutinized all of her boyfriends, claiming he didn't want his surrogate sister dating some loser.

"Nice to meet you, too," Wiz said. "Come in and make yourself comfortable."

"Where do the gifts go?" Victoria lifted a

beautifully wrapped box and he pointed to the long table to his left. He started closing the front door but she stopped him.

"Stan and Layla are right behind us," she said over her shoulder, guiding Tim farther into the house.

Stan knocked on the door with his cane. "If I didn't know any better, I would say you were trying to keep us out."

"Only you, man. It's a good thing you're with this beautiful woman. Hey there." He placed a kiss on Layla's cheek.

"You're right. She is beautiful."

"Oh stop. You two are going to make me blush." She grinned and leaned into Stan, her cheeks tinting.

"Olivia just said that she hoped you both were going to make it tonight."

Stan, one of the security specialists with the agency, had been injured while providing security detail to Natasha months earlier. Layla, Natasha's best friend and a nurse, had nurtured him back to health and they'd been together ever since.

Wiz spent the next hour making his rounds, greeting each guest and ensuring that glasses were full. He stopped near the archway that divided their dining room from the family room and took a swig from his beer. R & B music played in the background as everyone talked and laughed, having a good time.

Olivia's birthday party had grown bigger than they had planned, but as long as she was happy that was all that mattered to him.

That smile.

Dallas had said something to Olivia that brought out that smile that always made Wiz's heart turn to mush.

"Are you just going to stand here staring at Ollie all night?" Malik asked, his large hand wrapped around a glass holding dark liquor. Wiz assumed it was bourbon since it was his friend's drink of choice tonight. "You're watching her like she's a perp staking out the joint with plans to steal something."

Wiz shook his head and chuckled. "Man, the stuff that comes out of your mouth. If you must know, I'm looking at my beautiful wife because it seems as if she's fading. She's still not a hundred percent."

"Yeah, I did notice she looked a little green around the gills. I thought it was because she's a year older, but I guess not. When I mentioned it to her, she punched me." He rubbed his thick bicep as if she had really done damage to it.

Wiz laughed. "Man, you're a fool. You're lucky she didn't do more than that. Her self-defense skills are top notched." After the situation with Natasha and the guy who attacked her, Wiz had started teaching Olivia a few moves. She was already comfortable with handling a gun, but her self-defense skills had been lacking.

"Well, I wish she would share some of her moves with Natasha. Every time I try to teach her anything or get her to go to the gun range with me, she gives me that bullshit about her being in the business of saving lives, not taking them."

"Well, she is a doctor by trade."

"Yeah, yeah, whatever. That's just an excuse she uses. She needs to get serious about self-defense." Malik brought his drink to his lips and sipped. "So how did it go with the diamond-studded watch for Olivia? Did you tell her that it has a GPS in it?"

"Of course not. She loved it but would have had a

fit if she knew about the tracker. She already thinks I'm overprotective."

"Really? I wonder why she thinks that." Sarcasm dripped from Malik's words. "You have to admit, you are a little extreme with your possessiveness when it comes to her."

"You would be too if Tasha had a psycho sister who attracted trouble like honey attracts bees." He pointed his beer bottle at Natasha who was across the room. "You should be the last person to talk about someone being overprotective and possessive. Poor Tasha can barely take a step without you following behind her. And on that note, I'm going over there to rescue the love of my life from your brother."

"Why do you have your arms around my wife?" Wiz asked when he walked into the family room.

"As I understand it, she's not your wife yet. There's still a chance that I can steal her away from you," Hunter Graham said. "Besides, I think she's ready for a younger version of you."

A NBA superstar, Hunter had flown to Chicago for the day upon Malik's insistence to discuss him needing a security detail. Hunter had recently been called out by the media, claiming he had a gambling problem and has since had a few run-ins with the paparazzi.

"Careful, Hunter. You know Wiz don't play when it comes to Ollie. Many have overstepped and to this day we haven't seen hide nor hair of them," Malik remarked, joining the group, his glass held up saluting Wiz.

"Listen, to your big brother, man." Wiz nudged Hunter aside and wrapped his arm around Olivia. He placed a noisy kiss on her cheek. "She's all mine. Ain't that right, sweetheart?"

She glanced at him, that beautiful smile of hers squeezing his heart. He fell more and more in love with her each passing day.

"That's right. You're the only one for me."

She raised up on tiptoes and placed a sweet kiss against his lips.

Hunter's hand went to his heart. "Olivia, you wound me. I thought we had something special."

She laughed, snuggling closer to Wiz. He held her around the waist and stared down into her big, brown, tired eyes.

"Okay you guys, I'm stealing the birthday girl away for a minute." Wiz looped his arm around Olivia's shoulder. "Make yourselves at home and, Natasha, you're in charge."

"I think I can handle that." She grinned.

"Oh, wait." Olivia turned to the group. "Hunter, I hope you're planning to be at the wedding."

"Wouldn't miss it, babe, though you'll be breaking my heart marrying someone other than me."

She shook her head. "Considering the number of women vying for your attention, I'm sure you'll survive."

"Yeah, maybe," he grumbled, his sad expression a bit overkill in Wiz's opinion.

"I'm not sure where you're taking me, but can we stop in the kitchen?"

"Sure." When he went to her, he didn't really have a plan, he just wanted to check and make sure she was doing all right.

After grabbing a bottle of water from the cooler near the patio door, she leaned against the kitchen counter. She lifted her foot, twisting it back and forth.

He set down his bottle. "Why don't you sit for a while, or at least put on some flats?" he asked against her ear and kissed her on the neck. He rubbed his body against her backside, quickly realizing that was a bad idea when his body stirred to attention. "I'm sure no one will mind if you're not floating around the room, being the perfect hostess by trying to talk to everyone."

She reached back without turning and patted his cheek. "I'm fine. And if you don't stop grinding against me, you're going to start a little something."

"If that will get you off your feet, maybe I should."

She laughed and turned to face him. He blocked her in with his hands braced on the countertop on each side of her.

"Maybe you should." Her sauciness was a serious turn on. She placed her hand behind his head and pulled him close. She nibbled on his top lip and then pulled at his lower lip before slipping her tongue into his mouth.

He groaned and pulled her hard against his body. He would never get enough of her sweet mouth, but he knew that if they didn't stop, a certain part of his anatomy was going to reveal what was on his mind.

"Okay, maybe you are fine," he mumbled against her lips before pulling back.

"I told you." She grinned.

"God I love you." He cupped her cheek. "Promise me that you'll sit down for a little while."

"I love you, too, and I promise."

He didn't want to let her go, but when the doorbell rang, she insisted on answering the door.

He adjusted himself and watched Olivia glide across the room. She didn't seem to be limping as her hips swung left, then right seductively. She might have been thin, but that sexy ass of hers was shapely and enticing.

He lifted his beer bottle from the counter and brought it to his lips. Taking a swig, he almost choked when Olivia screamed.

What the …

He set the bottle down and rushed to the door, but stopped. Ice ran through his veins when Olivia appeared with her arm looped around the shoulder of the new arriver.

Keisha.

He could have sworn he heard Malik say shit, but he wasn't sure. All he could focus on was the woman who was bold enough to walk into his home as if she'd been invited.

"I can't believe you're here." Olivia wrapped her arm around Keisha and pulled her close again for a hug. "You look great. Everyone, if you hadn't noticed, this is my twin sister who I haven't seen in years."

Cheers and claps went up all around. Anger exploded inside of Wiz. All the chatter and music faded to the background as he charged across the room. It was like his body had a mind of its own and he had no control over what he was about to do. All he could see was Keisha standing just inside their front door with that fake smile spread across her lips.

He clenched and unclenched his fists, his hands itching to wrap around her neck and squeeze. When he got within ten feet of her and Olivia, the stupid grin slipped from Keisha's mouth and fear shone in her eyes. Suddenly, in a blur, several people came at him from all sides; Malik on his left and Victoria to his right. But then Olivia launched herself into his arms.

That's what stopped him from killing the woman who had defied him and walked into his home.

"Thank you, thank you, thank you," Olivia exclaimed against his neck, her voice filled with emotion. Her words of gratitude did very little to squelch the rage roaring through his body. In fact, he got angrier by the minute.

Wiz couldn't understand her. After all that they'd been through with Keisha, he couldn't understand how Olivia could forgive and forget and welcome her with open arms.

She released him and quickly ushered her sister farther into the house. Before he could form his next thought, Malik gripped Wiz's shoulder and forcefully escorted him from the room. They didn't stop until they were outside on the patio.

"What the hell is she doing here?" Wiz roared, stomping across the small yard. He didn't care that he was out in thirty degree weather with short sleeves, no hat, and no gloves. The crisp chill of the night couldn't cool the blistering fury burning through him. "I can't believe this shit!"

Malik, standing on the patio, burst out laughing.

Wiz charged at him, wanting to hit something or someone, only causing Malik to laugh harder. "What's wrong with you?"

"I'm sorry, man. This shit ain't funny. But you have to admit, the woman has balls. Only a nut case would come here knowing how you feel about her. She had to know there was a possibility that you would be ready to put a bullet in her head."

"And that's funny to you?" The tension coiled

inside Wiz was almost suffocating. He backed away from Malik. Pacing around the yard, he ran his hand over his head and down the back of his neck.

Malik finally stopped laughing and leaned against the brick exterior of the house, his arms folded across his chest. He knew his friend was waiting for him to calm the hell down, but Wiz didn't know if that was possible.

"You know what I can't believe? That your ass was going to attack Midnight with all of those people standing around," Malik said when Wiz stopped at the rectangular patio table and leaned on it, still trying to slow his erratic heartbeat.

Wiz couldn't believe it either. When he zoned in on her, it was as if his legs had a mind of their own and moved in her direction. Everyone else in the room faded to the background. He didn't know what he was thinking. No, actually he did know. He wanted her out of his home and away from his wife.

"So, what are you going to do about her? I could suggest a few ideas, but you'd be risking a life in prison if you choose either of them."

Wiz ignored his friend's sarcasm. Then again, he had a feeling those ideas were in line with some of the thoughts he was having.

"What I want to know is where Hank is? He was supposed to be watching Keisha!"

Wiz didn't care that his voice carried in the backyard. All he wanted to know was why the person assigned to keep an eye on the woman was nowhere to be found.

"I was on my way to tell you that Hank was trying to reach you."

Wiz straightened. "What? When?" He patted his

front pockets realizing he'd left his cell phone on his desk.

"About the same time Midnight showed up. He tried you a few times, but when you didn't get back to him he called me ... well, you know the rest."

Wiz resumed pacing. Hell, he had done more pacing in the past week than he'd done in all his life. Frustration ran through his veins. It was because of him she was still alive and able to wreak havoc on their lives again. It had been four days and he had yet to find anything to support her story.

He still couldn't believe Keisha was bold enough to show her face at their home. Not only that, the fact that she knew where they lived didn't sit well with him. He had purchased the home long after she disappeared.

He needed some answers and he needed them now.

"Where do you think you're going?" Malik's large body blocked the entrance.

"Where do you think? I want her out of my house!"

Malik shook his head. "You're not going back in there until I'm confident you're not going to strangle the woman."

Wiz stepped back and sighed. "I can't promise you that, but she can't stay here."

"Then what are you going to do with her?"

"After I get some answers, I'm kicking her ass out. Now move!"

Seconds ticked by before Malik step aside and Wiz went back inside, shaking off the cold that had soaked into his bones. Maybe it was good he'd been outside without the right clothes, the chilling air was getting colder by the minute. It did help get his head back on straight.

That thought was short lived when he spotted Keisha exiting their guest bathroom brushing her hand down the front of her long skirt.

Wiz walked the short distance down the hall and blocked her path.

"How did you know where we lived?" His voice was low and lethal. Her gaze darted around the enclosed space. When she took several steps back, he was comforted knowing he had instilled a little fear in her. He hated the person he became whenever she was around, but he had to make her understand a few things. He tolerated her in the past because of Olivia, but no longer. "I asked how did you know?"

She backed into a wall, unable to go anywhere, holding her hands out in front of her.

"Cameron, listen. I'm sorry for just showing up. I wanted to see my sister. Surely you can understand that—"

"Don't give me that shit!" he seethed, trying like crazy to keep his voice down. "I asked how you knew where we lived. You're not going anywhere until I get some answers."

"What's going on here?" Olivia halted anything else he was going to say. "Cameron?"

He took a few steps back. "I want her out of here. I want her out of my house."

"Your house?" Olivia narrowed her eyes. "Your house?" she repeated.

"You know what I mean." He mentally kicked himself for the slip. It had taken him months to convince her to sell her townhouse in D.C and make this house her permanent residence. Now he might have just undone the progress he had made. "She can't stay here."

Olivia stood before him, her gaze studying his face. She tilted her head as if something had just dawned on her.

"Can I speak to you in your office?" she finally asked. Without waiting for a response, she escorted Keisha back to the main living area.

Wiz made eye contact with Malik as he followed Olivia. A slight nod of his head toward Keisha and he knew his friend understood.

Keep an eye on her.

CHAPTER ELEVEN

Knowing that Wiz was close behind, Olivia stormed up the stairs, her every step landing with such a thud, the staircase vibrated.

I want her out of here. I want her out of my house.

Wiz's angry words played around in her head, pissing her off even more as she walked into *his* office.

The spacious room looked more like a high tech central command station. The number of computers and monitors strategically positioned around the room resembled a government facility, rather than a home-office. At the moment she was ticked off enough to take a bat to every single device.

How could he embarrass her like that? And why did he corner Keisha, acting like a madman?

Wiz stalked in and she moved farther into the room, hovering near the leather sofa. All evening she had felt his gaze on her. He had always been attentive and overprotective, but tonight was different. He seemed more worried and clingy.

And then there was Keisha's arrival. It was clear her presence surprised him as much as it surprised her.

"I should have known you had nothing to do with Keisha being here," she snapped the moment Wiz closed the office door. The chill that had radiated off him upon seeing her sister could have frozen Lake Michigan. He was beyond livid. "But I can't help but feel as if I'm missing something here. First of all, where did she come from? How is it that she just happened to come to *our* house tonight of all times?"

Wiz shook his head and walked over to his desk, perching on the corner of it.

"I don't know," he finally said. "That's what I was trying to find out when you found us in the hallway."

"Cameron, do not lie to me. We agreed that there would be no secrets between us." Guilt stabbed her in the chest at her last words. Here she was telling him not to hide anything from her, when she had gone behind his back to search for Keisha. "Just tell me."

He stood and glared at her. "I am telling you! I have no idea how she knew where we lived or that we would even be home and celebrating your birthday."

Olivia studied him. He was telling the truth. Or at least some of the truth.

She walked to one of the windows and stared into the night, her arms wrapped around her midsection, as though she was holding herself together. Rarely did he volunteer information. She wasn't sure if it was because of his military training, but she hadn't noticed the trait until after his first tour in Afghanistan. Soon after, she realized that if she wanted answers, she had to ask the right questions.

"After you refused to search for her, did you change your mind?" She turned to him.

"No."

"Did you know she was coming here tonight?"

"No," he said with more frustration.

"Have you seen her before tonight? Like recently?"

He hesitated. *Bingo.*

"Cameron, please tell me what's going on. I know you can't stand my sister. So how is it that you've seen her or have been in contact with her?"

He walked around his large oak desk and sank into his leather chair.

"She came to the agency Monday night asking for my help."

Olivia stood speechless. She wasn't sure what to say, but she didn't miss the way his greenish eyes turned to dark emeralds. He wasn't happy. As a matter of fact, he looked as if he were about ready to spit bullets.

Something else dawned on her. That was the day she had stopped by his office on her way to school.

"Your sister pretended to be you."

Olivia's head snapped up. "What?"

"She walked into the admin section of the building as if she belonged there." He sighed roughly, his anger barely under control. All types of thoughts clouded Olivia's mind. "She says she's in trouble and wants my help."

Unease crept through Olivia's body as she thought about the note that she had been carrying around. She had been tempted to read it, but decided not to. *What if the note was ...* She refused to finish the thought.

Feeling sick, she sat on the edge of the sofa

cushion.

"What kind of trouble? And why did she come to you?"

He lifted his eyes to her, disgust written over his face. "Why does Keisha do anything that she does?" He rose slowly from his seat. "I don't care why she came to me or what she wants. All I know is that I want her to stay the hell away from you and to stay out of our lives!"

"I need to talk to her," Olivia said, ignoring his comment.

"What? Why?"

"Why? Because, Cameron, it's been ten years. I'm not going to just turn her away without finding out where she's been or what's going on with her."

"Unbelievable!" Wiz swiped most of the items off his desk and onto the carpet with one smooth sweep of his arm.

Olivia jumped, her hand over her heart.

"Un-frickin-believable! I just don't get you. Hasn't her presence in our life wreaked enough havoc?"

"I'm not sending her on her way without answers. Besides, she doesn't look drunk or high. Maybe she's finally gotten herself together."

"Forget what she looks like. After all the shit she's put you through you're still believing anything she says! Did you miss the part where I said that she's in trouble?"

"No, I didn't." She stood, anger creeping faster through her body. "I also didn't miss you not giving me a straight answer about why'd she come to you. Or the fact that you didn't tell me days ago that you had been in contact with her!"

He glared at her as if she had lost her mind.

"You're kidding, right? That's what you're concerned about, that she came to me? You're not concerned about her setting another house on fire, stealing from you again, or letting some assholes drug you and then leave you for dead?"

Olivia said nothing. What could she say? Yes, Keisha had done all of those things and more, but Olivia had forgiven her. And just because she had forgiven her, didn't mean that she was letting her back into their lives. But of course she was curious about where her sister had been and what she'd been up to.

Wiz moved toward her, but stopped. "Do you have any idea how it felt to get a call from my dad saying that you were missing and I was thousands of miles away?" His voice hitched, deep heart-felt emotion strangling his words. "Do you know … what it was like on the ride back to the U.S.? Or what it was like when we found you in that drug house? I had to carry you out of there because you were unconscious, Olivia. I had no idea if you were even going to live long enough for me to get you to a hospital. Do you have *any* idea what that's like?"

Olivia released an uneven breath, trying to choose her words carefully, feeling overwhelmed by his words, his emotional state.

"No. No, I don't, and I'm so sorry for all that my sister has done and for how it affected you. How it has affected us. I'm trying to tell you that I don't plan on letting her back into our lives. I just want to have a conversation with her. But you know what, Cameron? I left that time in my life in the past. I can't keep holding onto that hurt, the feeling of betrayal and at times even fear. And neither can you."

He shook his head. "I don't believe this shit. After all of that, you still think there's hope for her? You still think you can save her."

"I'm not trying to save her. I just want to talk with her, and I don't understand why you're so concerned. It'll just be a conversation. Why are you so afraid of me talking to her?"

"Well, you know what? I can't do this anymore. I can't stand by and watch her screw up something else in our world." He snatched his keys and picked his cell phone off the carpet, leaving the rest of the mess on the floor. "Speak to her all you want, but not in this house! When I return, she better be gone."

"Where are you going?"

Olivia hurried behind him, barely keeping pace as he flew down the stairs. He left through the garage without looking back.

She turned to see Malik walking toward her.

"Malik, can you go after him? I'm afraid he's going to do something crazy."

"As long as Midnight is still here ... he won't."

Olivia frowned. "Midnight?"

He cursed under his breath and glanced away before turning back to her. "Your sister. As long as your sister is still here, Wiz won't do anything crazy. It's when she leaves you might need to worry." He strolled away, leaving her standing there.

Olivia stared after him. *What does that even mean?*

*

Wiz left the motel office fifty dollars lighter in exchange for a key to Keisha's room. Had it been anyone else, he would have been concerned about how easy it had been to get access.

He pulled the brim of his cap lower, and adjusted

the collar of his leather jacket as he hurried across the parking lot. The wind whipped around him, lifting dust, debris, and a light dusting of snow, but that didn't slow his steps. He had one thing on his mind—show Keisha what it felt like to have an uninvited guest in the place where she called home.

A new wave of fury surged through his veins at her boldness. She had to know he'd be out for blood. And that *I wanted to see my sister* crap hadn't helped her case. She was definitely running some type of game and he needed to find out what it was sooner than later.

After driving around for the past two hours trying to clear his head, he ended up at her motel. Probably not the smartest move considering the way he was feeling, but he needed to make something clear to Keisha once and for all.

Wiz glanced around the darkened parking lot before heading toward the cement stairs, taking them two at a time. He headed straight for room 214. After knocking and not getting a response, he checked his surroundings then eased the door open. His gun at his side, he stepped into the doorway, a small amount of light filtering into the room from the outside fixture. He was able to see enough to know he hadn't been her only visitor tonight. Drawers hung open, clothes littered the floor, and the mattress hung partially off the bed. Thieves rarely left behind items like the television, an iron that sat on the dresser, and even the digital clock on the bedside table hadn't been touched.

Clearly, someone had been looking for something, but what?

One last glance toward the stairs and he moved

farther into the cluttered space, letting the door close behind him. A sliver of light shone through the pair of dingy curtains hanging at the window, illuminating the room just enough for him to double check that he was alone.

Tucking his gun in the back of his waistband, Wiz flicked on the lamp sitting on the edge of the dresser, giving the room a little more light. He stood in the middle of the floor, slowly scanning the space. With gloved hands, he rummaged through an opened suitcase that sat on the other side of the bed, checking every pocket. He had no idea what he was looking for, but he'd know the moment he found it.

Next, he went through the pockets of a pair of jeans, pulling out receipts. Maybe they could tell him something.

He moved closer to the lamp and sifted through the small slips of paper, noting the dates. Well, they held answers to a couple of his questions. One, based on the gas receipts, she had driven from New York, and two, she had been in Chicago for at least three weeks. Longer than he had originally thought.

When he heard someone coming, he clicked off the lamp and pulled his gun from his waistband, holding it close to his side.

Seconds later, Keisha rushed into the room. She stopped just inside the door and peeked out the window. Wiz wasn't sure what she was looking for, but apparently she was satisfied that there was no threat beyond the window. Her shoulders relaxed and she breathed a sigh of relief.

He flipped on the light, ignoring her startled gasp. "I wouldn't get too comfortable if I were you."

"Oh my God, Cameron! You scared me to death."

Her hand covered her heart, but then she looked around. "What did you do to my room? How dare you just come in here—"

"It wasn't me." He tucked his gun away and leaned his hip against the dresser. "You have a lot of damn nerve. You show up at my house as if you belonged there and now cock an attitude about someone tossing this rat hole?"

"I ... I ca—"

"Sit down." He pointed to the only chair in the room, positioned near the window. He wasn't in the mood for bullshit and that's exactly what she was about to start spewing. When she just stood there, he snapped. "Sit your ass down!"

She plopped down into the chair and he tried to rein in his rage.

"What are you involved in? And this time be straight with me. No more of your bullshit."

She fidgeted with the hem of her short wool jacket that looked so much like one that Olivia owned. If she were here for the past few weeks, that was plenty of time to study Olivia's coming and goings as well as her style. What he wanted to know was why she was going through the trouble.

"Nothing," she finally answered. "I told you everything. I just need help getting out of the country. I know you're angry about me crashing the birthday celebration, but I wanted to see my sis—"

"Let me try a different approach." Wiz reached behind his back and pulled out his 9mm from the back of his waistband and a silencer from his pocket. He quickly attached it to the gun, ignoring her pleas to just listen to him.

"I'm going to ask you again. What are you

involved in?"

The fear in her eyes showed that she believed he would kill her. And at the moment, he couldn't say that he wouldn't.

"I told you the truth, Cameron. I did witness Dwight killing one of his boys and all I could think to do was run."

"So you ran to Chicago, the last place you should've come." With the safety still on, Wiz lifted the gun. He wouldn't kill her, but he wanted her to think that he was willing to do the deed if she didn't cooperate. He knew her well enough to know that to get her to come clean, she had to think her life was being threatened. Yet, even then, he'd known her to lie.

"I know there's more to this story of yours than you're telling. You have five seconds to start telling me the rest of it."

Just then his cell phone vibrated. He had planned to ignore it until it started vibrating again.

He pulled it out of his pocket without taking his eyes from Keisha. The cell stopped and then started again, meaning it was Malik.

"Yeah," Wiz answered.

"Where the hell are you?" Malik growled into the phone.

"I can't talk right now." Wiz watched Keisha fidget in her seat, glancing around as if looking to see what he'd found in her room.

"God, I hope you're not where I think you are. You cannot be that stupid." When Wiz said nothing, Malik continued. "Okay, since apparently you are, I'm going to save you from yourself. You have five minutes to get your ass out of there. Otherwise, we're coming to get you. The last thing you need is for that woman to scream rape, or some other shit. You know how she operates, Wiz. She'll do it. We'll find out what she's involved in, but not like this."

It wasn't often that Malik was the voice of reason, but he was right. Keisha wasn't going to volunteer any information. They would just have to wait it out.

"I'll be done in a minute." Wiz disconnected the phone to the sound of Malik yelling his name.

"Cameron, I've told you everything. You have to believe me."

"But I don't."

She stood. "I swear, I'm telling you the truth. I need your—"

"Enough!" He sliced his hand through the air. "I'm done, Keisha. As a matter of fact, I don't give a damn what you're involved in or with whom. I've had enough."

"You promised you would help me."

"The type of help you need, I can't give you. You need a damn shrink. But what I will do is give you one last warning. Stay the hell away from me and my wife or else … you will be sorry."

CHAPTER TWELVE

Once the last of her guests had left, Olivia sat in the semi-dark family room, jazz playing softly through the overhead speakers. Wiz, being the techie he was and loving anything electronic, had wired the house years ago to include an intercom, as well as a sound system throughout the 3500 square foot Tudor home.

She lifted the hot cup of herbal tea to her lips and took a careful sip. *My house.* Wiz's words bounced around her mind. He'd said them out of anger and she could tell he had regretted them the moment they left his mouth. But knowing that didn't make it easier to hear.

Technically, it was his house. After much discussion, regarding selling her townhouse in D.C, which until recently was her place of residence, she had finally agreed. Having the townhouse made sense when she did a lot of traveling on the East Coast because of her art. Now that she and Wiz were remarrying, they agreed that Chicago would be home.

Glancing around the space, she recalled the renovations that had gone on for the last two months. Unlike most Tudor style homes of that age, they had opened up most of the first floor, but still kept as much of the architectural detail as possible. She absolutely loved the dark, timber ceiling beams and wood trim, as well as the wrought iron details. It was truly a dream home. Too bad they wouldn't be keeping it. She wanted something that they could really call *theirs*.

Olivia took another sip of her hot tea, unable to stop thinking about Wiz. He still wasn't home and she was trying not to worry. She hated when they argued, but this time she had to stand her ground. Most times she appreciated his protective behavior. Yet, there were other times she didn't, like when he got into that alpha mode that drove her crazy. But that was him. He had been that way for as long as she'd known him.

Olivia lowered her cup, but stopped midway when she thought she heard a sound at the patio door. With the remote to their sound system, she turned down the music but didn't hear anything.

Relaxing against the sofa, she pointed the remote to the system and stopped.

There it was again. Someone was jiggling the handle.

With shaky hands, she set the cup on the table and quickly turned off the lamp next to the sofa, her heart pounding faster than the wings of a hummingbird.

It could be Wiz, but she would have heard the overhead garage door or at least saw the headlights through the family room window. No, Wiz wouldn't be messing around in the back of the house, especially at one in the morning.

She hurried to the hall closet near the stairs and pulled down the lock box that held a .45 ACP. If she was overreacting, so be it. She'd overreact with a weapon.

Gun in hand, adrenaline surged through her body as she eased around the corner leading to the kitchen. Thankfully there were no lights on except for a night light near the kitchen bar.

She crept along the wall. Though she was comfortable with a gun, the sudden thought of using it on someone made her blood pressure rise.

She swallowed hard and stood near the kitchen sink. The window over the sink wouldn't give her a complete view of the backyard, but she would be able to see some of it.

Easing the curtain back, her gaze darted back and forth. Seeing nothing, she released the curtain, but at the last second, thought she saw movement near the patio stairs.

Okay. Don't freak out.

Releasing a shaky breath, she lifted the curtain again and jumped back when she heard the garage door go up.

Heart pounding loudly in her ears, she hurried away from the sink and stood behind the door that led to the garage.

Please let it be Wiz, she thought. It had to be him. Surely no one would be able to open the overhead door without a remote or a code to the garage door opener keypad.

A car door slammed and seconds later, a key jiggled in the lock.

Olivia's stomach clinched. She lifted the gun and held it the way Wiz had showed her, with both hands.

A second later, the door swung open and the house alarm beeped several times waiting to be disarmed. It wasn't until she heard the alarm code being entered did she release the breath that she'd been holding and slowly lowered the gun.

When Wiz didn't flip on the kitchen light, like he usually did, her breath caught. She stayed behind the door as it closed slowly, her heart in her throat.

The sight of him should have made her relax, but she couldn't move. He stood stock-still. His hand was behind his back, no doubt either reaching for a gun or holding one in his hand. His keen senses never ceased to amaze her.

Without a word, his sharp eyes quickly scanned her body, before settling on the gun at her side. His questioning gaze moved to her eyes.

"I'm okay." She released a sigh of relief.

The adrenaline racing through her body only moments ago skidded to a sudden halt, and she would have slid to the floor had Wiz not reached out for her.

"What happened?" He tucked the gun he'd been holding in the back of his waistband and quickly gathered her in his arms, disarming her at the same time.

He sat her gun on the kitchen counter, holding her tightly against his body as he glanced around the living space.

Lifting her effortlessly, he laid her on the sofa and placed his gun on the coffee table before sitting on the edge of the table facing her.

Pushing hair away from her face, he studied her, concern in his eyes.

"Tell me what happened," he said calmly, though

she knew his heart was racing just as fast as hers. Whatever skills they had taught him during his military days were still as acute as they had been when he was active duty.

Olivia shook her head, feeling a little silly. "Nothing," she finally answered. "I thought I heard something in the backyard, but I don't think—"

Before she could finish her sentence, he was out of his seat. With his gun in hand, he headed to the door that led to the backyard, not bothering with the lights.

She tiptoed behind him, careful to stay out of sight and out of the way. He glanced out the door window before disappearing outside.

Olivia moved back to the family room and laid her head on the arm of the sofa, taking several cleansing breath.

Maybe she had been overreacting, but she could have sworn she saw movement out back.

Wiz reentered the house a short while later.

She lifted slightly. "Did you see anything?"

He shook his head. "If someone was out there, they're long gone." He set his gun on the counter, but returned hers to the lock box.

Early in their marriage when he had first showed her his gun collection, she freaked. She hated guns. But he insisted she learn how to use one. She got more comfortable with them, but vowed she would never touch one unless he was nearby. Yet, when he enlisted in the Navy and was gone more than he was home, not only did she get used to having them in the house, he bought her the .45.

"Tell me what happen," he said, approaching the sofa. She started to lift up, but he stopped her with a hand on her hip. "Stay here." He sat on the edge.

"I was waiting for you." She told him how she had been drinking tea and heard someone at the patio door or thought she had. She went through the whole story to the point of him walking through the garage door.

"I'll check the surveillance footage in a few minutes." He frowned and caressed her cheek with the pad of his thumb. Her eyes drifted closed, savoring his touch. "Are you sure you're okay?"

Olivia opened her eyes. His frown deepened as he touched the back of his hand to her forehead and then to the side, near her temple. He was probably checking for a fever. Though she felt a little warm, it probably had more to do with the hot tea and the excitement a few minutes ago more than anything else.

"I'm fine."

She moved her legs and curled them underneath her. He sat back on the sofa, his hand now resting on her thigh.

"We need to talk."

"Yeah, I know." He laid his head back, exhaustion radiating off of him.

"Cameron, I know seeing my sister again upset you and I'm sure it doesn't help that I was glad to see her." When he said nothing, she continued. "But you can't just walk out on me every time we have a disagreement. It doesn't help anything and it's hurtful."

He gripped her fingers and brought her hand to his lips, kissing the back of it.

"I'm sorry. I would never do anything to intentionally hurt you."

"I know. Baby, you're my everything and I hate

when we argue. But if we are going to make our marriage work, we can't walk out on each other when we don't agree on something."

"I know, but your sister—"

"No." She halted his words and shook her head before turning more toward him. "We're not talking about her for the rest of the night. She's been the topic of too many conversations between us lately. Tonight I want this conversation to be about us. Just you and me."

No way was she going to tell him that she had agreed to meet Keisha for brunch the next day. He would be furious. She'd admit he had a right to be, but this was something she had to do for her own piece of mind.

"So what else do you want to talk about?" Wiz asked, pulling her into his arms and kissing the top of her head.

"How about if we discuss our wedding plans?"

"Are you going to make my evening by telling me that you've changed your mind about a formal ceremony and are willing to go to the courthouse?"

She pinched his stomach, barely able to grasp any skin thanks to his muscular abs.

"Ow!" He flinched, laughing. "What? I thought that's what you wanted to discuss."

"No. And you know we've been there and done that already. This time, we do the small church wedding with our closest friends and family. Besides, your dad and stepmother have already made arrangements to be back in the country. They're excited about being here for the ceremony." She couldn't wait to see them. Wiz's dad had remarried a few years ago and couldn't have picked a better mate.

Elaine was one of the sweetest people Olivia had ever met and was perfect for Andrew. Now that they had moved to Fort Lauderdale for retirement and traveled a lot, she didn't get to see them as often.

"Yeah, I talked to dad this morning. He said you asked him to walk you down the aisle."

"He's been like a father to me since my dad died. It was like a no brainer."

"I'm glad you asked him. He doesn't think my sister will ever get married, so you might be his only shot at marrying off a daughter."

It was Olivia's turn to laugh. "He's probably right." Carmen, Wiz's sister, loved being single and traveling. She was currently living in Brazil. As a reporter, her career took her all over the world.

"Tomorrow, Tasha and I are going to take care of some last minute wedding details, including finalizing things for the reception." Olivia snuggled closer, knowing Wiz was going to hate the next part of their conversation. "After I get off of work Wednesday, I want you and me to do some wedding cake tasting."

His brows drew together. "What?"

"The woman who owns the bakery and will be making our wedding cake, suggested we stop by and taste a few samples. That'll help us decide which one we want to go with."

"Come on," he groaned, sounding like a two year old. "Can't you and Tasha do it? I honestly don't care what type of cake we have. Just pick the one you want. I'm sure it'll be great."

She released an exaggerated sigh. He hated stuff like this, but she was determined to get him involved in some of the planning. Since she had waited until the last possible minute to finalize everything, they needed to do this as soon as possible.

"I don't want Tasha to help pick one. I want *you*." She looked at him pointedly knowing he would cave.

The left corner of his mouth tilted up and he shook his head. She knew she had him.

"All right, *Ollie*, I'll go, but it's going to cost you."

She punched him in the chest.

"Ow, woman! I don't think you realize how hard you hit."

"Well, don't call me Ollie. You know I hate that name. Besides, only Malik can call me that."

He lifted an amused eyebrow and burst out laughing.

"Oh really?" The wicked look in his eyes had her scooting away from him, giggling. Each move back she made, he moved forward crawling on the sofa.

"Yes and ... ooh ..." she purred as he slipped his large hand under her sleep shirt, heat rose within her when his hand made contact with her breast. She moaned as he caressed her with such gentleness and her eyes drifted closed.

"You feel so damn good." He crushed his mouth over hers and his hand moved with more purpose. Stroking. Kneading. Tweaking.

Her nipples hardened under the heat of his caress and currents of desire shot to the tips of her toes. She didn't know what it was about him. One touch and she felt as if she would leap out of her skin. Adrenaline pumped through her veins and her heart rate amped up with every flick of his finger against her sensitive peaks.

She tugged on the front of his shirt, pulling him closer, needing to touch him, feel him against her. She whimpered when he pinched one of her nipples, his tongue continuing to explore the inner recesses of her mouth. His hand went lower, but got tangled in her shirt.

He yanked his mouth from hers panting. "This thing is in the way and I need to feel all of you."

"Funny, I was just thinking the same thing. You have on way too many clothes." She jerked on his polo shirt.

He lifted up. "You're right."

He stood next to the sofa, toed off his shoes and quickly undressed, his muscles bunching with each move. A slow smile inched across Olivia's mouth at the sight of him.

God, he has an amazing body.

Her gaze followed his every move.

"Now where was I?"

Sitting on the side of her, he eased the sleep shirt over her head, leaving her naked except for red, satin panties. His gaze did a slow drag down her body and warmth shot through her at the longing brimming in his eyes. There were moments like now that her heart swelled with love for him. Not only did he always make her feel safe, but when his gaze took her in the way it was doing now, she felt cherished and desired.

His hand seared a tantalizing path from her neck, down between her breasts, and over her belly, not stopping until he reached the thin lacy material.

"These need to come off." He slid her panties down her legs and tossed them to the floor.

"You're so beautiful." The huskiness of his voice matched the passion swirling in his eyes. "I wanted to take this slow, but..."

Hovering above her, he braced his hands near her head and nudged her thighs apart with his knees. She breathed in his fresh scent and moaned when their lips touched. A wave of contentment settled in her soul. This sweet, loving man was all hers and she melted a little inside thinking about how special he was to her.

Her palms glided over his shoulders and down his back over his sinewy muscles, delighting in the way they contracted beneath her hands. He belonged to her and she wanted all of him.

She reached between their bodies and wrapped her hand around his penis. "I don't want to take things slow tonight," she murmured against his mouth.

A low growl rumbled in his throat when she slid her hand up and down his length, squeezing and stroking, enjoying the way he grew within her grasp. She added more pressure and the heat from his body transferred to hers as he moved against her palm.

He felt so good.

She glided the pad of her thumb slowly over his velvet tip, moisture coating her finger. Wiz cursed under his breath when she added more pressure. He shivered and jerked out of her hold, his breathing labored.

"Okay. Okay. Okay."

He grabbed hold of her hands and lifted them above her head. Without warning, he plunged inside of her. She sucked in a breath, her back arching off of the sofa as her body slowly adjusted to him.

"Ohhh," she said on a breath as he began moving inside of her.

He stared down at her with lust-filled eyes and then his gaze moved to her mouth. Kissing her sweetly, he rocked his hips and they moved to their own beat.

This was how she wanted to spend the last moments of her birthday, not arguing with him, but having him buried deep inside of her. He was the only man she had ever been with and she couldn't imagine ever sharing something so special with another.

Wiz broke off the kiss and released her hands. Gripping her hips, he plunged deeper. Passion pulsed through her like warm honey and heat spread throughout her body as he increased the pace.

"Ca ... Cameron," she panted, his hold on her hips tighter, his moves more jerky. On the verge of an orgasm, she matched him stroke for stroke, barely able to hold on to his sweat, slicked arms. She squeezed her thighs together, tightening around him as he continued to thump in and out of her. Faster. Harder. Deeper.

"That's it," Wiz growled, his fingers digging into her skin.

An electric current seemed to arc through her. "Cameron!" she screamed, her body convulsed against him as she clung to his shoulders. Her world spun on it's axis as a wave of sensation hurtled her beyond the point of no return.

With one last powerful thrust, he growled her name as his body trembled and he collapsed on top her.

Minutes ticked by with neither of them able to speak. Their labored breaths filled the quietness in the house and Olivia wrapped her arms around Wiz's shoulders.

"I love you so much," she whispered close to his ear.

*

An hour later, they were settled in their bed and Wiz pulled the sheet over their naked bodies. Olivia snuggled into the crook of his arm, her hand resting on his chest and her leg across his thigh.

"I'm sorry about what happened earlier. I definitely didn't plan on ruining your birthday celebration with an argument," he said. "But I hope you understand that it's my job to keep you not only happy, but also safe."

"After the way we just made up, I am beyond happy and I do feel safe. Remember, I'm not the young, naïve person I once was and I'm not trying to rebuild a relationship with Keisha. So let's not ruin a wonderful end to the day discussing her."

That was cool with him. The last person he wanted to talk or think about was her sister.

A short while later, after Olivia had fallen asleep, Wiz eased out of the bed and slipped into a pair of pajama bottoms. He had already planned to look through their home's surveillance after talking with Keisha. But finding out Olivia had heard something or someone on the patio, it couldn't wait.

The automatic lights flickered on when he stepped into his office. His gaze immediately went to the floor where the items from his desk lay. Quickly picking everything up that wasn't broken, he set it all back in its place.

Clearing the desk that way had been a stupid move. Although, it seemed his night was filled with a lot of stupid moves.

Wiz sat at his desk. Logging into his laptop, he pulled up the cameras around the outside of the house. He had them installed in various light fixtures on the property.

The surveillance software opened and Wiz began his search.

Why would Keisha wait weeks before revealing that she was in the city? And why was she suddenly dressing like Olivia? More importantly, who the hell had been lurking around their backyard tonight?

So many questions and not enough answers.

"All right, let's see what we have here," he muttered into the quietness of the room. He went back a few weeks to the approximate day Keisha had returned to Chicago.

They lived on a quiet street, with not much traffic, and scrolling through the security footage proved that up until two weeks ago. One thing that stood out was a small gray car that drove by daily, slowing down in front of their house every time it passed.

The vehicle didn't look familiar, but that didn't mean it didn't belong to someone in the neighborhood. It wasn't until Wiz spotted the same car sitting across the street one house down did he think otherwise.

He zoomed in. He couldn't make out the person behind the steering wheel. Based on their build, it was a woman, but he couldn't see her face. And despite Illinois requiring license plates being on the front and back of the car, this vehicle didn't have one on the front.

He switched to a different camera, hoping to get a shot of the back of the vehicle in order to see the license plate number.

Damn. No plates.

Wiz sat back in his seat and rubbed his eyes. His gut told him it was Keisha, but he didn't have any proof. No one could ever accuse her of not being street smart. At some point, she would screw up and he'd be right there to catch her.

He scrolled through footage from the camera at the back of the house. At first, there was nothing, but then the camera picked up a lone, dark figure.

The hairs on the back of Wiz's neck stood at attention when a tall, lanky man, dressed in all black, wiggled the handle on the patio door.

Shit.

The thought of Olivia being in the house alone with some creep roaming around the back trying to get in sent a rush of heat through Wiz's body. Zoning in, he didn't have a good shot of the man's face, but he froze the image. Hopefully his facial recognition software would be able to get a match.

First Keisha shows up at their house and now some random guy. Maybe the two situations weren't connected, but Wiz had a feeling they were. Now all he had to do was make the connection ... without anyone getting hurt.

CHAPTER THIRTEEN

Late the next morning, Olivia walked into the restaurant and did a quick glance around looking for Keisha.

"Hi, table for one?" the hostess asked when Olivia approached the podium.

"Actually, I'll need a table for two. I'm meeting someone."

"Okay, would you like to be seated now or wait for your party?"

Considering there weren't many empty tables, Olivia figured she should snag one before they were gone.

"Now is good, and if you have a table near the back, that would be great."

The young brunette gathered two menus. "Sure, right this way please."

Olivia followed her into the dining room that was buzzing with conversation. When they neared a table where three men were seated, one of them offered her a seductive smile, his appreciative gaze traveling down her body.

She nodded a greeting, but didn't return the smile. No need to encourage him. The man looked a little young, but she had to admit that now that she was thirty-five, it felt good to know that she could still turn a man's head.

Olivia groaned when the hostess stopped at an empty table next to the group of men.

"Is this okay for you?" she asked.

"This is fine. Thanks."

She set the menus on the table. "Your server will be right with you."

Olivia slipped out of her wool coat and laid it across the back of one of the extra chairs. She took the seat that faced the bulk of the dining area and hoped her sister would show. With Keisha, she couldn't be too sure.

The note in her handbag came to mind. She wanted so bad to believe that her sister had gotten her act together.

"Damn, there's two of them," one of the men from the next table murmured.

Olivia glanced up. Keisha walked toward her, looking as if she had just stepped off the cover of *Vogue* magazine. The fitted, white lace top and long, flirty skirt were artsy and chic rolled into one. The red leather jacket hanging open with matching high heel boots and handbag set the outfit off perfectly. And the extra swing of Keisha's hips ensured that she would get the attention she clearly was going for.

"Hey, sis, sorry I'm late."

"No problem. I just got here."

Olivia wasn't sure how to greet her. She was a

hugger, but based on Keisha's reaction last night, she still wasn't into hugging.

Keisha eased out of her jacket and draped it on the back of her chair. Olivia just shook her head as her sister adjusted her clothes, which were already perfectly in place, and put on a show of sitting down. She definitely had the attention of the men at the next table.

"Whew." She leaned forward. "Those are some cuties over there, but I guess you probably didn't notice since Cameron has you on lock down." The snarkiness behind her words and the way she twisted her mouth in disapproval had Olivia holding her tongue.

Well, I guess some things haven't changed.

As Keisha studied the menu, Olivia did a thorough perusal of her sister's long, straight hair, conservative make-up, and sensible jewelry. She had noticed the change last night. It was like looking in the mirror at herself. Olivia changed her look often until about a year ago when she let her hair grow out.

There was a time when her sister would do everything she could not to look like Olivia. Yet, last night and today not only were their faces the same, so was their style of dress. Olivia had to admit that this new Keisha was a little unnerving for more reasons than one.

The server approached their table and they placed their order.

"I'm glad you found me last night," Olivia said when the server walked away. "I was actually going to hire someone to search for you." She pulled out the white envelope from the side pocket of her handbag, but stopped when a strange expression covered her sister's face. "What?"

"I'm still stuck on the fact that you were going to hire someone to find me. Does Cameron know?"

"No."

Keisha let out a humorless laugh. "Of course your master wouldn't have allowed it, huh? I guess you're probably still jumping whenever he says jump, too."

Olivia shook her head, feeling like Boo Boo the Fool for even wanting to have a conversation with her sister. "Your trifling ass hasn't changed one bit. You're still the same mean-spirited, selfish, cold-hearted bitch you've always been. I actually thought that just maybe I could have an adult conversation with my sister, but apparently not. And why the need to dress like me? Surely you must know that you will never be me."

Olivia hated stooping to Keisha's level. She prided herself on keeping her cool and treating people the way she wanted to be treated, but her sister brought out the worst in everyone.

"Wow, I see someone has a backbone now. What happened? Cameron finally started letting you make your own decisions?"

"You're a real piece of work. You have your nose turned up so high, like Cameron is some overbearing asshole, yet you went to him for help. Why is that, Keisha?"

The self-righteous grin slipped from her sister's lips. "He owed me."

Olivia's skin crawled with the bite behind Keisha's words. Last night, when she and Wiz argued about Keisha's sudden appearance, Olivia had a feeling Wiz was holding something back.

"He owed you what?"

Her sister hesitated, her gaze everywhere but on Olivia.

What the heck is going on?

Keisha sighed when she finally returned her attention to the conversation. "Look, he's always treated me like crap, but I knew he had connections. I'd like to relocate to Europe or anywhere oversees. I thought he would be able to make some calls and help me out."

Olivia studied her sister, knowing there was something she wasn't telling her.

"So you going to his office, pretending to be me had nothing to do with this?" Olivia held up the note she had received from their childhood friend weeks ago.

Keisha narrowed her eyes. "What's that?"

Olivia handed it to her.

"I'm not sure if you knew, but Donna from the old neighborhood bought Gramma's old house after Gramma died. Some guy stopped by looking for you, and when she told him that she might be able to get a message to you, he handed her that note. Since I hadn't seen you in years, I opened it."

Actually, Olivia hadn't opened it until last night after everyone had left the party. When Cameron told her that Keisha was in some type of trouble, Olivia got curious. The message was short. *You have something that belongs to me. B.*

Her sister stared at the writing on the outside of the envelope, her first name and last initial scribbled across the front. She skimmed the note.

"Has anyone else seen this?" She folded the paper and stuffed it in her oversized handbag. "Does Cameron know about it?"

"No, and why would you care if he has seen it?"

Her sister glanced around with worried eyes.

"Because he already hates me. If he has any idea that ... oh, never mind."

Olivia knew why *she* hadn't shown Wiz the note. He would have looked at it as a threat to Olivia, since everything her sister was involved in often spilled over to her life. But Olivia couldn't understand why Keisha would care what Wiz thought. He tolerated her at best early in their marriage, but toward the end, his feelings for her went beyond hate, especially after the drug house incident.

Olivia would never forget when she woke up in the hospital after that horrible night. The first person she saw when she opened her eyes had been Wiz and she almost didn't recognize him. Disheveled, pale, and considering how thin he looked, it was clear he hadn't been eating. She hadn't seen him in a few months, not since he had left on one of his secret missions.

But what she remembered most was when their gazes connected. She saw the strain on his face and tears in his eyes. That's when she knew. That's when she knew that she had lost their baby.

Olivia shivered at the memory. She hadn't thought she would ever recover emotionally, blaming her sister, the hospital, and then Wiz for losing their baby girl. After months in therapy, she was finally able to stop blaming Wiz for not being in the country during her pregnancy. She also felt that he could have stopped her from going to Keisha's rescue.

Olivia eventually realized that it had been her decision to risk her and their baby's life that night in order to save her sister. For years, Olivia faulted herself, but Wiz had never blamed her. He blamed Keisha.

The server came with their meals and Olivia was glad for the distraction. They talked about the weather and the birthday party, and for long stretches, ate in silence.

"By your reaction, I assume you know what that note was about. Care to fill me in?"

"It's nothing for you to be concerned about." Keisha stabbed at one of her sausage links, cut it in half, and shoved a piece into her mouth.

"So where have you been, Keisha?"

"What do you mean?"

"Where have you been living?"

She hesitated, and Olivia wondered why she would have to think about the question.

"I've been all over. I left Chicago years ago and did a little traveling here and there before arriving in New York."

"How long will you be in Chicago? Are you working here?"

"I ... what's with all of the questions?" Keisha set her fork down, pushed her plate back, and folded her arms on the table. "Is that why you suggested we get together, so that you could ask me fifty-million questions?"

"Keisha, I haven't seen you in ten years. Of course I'm going to have questions. I think of you often. Wonder how you are, if you're safe. We didn't leave off on the best of terms and," she shrugged, "I guess I was just concerned."

"You weren't that concerned when you told me to never call you again and to stay out of your life," she seethed, her breathing coming in short spurts. "You knew I wasn't working and didn't have a place to live. Yet you discarded me like an old pair of tennis shoes."

Yep, this was the Keisha Olivia remembered. The arrogant person who thought the world revolved around her and the person who never took responsibility for her own actions.

What was I thinking? Why the heck did I think I could talk to her?

The hate in Keisha's eyes was like a dagger to Olivia's heart. How could she have thought that someone like Keisha could change?

"Keisha, I seem to remember the situation and the conversation going a little different back then." Olivia lowered her voice when a few people glanced their way. She had to say her peace because this would be the last time she saw Keisha. "I think it all started with me going out in the middle of the night to search for you and pay off your *drug* dealer. Oh, and if that wasn't bad enough when you refused to leave with me, *you* allowed someone to drug me and then you left me there. My own sister left me in a house barely conscious with drug addicts."

"Well you should have—"

"I lost a whole lot more than you that night, Keisha," Olivia said through gritted teeth, willing herself not to shed a tear. "I also lost my baby that night. My little girl."

Olivia recalled the day she had shared her pregnancy news with her sister. It was one of few days Keisha wasn't high. At the time, Keisha was staying with her while Wiz was away. Unlike most sisters upon hearing that type of news, she showed no love. Her response had been "don't expect me to babysit."

Even now, there was no remorse and no apology. Not that an apology would have made Olivia feel any better.

"You have a perfect life." Bitterness laced each word. "You have always had it made. Brains, talent, and you even landed the great guy. The man still worships the ground you walk on. He caters to your every need and treats you like some damn princess, even after you divorced him," she spat out, the venom returning to her words. "Well, Olivia, I had nothing. Even now, I have nothing. So forgive me if I'm not feeling any love for you right now."

Olivia had always known her sister was jealous of her, but had no idea she held this type of animosity.

"Your life could have been different had you made different choices. So don't blame me for all the bad in your life. *You* brought all that on yourself. How many times did I try saving you, only to be pulled into your mess?" A shiver ran through Olivia's body remembering the condition of the drug house that she'd been lured to. She hadn't been sure what to expect, but was glad that she had told her father-in-law about having to go and help Keisha out of a jam. Otherwise, Wiz might not have known where to start looking for her. Like always, he had saved her from some mess her sister had pulled her in to.

Right now, all she wanted to do was get away from Keisha.

"Excuse me for a minute. I'm going to the lady's room."

"Take your time," Keisha mumbled and turned her attention to the guys at the other table.

Unbelievable.

Olivia headed to the bathroom, but slowed when she spotted Travis, one of the agency's security specialists, sitting alone at a table for two eating pancakes.

She offered a small smile. She wasn't sure if Wiz had orchestrated the coincidence or if Travis just happened to be there.

He nodded a greeting in her direction and went back to eating.

Olivia kept walking. She hurried to the bathroom hoping it was empty so she could pull herself together. How could she be so foolish for thinking Keisha had changed? She owed Wiz a huge apology.

God, what was I thinking? She knew what she was thinking. One, she was concerned about her sister's well-being, and two, she really had hoped they could talk like civilized people.

Well, that wasn't going to happen.

She dabbed at her eyes and blew out a breath. She might not have a sister, but she still had Wiz and his family.

On the way back to her table, Travis was no longer at the table he had occupied moments ago. Apparently, Wiz hadn't put protection on her.

She smiled. She knew him well enough to know that he did probably think about it.

When she returned to the table, her sister was smiling at a business card in her hand.

"What's that?" Olivia asked, feeling refreshed and back in control of her emotions.

"A telephone number. Nice to know I can still get some digits."

Olivia didn't comment. She was so glad to be out of the dating scene.

Thinking about Keisha's words from earlier, Olivia was reminded of what an amazing man she had. Her sister was right when she said that Wiz treated her like a princess. She never doubted his love for her, not even while they were divorced.

Thank God Wiz didn't give up on her. He didn't give up on them. More than once he had told her that he wanted to fight the divorce, but had felt guilty for being away from her more than he was with her. In the past three years, he had proposed marriage three times. The last time, she had said yes. She was finally ready to put their past in the past and focus on a future with him.

Her father-in-law's words from months ago came to mind. "Why deprive yourself of the joys of marriage with the man you love, for fear of him being taken away from you? We all have to go sometime, but in the meantime …"

She'd been living life differently ever since.

Olivia reached for her glass of orange juice, but stopped before the liquid touched her lips.

Never leave your drink unattended, she remembered the self-defense instructor at Supreme Security saying. And Olivia didn't trust her sister.

Their server approached the table. "Can I get you ladies anything else?"

"Just the check please," Olivia said.

"Will this be on one check or two?"

"One," she and Keisha answered in unison.

Olivia lifted an eyebrow to her sister. *Well, this is a first.* She couldn't ever remember Keisha treating her to a meal.

Keisha shrugged. "What? I figured this was your treat since it was your invitation."

"Of course. I wouldn't expect you to pay for anything," Olivia mumbled, more than ready to get away from her sister.

They stood, preparing to leave. "Oh, can we swing by your house?"

Olivia frowned. "Why?"

"I think I left my makeup bag there last night. I would have called you to bring it, but I didn't have your telephone number."

After the fight she and Wiz had the day before, there was no way she was taking Keisha to their house. As a matter of fact, like Wiz, Olivia didn't trust Keisha.

"Unfortunately, I don't have time right now. I have another appointment, but let's exchange numbers and I'll call you if I find it."

They both pulled out their cell phones and added the contact information. Olivia didn't see them as ever being close again. She couldn't even see them talking much, but she was glad that they would be able to keep in touch if ever they wanted to.

"Well, I'm only going to be in town for another day or two. And I'm not sure exactly where I left the bag. It would probably be better if I swung by and—"

"If it's there, I'm sure I'll find it. I'll call you."

Keisha huffed but dropped the subject.

They walked toward the front door, and Olivia smiled when she saw Travis leaning against a wall near the exit. Dressed in a leather jacket, with a matching cap pulled low over his eyes, dark jeans, and black Timberlands he acted as if he didn't have a care in the world.

Now she knew Wiz had sent him.

"Well, hello handsome," Keisha flirted, flashing

him a sexy smile.

Travis touched the brim of his cap and nodded. "Ma'am."

Keisha scowled at him. "I got your damn, ma'am."

Olivia burst out laughing when Keisha stormed out of the restaurant. She couldn't help it. The look on her sister's face was priceless.

Olivia mouthed a "thank you" to Travis when he smile and winked at her.

Yeah, Wiz was right. Malik and the gang were her family.

CHAPTER FOURTEEN

Once Olivia climbed into her car, she activated her Bluetooth to call Wiz.

"Good afternoon, Supreme Security, this is Stacy. How may I direct your call?"

"Hi Stacy, this is Olivia. Is Cameron in his office? He's not answering his cell phone." Olivia had to get used to someone else answering besides Victoria on the weekends, since she now only worked Mondays through Fridays.

"Oh hi, Olivia. Actually, he's right here at my desk. Hold on and he'll take the call in his office."

Seconds later, he came on the line. "Hey, babe."

"Hey yourself." She turned on the heat in the car and rubbed her palms together to warm them.

"What's going on?"

"Well, first of all thanks for the security detail. I hope you're not mad that I didn't tell you that I was meeting Keisha for brunch. I just didn't want another argument."

"Yeah, I know and I can't say that I blame you. But I hope one day you'll understand that my only concern is you. I just don't trust her."

"Yeah, I know. So how did you find out I was going to be meeting with her this morning?"

"Malik. He overheard the two of you talking before she left the party."

Olivia smiled to herself. "You guys are good. You both are definitely in the right business."

Wiz chuckled. "I'm glad you think so." Paper rustled in the background.

If Olivia didn't have plans with Natasha for the rest of the afternoon, she would surprise Wiz with a visit to his office. She was sure he'd enjoy a repeat of Monday.

"So how was brunch?"

"It was … enlightening."

Olivia was glad Keisha appeared to be clean, but that edginess she wore like a badge of honor was still intact. By the time they said their good-byes, Olivia felt confident in knowing that she had done all she could do for her sister.

"Enlightening, huh? Does that mean you two are best friends now?"

"No. It means that I won't be making an effort to see her again."

"I see. Well, though my feelings for your sister haven't changed, I'm glad you have some closure."

Closure. That was a good way of looking at her time with Keisha. Now Olivia could move on with her life.

"By the way, I'm really proud of you."

Olivia grinned like a little kid. "Really? Why?"

"Travis mentioned how you looked around the parking lot before exiting your car this morning, and then again as you approached the restaurant. And did you think Keisha had put something in your juice or was it just intuition that kept you from drinking from the glass when you returned to the table?"

Wow, their team really was good if Travis saw all of that.

"I guess some of the self-defense I've learned over the years is starting to stick."

After Wiz's first tour in Iraq, he had drilled many self-defense tips into her. Then she took a course that Supreme Security offered and now some of the techniques learned seemed second nature.

Part of her didn't want to know, but she had to ask. "So did Travis see her put anything in my drink?"

"No. She didn't touch the glass or the food left on your plate."

Olivia sighed in relief. Her opinion of her sister already wasn't that high. Had she done anything to her food or drink, that would have definitely been the last straw for Olivia.

"So where you headed?" Wiz asked.

"I'm on my way to get Tasha. Oh, and before I forget, can you call off Travis? I don't think I need a security detail to go dress shopping."

He hesitated but eventually said, "Okay, but I can't guarantee that Malik won't have someone on Tasha."

"*Oh great.*"

Wiz laughed. "In his defense, he's backed off a lot. He normally doesn't put someone on her unless she asks."

"Well, I need to call her now and tell her not to make *the call.*"

*

Wiz disconnected from Olivia and called Travis.

"Yeah," he answered on the first ring.

"Man, thanks again for looking out for Olivia for me. I owe you one." Despite having part of the day off, Travis hadn't hesitated when Wiz asked if he could follow Olivia.

"The pleasure was mine. A free meal to watch two beautiful women, it wasn't exactly a hardship. But I have to ask, doesn't it freak you out that another human being has your woman's face? I mean, if you're in the same room with them, aren't you afraid you'll get them mixed up?"

Wiz chuckled. "No. For one, I try never to be in the same space as Keisha. And two, if you look into their eyes, you'll be able to tell the difference between them."

"Gotcha."

"But my advice to you is to stay away from twins."

"Yeah, that's probably some good advice. I can see myself screwing that shit up every time."

Wiz laughed, knowing Travis the playboy spoke the truth. Wiz found out early on that Travis was a babe magnet. With his youthful, charming ways, and that dangerous, bad-boy persona he had going for him, Travis drew women to him like a moth to light. The agency had used his talent on several cases over the past year to get information or to get into places they wouldn't ordinarily be able to get into easily.

"Wiz, something else I forgot to mention. Your woman gave her sister a note while they were eating."

"And?"

"And whatever was on it freaked your sister-in-law out. After she read it, she glanced around the restaurant as if expecting someone to make an appearance."

Interesting.

Wiz wasn't sure what to make of this new information. What could Olivia have given Keisha that would make her nervous?

"All right, thanks, man. I'll talk to you later."

Wiz tucked his cell phone away, glad Olivia was done with her sister. But as long as Keisha was in Chicago, he wouldn't rest easy.

He stared out the window. Considering the gray skies, it appeared the weatherman would be correct about the city getting some snow. He glanced down at the busy traffic, his mind going back to the conversation with Travis. Wiz wasn't sure what Keisha said or did to make Olivia change her mind about rekindling their relationship. His wife had a high tolerance level for people. Even if they were dishing bullshit, she still tried to find the good in everyone. Apparently, she'd finally had enough of her sister's BS.

"Wiz?"

Wiz glanced over his shoulder to find Raeanna standing in the doorway with her laptop open.

"Hey. Come in."

"I was going through the jewelry store's surveillance footage and found something."

They sat at the round table and she turned the screen toward him.

"Who does that look like?" she asked of the dark-skinned woman whose face was frozen on the screen wearing a blonde, shoulder-length wig. In this shot, he could only see her profile, but he knew exactly who it was.

"That's Keisha."

What caught his attention though, was the small

velvet bag in her hand.

Raeanna remained silent as he rewound the video, watching the scene play out. Keisha emptied the contents of the pouch onto a small, velvet-lined tray that Clayton placed in front of her.

Keisha's trying to sell him diamonds.

The way the store manager's gaze darted around the store made Wiz wonder what they were saying and why he was jumpy. Keisha's finger tapped vigorously on the glass counter as if trying to get her point across about something. The way they faced off, it seemed they knew each other.

The conversation became more heated when Clayton scooped up the stones and slid them back into the pouch, handing them to her. Clayton peeked at his watch for the second time in minutes.

Is he expecting someone?

Suddenly, Clayton stopped talking to Keisha and pointed to the door. After a slight hesitation, she stormed out. Seconds later, Gary entered from the back.

Wiz sat back in his seat, frustration lodged in his chest. He still had more questions than answers when it came to Keisha. Like where did she get diamonds? Assuming they were real.

No, soon as the thought entered his mind, he recalled her fiancé. Wiz had done some digging, but no Dwight Watson came up as a diamond dealer. Unless he wasn't legit. Which was probably the case considering the type of people Keisha attracted.

But why was she trying to sell them at Gary's place? Normally he didn't buy diamonds from random people, only those who were bona fide diamond dealers. Wiz couldn't say the same for

Clayton. If they proved he was stealing from Gary, that could also mean he was doing some deals on the side.

No wonder someone had ransacked Keisha's motel room. They were probably looking for the diamonds.

A sick feeling swirled in Wiz's gut. This explained why she was on the run. Diamonds. Probably stolen diamonds. Only a few types of people had diamonds laying around for someone to easily steal and most of them weren't good people.

And she brought this shit here.

Raeanna moved next to him, jarring him out of his thoughts. He had almost forgotten she was there.

"I know they're twins, but God she looks so much like Olivia," Raeanna said. "At the party, when she walked in, I thought my eyes were playing tricks on me. Until I remembered …"

When she stopped, Wiz glanced at her. "Until you remembered what?"

She shook her head. "Nothing. Don't mind me. I'm just rambling. I got home so late last night. I guess I'm not fully awake."

Wiz folded his arms. "Until you remembered what, Raeanna?"

He wasn't buying her lame excuse. He had seen her pull all-nighters hacking into a company's system with no problem of sleep deprivation.

She's hiding something.

"Until you remembered what?" he repeated.

She twirled a strand of hair around her finger. Just when Wiz thought she wouldn't respond, she spoke.

"I'd rather not say."

Wiz frowned, now concerned that she was withholding something that had to do with Olivia.

"Raeanna, my wife's life might be in danger. If you know something, anything, start talking."

"I promised her I wouldn't say anything."

"Her who?"

"Olivia."

"Does this little secret have anything to do with Keisha? If it does, I need to know. Now!"

She trembled. The hardness of his tone left no doubt that he had reached the limit of his patience.

"I ... th-that," she stuttered, "that day I spent at your house, she asked me to search for her twin sister. I never knew she had a twin. So to see them suddenly standing next to each other was weird."

Annoyance rose inside Wiz. Olivia had gone behind his back to try to find Keisha. Sneaky she was not. So this new development was a little mind boggling.

"Did she say why she wanted you to locate her?"

"She hadn't seen Keisha in a while and said she was worried about her. She wanted to make sure her sister wasn't in any type of trouble."

Why would she all of sudden be worried about Keisha's well-being? So all of that forgiveness crap she spewed the night of their engagement party was bullshit. She had an ulterior motive for wanting him to search for her sister.

"Wiz, please don't tell her that I told you."

"I won't." If Olivia wanted to keep secrets, fine. God knows he had enough of his own. His only concern was that she might be keeping something from him that could get her killed.

His cell phone chirped.

"Hello."

"I lost Midnight," Stan huffed on the other end. "I'm sure she didn't see me, but somehow I think she knew she was being followed."

Wiz sighed. "She probably was, by someone other than you."

CHAPTER FIFTEEN

Natasha's hands flew to her mouth when Olivia strolled out of the bridal shop's dressing room.

Olivia couldn't help the smile that spread across her lips as she stepped up on the platform in front of the large mirror. The beautiful gown was even more gorgeous than the first time she tried it on.

"It's perfect," she said, twisting back and forth to get a good view of every angle.

The rhinestones covering the high collar and the bodice glittered under the store's fluorescent lights like stars in a darken sky. And she absolutely adored the way the skirt flared out. The abundance of tulle beneath the satin material made it look like a dress a Disney princess would wear. After getting married the first time in a simple white sundress, Olivia had vowed that she'd go all out this time. Back then they didn't have the money for anything lavish, but now she had more than enough money to buy whatever she wanted.

"You look amazing." Natasha moved closer to the right side of the platform.

The tailor stood to her left and fluffed the skirt of the dress as if it needed it. "Except for maybe some teardrop diamond earrings, you don't need anything else. The dress is so elegant it stands out all by itself."

"I agree." Olivia couldn't help grinning. In a month she'll be remarrying the only man she'd ever loved. She felt like the luckiest woman in the world. "All I need now is a veil and the shoes."

"And flowers for the church, the bouquets, party favors, and a host of other things. Oh, and did I mention cake?" Natasha said sarcastically as she stared down at Olivia's list of things to do. To say she was behind in pulling everything together was an understatement. But as long as she got the dress out of the way, she had no doubt the rest would be a breeze.

"Speaking of cake, when are you and Wiz going cake tasting?"

"Wednesday. Although I think I already know the flavor I want. I just want to torture him a little." She grinned. "He couldn't care less what we have for the reception. I just want him to participate in some aspect of the process."

"I am so not looking forward to planning me and Malik's wedding." Natasha shivered. "I think it'll be easier to get married in Vegas than to try to get him to do anything as it relates to our wedding."

Laughing, Olivia gathered the skirt of her dress and stepped down from the platform. "Probably, but I can't wait. I can hear him cursing already."

Natasha rolled her eyes. "Yeah. Me too."

A short while later, they hurried to Olivia's car and

jumped in.

"I can't believe it's trying to snow again." Olivia put the heat on full blast and rubbed her hands together.

"Ah yes, Chicago in the winter. Gotta love it."

Olivia loved Chicago, but the winters could be brutal. It was still early in the season, yet it felt like January instead of November.

"I need to get us home before this snow starts sticking. This is definitely not a vehicle meant to be driven in this type of weather." She had always owned a sports car and the new Mustang Wiz had bought for her a couple of months ago was her dream vehicle. But not when there was snow on the ground.

Olivia leaned forward in her seat trying to see better out the front window as the windshield wipers swished back and forth. The rain/snow mix was still just that, but the snow was starting to win out. So far it wasn't sticking.

She drove west and slowed to turn onto Halsted when she noticed a dark SUV riding her bumper.

Back off, jerk. She couldn't believe the way some drivers drove despite the inclement weather. She was driving the speed limit and had no intention of going any faster. If he was in such a hurry, he could go around.

"You okay?" Natasha asked just as her cell phone rang.

"I'm good." Olivia divided her attention between Natasha and the road as she merged into traffic on the 94. "I thought you were off today. Your staff has been blowing up your cell all afternoon."

"I know, right?" She dug her phone out of the side pocket of her large Coach bag. "I took yesterday off without much notice and threw everyone for a loop. This is my payback." She held up her phone just before answering.

Olivia exited the highway and turned right onto North Avenue, surprised to see the same SUV behind her. It wouldn't have been so bad if it wasn't still riding her bumper.

Wait ... is he following me?

Unease course through her veins. After all the tips and warnings Wiz had drilled into her, she was pretty sure this person was following them. It wasn't one of the agency's vehicles since the truck didn't have the standard decal in the upper left hand corner. That was the only way the drivers could enter the company's underground garage.

Olivia was glad Natasha was busy on her call and had now pulled out her tablet. Since she wasn't paying attention, Olivia decided to try something.

She made the next right into a residential neighborhood, then went a block and made another right. Sure enough, the SUV was still on her tail.

Heart thumping a shaky beat, Olivia made another turn and panic crawled up her spine. The last thing she wanted to do was freak Natasha out. After her ordeal months ago, she was just getting comfortable again going out without being escorted by Malik or one of the agency's bodyguards.

Okay, just stay calm.

Maybe she was being paranoid. It didn't help that Wiz's fears about Keisha's appearance were at the forefront of her mind.

Olivia made another right.

They're definitely following us.

"Where are we going?" Natasha asked, her cell

phone to her ear with her hand over the mouthpiece.

Oh crap. Think.

"Um, one of the professors at the university mentioned a bakery to me. I thought she said it was around here, but maybe not." Olivia hated lying, but the last thing she wanted to tell Natasha was that they were being followed.

Natasha took a quick glance around. "I don't think I've ever seen a bakery around ... yes, yes, I'm still here." She went back to her telephone conversation.

Now that the rain/snow mix had turned to all snow falling, Olivia was more anxious than ever to get off the road. With her heart racing, she slowed down to get a feel of their location, trying to decide what to do. The person in the vehicle hadn't really done anything to her except maybe freak her out, so calling 911 was out.

She folded her bottom lip between her teeth as she waited for the light to turn green.

"Wow, it's really starting to come down out here," Natasha said when she finished her call and put away her tablet.

Olivia kept driving, but not as fast as before. Ice cold fear gripped her as she slowed, the back of her car sliding slightly to the right before she could straighten it. The roads were starting to get slick. She might've been an excellent driver, but her nerves were wound tight not knowing the intent of the person following them.

"I'm going to call Cameron to see if he's still at the office. If so, I'll park this car there and have him take us home. Mustangs are definitely not conducive to this weather."

"Actually, that's a good idea since Malik is still

there. That'll save you a trip to our house."

Olivia activated the car's Bluetooth, but kept an eye on the SUV.

"Hey, sweetheart. What's going on?" Olivia sighed with relief when Wiz picked up on the first ring, his deep voice coming through the car speakers loud and clear.

"Wiz," she started, trying to keep her voice steady despite the unease crawling up her back. The SUV swerved into the left lane. When it crept alongside of them, Olivia slowed hoping it had finally decided to go around them. Giving another quick glance at the vehicle, she took in the dark tinted windows. All she could think about was the number of movies she'd seen when the passenger side window goes down and a gun appears.

"Olivia?"

"I'm … I"m here." She gripped the steering wheel tighter. "Natasha and I are near the office and I think we're going to come there."

He hesitated and then said, "Pull into the circular drive and I'll meet you out front."

*

Wiz disconnected the call deep in thought as he tapped his pen against the top of the conference table. Disturbed by Olivia's call, he replayed the conversation over in his head.

Something's not right.

He went to his desk and logged into his computer.

"What's going on?" Malik asked. He, Raeanna, and Wiz had been discussing the jewelry store case and next steps. "Is everything all right?"

"I'm not sure. Olivia called to say that she and Natasha were on their way here."

"And?"

"And she called me Wiz." He didn't have to say anything else to Malik. That said it all. Olivia never called him Wiz. As a matter of fact, she thought it was a stupid nickname. "I'm pulling up the app so that I can access the GPS on her car to see exactly where they are."

Malik stood and pulled out his cell.

"Hold up, Tree. Don't call." He knew he was getting ready to call Natasha. "It might be nothing. Besides, if they were having a problem, I'm sure Tasha would've called you."

Wiz met Malik's gaze and knew he wasn't buying it.

Olivia's location came on the screen. "They're about two blocks away."

Malik was out the door before Wiz could finish the sentence.

Wiz grabbed his gun from the top drawer of his desk and placed it in the back of his waistband underneath his sweater. He hoped they were all right, but these days, he wasn't taking any chances.

Before he walked out of his office, Raeanna stopped him.

"Do you need me to do anything?"

"Yeah. Travis is here somewhere. Have him or either Hank to meet me out front."

Minutes later, Wiz and Malik walked out the front door just as Olivia's car came around the corner. She pulled into the circular drive.

Wiz was at her door before she could come to a complete stop. "Hey."

She practically leapt into his arms. He didn't know what the hell had spooked her, but the way she trembled against him it was something serious.

"Okay. Does anyone want to tell me what's going on? First Olivia was acting weird and now you guys are hovering," Natasha said when Malik helped her out of the car.

Before Olivia could respond to Natasha, Travis showed up.

"What's going on?" he asked, his gaze going from Wiz to Malik.

"I need you to pull Olivia's car into the garage. Put it in the employee's section," Wiz instructed, maintaining his hold around Olivia.

Travis moved around the car to the driver's side. "No prob."

"Do you need anything from the car before he takes it?" Wiz asked Olivia, placing a kiss against her temple, anxious to find out what happened.

"We have a couple of bags in the trunk." Olivia's voice was a little shaky, but that could've been caused by the wind that had just picked up.

He and Malik grabbed the bags and escorted her and Natasha inside. The moment they walked in, Natasha's cell rang and Malik escorted her to his office.

With his hand at the small of Olivia's back, Wiz guided her into his office, not surprised to see Raeanna still there.

"Hey, Olivia."

"Hi, Raeanna." Olivia walked across the room and gave her a hug. "It's good seeing you."

"You too." Raeanna closed her laptop. "I'll get out of the way so you guys can have some privacy."

"Actually, maybe you should stay." Olivia moved back to Wiz's side and grabbed hold of his hand. "I

179

didn't want to say anything around Tasha, but someone was following us."

"What?" He tensed. He closed his office door while Olivia told them about the SUV.

"God, baby." He cupped her face between his hands and brought his mouth close to hers. "I'm glad you're all right. Let's see what we can find out." He kissed her again, and then moved to the conference table where Raeanna had her laptop. "See if you can tap into the city's cameras in that area."

Olivia gasped and moved closer to them. "You guys can do stuff like that?"

"For me, only sometimes," Raeanna said, "but your husband is a *wiz*." She grinned, her fingers flying across the keys as she typed.

A few minutes later, they were in.

"Okay, there." They switched from one frame to another following Olivia's car.

"I think we might be able to speed up the footage some." Raeanna's fingers went to work again.

The three of them watched. There were plenty of opportunities for the driver to go around Olivia, which made it clear that the truck was following them. A hard knot formed in Wiz's stomach when the vehicle pulled up on the side of Olivia's car. They drove along the side of her, speeding up and slowing down whenever she did for at least a block. When Olivia made one of her right turns, the SUV almost caused an accident to get back into the other lane to follow her.

Wiz cursed under his breath. He was trying like hell to keep his rage intact, especially when the SUV rode her bumper, getting too close.

Wiz pulled Olivia back against him, needing to

touch her.

"How long did you notice him following you?" he asked close to her ear.

"Maybe after we were a couple of blocks from the bridal shop. Then again when we exited the expressway. He followed us until we pulled up in front of the building." She snuggled closer. "At first I wasn't sure if we were being followed, but when I did those two right turns and he was still behind me, I was pretty sure."

"You did good, babe." He kissed her cheek, glad she had kept her cool—not that he was surprised. She was an amazing woman.

Someone knocked on the door before it flew open.

"So what's going on?" Malik stepped in, closing the door behind him.

"Where's Tasha?" Wiz asked.

"In my office on the phone." He walked over to Olivia. "You okay?" He hugged her.

Olivia nodded against his chest.

Wiz filled Malik in on everything, watching his jaw twitch the more he heard.

"Olivia didn't say anything over the phone for fear of spooking Tasha."

"I appreciate that. She still has occasional nightmares from her ordeal."

"Rae, pull up the cameras on the east and south side of this building," Malik instructed, and sat in the chair next to her. "I want to see if we can get a plate number on the SUV."

When they couldn't get a good shot, Wiz had Raeanna go back to the city cameras.

"Why don't you lie down on the sofa," he said to

Olivia. She looked exhausted. He ushered her over before she could refuse. When she laid down with no argument, he knew the adrenaline was starting to wear off.

"I was so scared."

"I know." He caressed her cheek. She'd had one too many scares in the past couple of weeks and he didn't like it. "Do you realize you called me Wiz earlier?"

Her mouth twisted, trying to hide a smile. "Figures you'd catch that."

He chuckled. "Yeah, I caught it. That's what first tipped me off that something was wrong."

"It wasn't intentional. It just flew out of my mouth when you picked up. I have never been so happy to hear your voice. It actually helped me relax a little, like you were there with me."

"Stop. There." Malik's voice carried across the room. "What is that? G, 3, 2 ..." His voice trailed off and Raeanna went back a couple of frames.

Even with a partial plate number, they might be able to find the vehicle with the help of some friends at the Chicago Police Department.

An hour later, Wiz and Olivia were heading home. Besides the swooshing sound of the windshield wipers swiping away the snow, soft jazz played through the speakers.

Stealing a glance at Olivia, Wiz wondered what she was thinking about. Her eyes were closed, but the death grip she had on the door handle told him that she wasn't asleep.

"Do you think this has anything to do with Keisha?" Olivia asked without opening her eyes.

"Am I driving too fast for you? Why are you still

tense?" he asked instead of answering her question. At some point, he was going to have to ask if she knew why Keisha was in town.

"No, you're fine. I'm just really tired." She finally opened her eyes. "I noticed you didn't answer the question. So that means you do think she had something to do with the person following me this afternoon."

Wiz cracked a smile. Very little got by her. "Maybe."

"So that's a yes." She sat up a little straighter, wringing her hands in her lap.

Wiz checked his mirrors, making sure there wasn't a repeat of earlier.

"No, that's a maybe. I'm not sure. We had someone keeping track of Keisha while she's in Chicago, but she disappeared."

"I have her telephone number. I can call and see if she's still in the city."

A little taken back, Wiz wondered what else he didn't know.

"Yeah. I want you to call her, but don't use your cell. I have an encrypted one at the house."

"I should have listened to you about her. I should have known she was involved in something."

"Why do you say that? Did she say something to you?"

Olivia hesitated. "A few weeks ago I got a call from Donna from the old neighborhood. She said someone had left a note for Keisha and she wondered if I had seen her lately. Since I hadn't, I was a little curious about the note and went by there and picked it up."

Wiz mentally braced himself before he asked the

next question. "What did this note say?"

She glanced out the passenger side window. "I didn't read it until last night. It said, *You have something that belongs to me.*"

Wiz gripped the steering wheel tighter, struggling to maintain control. He knew there was more to Olivia's request to find her sister. He should have pressed her harder, but at the time, all he could think about was blocking anything relating to Keisha out of his mind. What he couldn't figure out, though, was why Keisha hadn't told Olivia about that night he held a knife to her throat. He knew her well enough to know that she would use it against him at some point. Which is why he needed to tell Olivia himself ... soon.

"I should have told you about the note weeks ago, but I knew you would freak out."

Yeah. Like he hadn't almost lost his mind at just the mention of her sister.

"You're right, I would have." He stopped at a traffic light and squeezed her hand. "Had you showed me that note, we wouldn't be here."

"What do you mean?"

"I mean I would have hauled ass and taken you far away from here, disappearing like Q and Alandra. Olivia, that note might've been meant for your sister, but it could easily turn into a threat toward you. The last thing I wanted when you first mentioned Keisha's name was to drag her drama back into our lives."

Silence fell between them. Wiz still entertained the thought of getting Olivia out of town. Maybe even out of the country. He had already lost his mother because of a senseless crime. There was no way he was going to lose his wife due to some nonsense brought on by her sister.

"Did the note say who it was from?"

"It was a couple of initials, but I can't remember what they were." She released a frustrated sigh. "Cameron, I'm sorry ... for everything. I know I've apologized in the past for Keisha, but I had hoped," she paused, "I guess I had hoped that by now she was doing something with her life. That she could be the sister she was before our parents died."

"You don't have to apologize to me. I know you have a big heart, which is one of many things I love about you. But, sweetie, sometimes I think you forget that you and Keisha are identical twins. As it relates to that note, if someone is after her, but see you, they're going to think that you two are one in the same."

By the faraway look on her face, it was safe to say that she hadn't thought about that.

"Before your party, most people didn't know you had a twin. And I doubt Keisha has broadcasted that bit of info to anyone she knows."

"So you think she intentionally started dressing like me because of whatever she's involved in?"

"Yes, and whatever trouble she's gotten herself into, she's brought it to our doorstep."

CHAPTER SIXTEEN

Olivia kept glancing at the clock, anxious for her afternoon session to end. This was the last day of class before final exams. But that's not what she was anxious about. She and Wiz were spending the evening together, starting with stopping by a bakery that would be making their wedding cake. In a few weeks, she would be walking down the aisle to marry the man of her dreams.

"All right, you guys. That's it for today." She placed her palms on her desk and faced the class. "You have everything you need to be successful on your exam next week. If you have any questions, feel free to email me anytime leading up to Monday. Enjoy the rest of your day."

Her students filed out of the classroom, except for two who came up to the desk and Travis, who was camped out in the back of the room. At twenty-three, he blended in with the other students in the class and even dressed similar. Needless to say, that with his bad-boy persona, he had caught the eye of many of the female students. If anyone thought it weird that he'd been hanging around her the last few days, no one said anything.

After the SUV incident the other day, Wiz told her that he wanted someone with her at all times. Considering how freaked out she had been, she didn't argue. As a matter of fact, it wasn't as inconvenient as she thought it would be. When she wasn't in class, either Wiz or Victoria shadowed her around town. She was enjoying the company and not having to drive herself anywhere made the arrangement something she could easily get used to.

"Mrs. Miller, here is the assignment from Monday," Terry, one of her more vocal students said, handing her a drawing and a report. "I know it's late, but figured better late than never."

"Thanks, Terry. Yes, it's better late than never, but seeing that it's two days late, you're starting with a C, so hopefully this is an A paper."

"Yeah, I hope so, too." He turned, his slow gait heading to the door.

Olivia shook her head. He had so much potential and talent. Too bad he didn't apply himself.

"Hey, Amanda. What can I do for you?" Olivia asked as she stuffed papers into her oversized bag.

"I just wanted to let you know that I contacted your agent and I have a meeting with him in two weeks," she stated, the grin on her face spreading as wide as a rainbow.

Olivia moved around the desk and hugged her. "That is wonderful! I'm so glad you followed through and sent him some of your work."

"Me too, and I know it didn't hurt that you put in

a good word for me."

When Olivia stepped back around her desk, she noticed Amanda's creepy brother standing in the doorway.

A chill crept through her and she cast a discreet glance at Travis who was sitting up straighter. He looked as if he was focused on the papers in front of him, but she knew better. The agency had some of the most elite security specialists in the business and Travis was one of the best.

Olivia's eyes went back to their visitor.

Amanda followed Olivia's gaze and glanced over her shoulder, sighing dramatically.

"Corin, I told you I'd come out right after class." Her brother continued to stare at Olivia, making her even more uncomfortable.

Travis slowly made his way to the front, pretending to be looking over the papers in his hand.

"Well, I guess I better be going." The sparkle in Amanda's eyes had dimmed now that her brother was there. "Thanks again for everything. I'll let you know how the meeting goes."

"I'd like that. Take care and good luck on your exams next week."

One last glance at the door, and Olivia made eye contact with the brother. She hated the way he looked at her, causing goosebumps to pop up on her arms. When he moved away from the door, Olivia released a deep sigh.

"Are you okay?" Travis asked, his voice low and calm.

She nodded. "He makes me so uncomfortable."

"You've seen him before?"

"Yeah, Amanda, the student who just left, he's her

brother and she introduced us weeks ago. That first time, he stared at me as if he was trying to figure out where he knew me from, but I know we've never met. But this time the way he looked at me …" She shivered and waved it off. "It doesn't matter. He's gone."

Travis studied her a while longer, giving her one of those *I'm not convinced* looks that she often got from Wiz.

"All right," he finally said. "If you're ready to go we can head out. I'll make sure your admirer is not around before we leave. Oh, and I just got a text from Wiz, he's outside."

"Okay, give me a minute."

She hurried and put the remaining papers into her bag, excited about spending the rest of the day with her man. She had some surprises planned for him this evening that were making her more eager than a kid on Christmas Eve.

"I'm ready."

*

Wiz pulled up near the door where Olivia would be exiting. Until Keisha was out of town and out of their lives again, he wasn't taking any chances with Olivia's safety.

Thanks to the help of a friend with the CPD, they did determine the vehicle that had been following Olivia had been stolen. Of course. Wiz wanted to believe that the SUV had some kids in it who were just goofing around, but his gut told him otherwise.

He glanced back at the university's entrance, wondering what was taking so long. They should have been out by now.

His cell phone chirped. *Travis.*

On our way. A student's brother seems interested in O. Makes her uncomfortable – more than once. Tattoo of serpent on right hand.

Wiz lifted his head and stared out the front window. He filled in the blanks of Travis's messages. Olivia possibly has an admirer. An unwanted admirer. One who makes her uncomfortable. The part that made Wiz uncomfortable, though, was the tat on the hand.

Cidal Boyz.

Okay. He texted back. He was definitely going to have to talk to Olivia. It rubbed him the wrong way that any man would be showing a blatant interest in her, but one of the Cidal Boyz's interest triggered all types of warning bells.

He glanced back at the building's entrance in time to see Travis and Olivia exit. He appreciated how vigilant Travis was being, taking in their surroundings while staying close to Olivia as they made quick work of getting to Wiz's truck.

Wiz climbed out of the vehicle.

"Hi, baby." Olivia walked into his arms, greeting him with a kiss.

"Hey yourself." He gave her a hug before helping her into the truck. He closed the door and met Travis's gaze, giving him a fist bump. "Thanks, man."

"Anytime." Travis lifted the collar on his black jacket, stuffed his hands into his pockets, and headed down the street in the opposite direction.

"So how was your day?" Wiz steered the truck in the direction of the bakery. He had finally given in to the cake tasting that Olivia wanted to do. Now all he had to do was try not to complain about it for the next hour.

"It was pretty good. I can't believe the semester is almost over." She snuggled deeper into the soft, leather seats, hugging herself.

Wiz turned up the heat and slowed at a traffic light, checking his mirrors without being too obvious. No one was following them, but now that he knew one of the Cidal Boyz was interested in Olivia, he planned to be extra cautious.

"Seems the semester went pretty fast," he said, splitting his attention between her and the road.

While riding, they discussed their wedding plans and the guest list, and Wiz told her that he had made the final arrangements for their honeymoon in Figi. Considering the stress of the last few weeks, he was glad to see her excited about their plans.

"I'm looking forward to this break from school."

"Speaking of school, I heard you have an admirer."

Shaking her head, she smirked at him. "Let me guess, Travis. Does that man notice everything?"

"Pretty much, but that's his job. So tell me about this guy. Does he have a name?"

"Why? So you can do a background check on him?" She pursed her lips, turning more to face him.

"Well, yeah. Some rough looking brotha shows an interest in my woman, more than once, I want to know who he is."

Olivia puffed out a breath. "He's Amanda's brother, but I can't remember his name. And you have nothing to worry about. I'm not interested in youngins when I'm about to marry a real man." She wiggled her eyebrows.

Wiz chuckled. "That's good to know. I would hate to have to hunt him down and whoop his ass."

She narrowed her eyes, her brows drawn together. "You really have to stop hanging out with Malik. You're starting to sound more and more like him." They both laughed.

"So what is it about this kid that makes you uncomfortable? Has he said or done anything to you?"

"No. It's the way he looks at me that kinda weirds me out. The first time, he acted as if he was trying to figure out where he knew me from, but today was different. Today he glared almost menacing like. Maybe it was because Amanda wasn't ready to leave." She shrugged. "I don't know. It's not that serious."

Wiz didn't respond, but for him, this was serious. Not just because she had caught this guy's attention, but also because too much had happened recently for him not to take everything seriously.

Twenty minutes later, they pulled onto the street where the bakery was located. Unable to find a parking spot right in front of the building, Wiz parked a half a block up. He hurried around the car to the passenger side and opened the door for Olivia. Staying close, his gaze swept the area from the park cars to neighboring businesses.

Olivia slowed when they reached the door. "You're really uptight. Did something happen?"

God. He and Malik really should hire her for one of their security details considering how perceptive she was.

"Everything's fine," he said instead of telling her that a sense of foreboding was churning in his gut.

Anxious to get her inside, he placed his hand at the small of her back and opened the door. They stepped into the well-lit hallway. There were stairs going up

192

and a long hall in front of them. The bakery was through the door on the right.

"Come on, let's go in and get this over with," he mumbled.

Olivia pulled up short, her arms folded across her chest. "We're not going in if you're going to act like this. I've only asked two things of you regarding the wedding. Get fitted for a tux and help me decide on a cake for the reception. I can't believe you're grumbling about doing this."

Wiz glanced over his shoulder. The all glass door was making him uneasy, but she was right. He honestly didn't see the point of cake tasting.

He pulled her into his arms and kissed her on the lips. "I'm sorry. You're right. You haven't asked much of me and I know how important this is to you."

"This should be important to you, too. This is the last time we're getting married and I want it to be memorable and special."

"Sweetheart, as long as you're there, it will be special." He slipped a finger under her chin and lifted, forcing her eyes to meet his. "I won't say anything else negative. Let's go in here and eat some cake."

A slow smile tilted the corner of her mouth. "Okay, and if you cooperate without complaining, then I have a surprise for you after we leave here."

His eyebrow lifted. "Oh really? And what would that be?" He actually didn't care what she planned, he loved her surprises. The last one had been a few weeks ago when she called him to their bedroom. He had strolled into the room, the lights were dimmed, a roaring fire in the fireplace, and she was posing in the bathroom doorway. He still had fantasies about her wearing that killer dominatrix outfit with the thigh high boots. That memory alone had him wishing they were home right now.

"Let's just say, you're going to be blown away," Olivia said, a sly smile spread across her tempting lips.

"Well all right, woman. Let's get in here. We don't want to keep the baker waiting."

Olivia laughed as they stepped inside the bakery, but Wiz stayed vigilant. The wall of glass windows didn't offer much protection, but he would just have to keep his wife happy while keeping an eye outside.

"You're doing it again," Olivia whispered.

"What?"

"Acting like something is wrong. I know you, Cameron. If we're not safe, we can just reschedule."

He sighed and rubbed his forehead. Maybe it's nothing. He didn't want to pull her out of here if there was no threat, and so far, all seemed fine. But his gut rarely lied.

"No, let's do this. Besides, I don't want you trying to back out of giving me my surprise."

She grinned and kissed him on the cheek. "Yeah, you *really* want to experience this surprise."

"Hello. May I help you?" the lady behind the counter asked, her raspy voice sounding as if she were a pack a day smoker.

Olivia stepped forward. "Hi, we're the Millers and we have an appointment for a tasting."

"Oh yes. Let me get Edna."

Moments later, an older woman with short gray hair, smooth mocha skin, and a pleasant smile came from the back.

"Hi. I'm Edna. Welcome."

"Thank you. I'm Olivia and this is my fiancé, Cameron."

Wiz hadn't ever heard her refer to him as her fiancé. For him, she was his wife and that's how he introduced her. He guessed it would be weird to introduce him the same way considering they were there to pick out a cake for their wedding reception.

"I've been expecting you. If you'll step over here to the bar, we can get started."

They walked past a large, glass display case. Wiz wasn't really a sweet eater, but he had to admit the cakes, cupcakes, and cookies on display looked impressive.

"Thanks again for your willingness to stay open a little later for us. I appreciate your flexibility," Olivia said.

"It's my pleasure. Your big day is coming up quick. You must be getting pretty excited." The baker and Olivia discussed the plans for the reception.

Wiz gave a quick glance at the windows again. It gave him some comfort that he and Olivia weren't sitting directly in front of the glass.

He waited until she sat on one of the bar stools and he slid onto the one next to her.

Edna set a tray on the low counter in front of them that held small bite-sized cake in three short rows. Next to the tray, she placed two small slips of paper with four lines of cake flavors, a box to check in front of each one. Wiz was surprised at how formal the process was. He had expected to come in, get handed a few bites of cakes to taste, and then pick one. So far, it seemed the process would be a little more involved.

Edna pointed to the two small pieces of cake on the left side of the tray. "Okay, here we have the yellow cake with raspberry filling and buttercream between the layers and on top. These two are traditional flavors, with a cream cheese frosting." She identified another flavor, and by the time she was done describing each one, Wiz was ready to get started with the tasting.

"I like the second one the best. The one with the strawberries in between the layers," Wiz said after they had tried all the samples. Turned out the experience wasn't as painful as he had originally thought. "What about you, babe?"

"I agree. The second one. They all were amazing, but that one reminded me of strawberry shortcake."

Wiz's phone chirped with a text message. Five minutes earlier, it had vibrated in his pocket, but he had ignored the call.

"Excuse me for a minute. I need to take this."

He glanced at his cell.

911

Speed dialing Malik, Wiz stepped out into the hallway.

"You'll never guess who the hell Midnight's fiancé is," Malik said by way of a greeting.

"Who?"

"Dwight *"Bishop"* Watson, leader of the Cidal Boyz."

Shit.

Wiz's mind immediately went back to Travis' text. There was no way the mention of the Cidal Boyz twice in one night was a coincidence, especially since he didn't believe in coincidences. This was one of the largest gangs in the country with a presence in not only New York and Detroit, but also Chicago.

Standing in the hallway talking to Malik on the phone, Wiz reached under his pant leg and removed the Sig Sauer P227 from his ankle holster. He placed the gun in the back of his waistband, beneath his jacket. When Keisha mentioned her fiancé's name, Wiz hadn't put it together that she was with *Bishop.* The guy was intelligent and rumored to have connections to organized crime.

"What the hell is she involved in?" Wiz said more to himself than Malik, his gaze traveling to where Olivia sat on the bar stool still talking with the bakery owner. His mind drifted back to Keisha and everything he had gathered on her since her return.

Diamonds.

His *oh-shit* meter flew off the charts. He had been so distracted the last few weeks that he wasn't thinking straight and hadn't put anything together.

"Talk to me, man. What are you thinking?"

"I'm thinking Keisha might have stolen diamonds from her *fiancé.*"

Silence filled the phone line before Malik said, "And she's on the run with him hot on her trail."

And she looks just like Olivia.

*

Wiz stepped back into the bakery, worried lines gracing his forehead. Olivia wasn't sure who he'd been on the telephone with, but whatever was discussed, hadn't been good.

"Are we all set?" he asked.

"Yep. We just need to pay the deposit and then we can leave."

"Sounds good."

The bakery owner went over everything she'd told Olivia and Wiz took care of the deposit. Olivia continued to watch him.

"Ready to go?" he asked, shoving his wallet into

his pocket.

"Ready when you are, my dear."

With a hand at the small of her back, he led her to the door. He gave the hallway a cursory glance before escorting her out of the bakery. She knew him well enough to notice when he was on alert and right now, his movements mirrored those of the secret service guarding the President of the United States. When they reached the outside door, everything within her tightened, his trepidation seeped into her soul.

"What's wrong, Cameron?" She looped her arm through his as he peered through the glass door before they stepped out. She always felt safe in his presence, but when he was tense and closed mouth, she got a little nervous.

The sun had set and the streetlights were on except for the one a few yards from the entrance, and one directly across from the bakery. Outside of that, nothing seemed out of the ordinary.

"You're starting to scare me." She stopped, her heart pounding faster than it probably should.

"Nah, sweetie." He slid his arm around her waist, pulling her close and placing a kiss against her temple. "Just checking our surroundings. You know, force of habit."

She released the breath she'd been holding. "You would think I would be used to your obsessive behavior, but I guess I'm not."

He pushed the door open, the cold air slapping them in the face the moment they stepped outside. There weren't many people on the street and the few that were, moved with purpose. No doubt to hurry and get out of the cold. Olivia was just glad it wasn't snowing, but the bite of Jack Frost was real. In just the little while that they were in the bakery, the temperature had dropped at least ten degrees.

"Cameron, if everything is okay, why are you acting so strange?" Olivia cast a worried gaze in his direction as they hurried down the street. "And don't lie to me."

He chuckled, still very in tuned with their surroundings. "Would I lie to you?"

"Yes, if you thought it was something that would worry me."

He gave a slight shrug. "True."

When it seemed he wouldn't elaborate, she said, "So?"

"So, I'm just being careful." He continued glancing around, his hold on her even tighter. "Besides that, it's cold out ..." His words trailed off and she followed his gaze to a dark, four-door sedan creeping up the street behind them. The car moved slower and Wiz picked up speed. Granted the car's dark windows and chrome rims were eye catching, yet she didn't understand his fascination with the vehicle.

"Cameron," she said, practically jogging alongside of him to keep up as they headed toward his truck, weaving around a few people. "I understand you're being careful, but this is getting ridicu—"

"Gun! Get down!" he yelled.

He pushed Olivia to the ground. Her arms shot out to help soften the impending fall and a sharp pain burst through her shoulder, another to her hip the moment she made contact with the concrete. Her head barely missed the pavement.

Gunshots rang out.

It was as if everything happened in slow motion. Wiz pulled the gun from behind his back and returned fire. Her screams mixed with the chaotic scene of others running for cover. Bullets pinging off nearby cars and buildings had her lifting her hands to cover her head.

Barely able to breathe, Olivia struggled under Wiz's weight as he kept her pinned to the ground. She couldn't stop screaming.

"Cameron!" she yelled when a window exploded behind them, sprinkling shards of glass on her head and face. Fear clawed through her body. Tears blurred her vision. She bucked against Wiz's weight, unable to move or see anything.

God, please help us.

Suddenly Wiz grabbed her around the waist. "We have to move!" She barely heard him, screams and gunfire muffling his words. She quickly rose to her knees. When she tried to stand, her legs wobbled. He got beneath her armpit, and practically carried her until she got her footing. They ran crouched down, slowing periodically behind parked cars and trees.

Bullets came more rapidly.

Wiz stumbled and cursed under his breath, his grip loosening from around her. "We need to get to the truck," he ground out, his breathing more ragged.

He cursed again. This time dropping his arms from around her. "Run!" He pushed her toward the truck and returned fire as he ran behind her, ducking and dodging flying bullets.

When he slowed, no longer returning fire, Olivia grabbed hold of the arm of his jacket and pulled him the rest of the way. They dropped down near the back wheel of his truck.

Her pulse thundered in her ears.

The shooter's vehicle screeched away, but not

before more shots rang out and one of the windows in Wiz's truck shattered. He flinched at the sound, pulling her tighter against his body.

"Ohmigod! Ohmigod!" Olivia cried, breathing hard, her body shaking. "We have to get out of here!"

She half stood, but Wiz pulled her back down. "Sirens in the distance. They're gone," he panted, his voice strained. He turned slightly toward her, his hands framing her face. "Are you hurt?" he asked in a rush. His eyes went wide and she followed his gaze, seeing the blood on the front of her coat.

"Oh damn. You've been hit!" He frantically clawed at her coat, trying to get it opened.

"Baby, it's not me," she cried, pushing his hands away and pulling at his jacket the way he had just done to her. Besides being sore and feeling a sting on her shoulder and hip, she was shaken, but okay. But if this wasn't her blood on her coat ... Her heart stopped.

Oh God. She sobbed, trying to keep it together as fear swirled inside of her, afraid of what she'd find under his jacket.

His face paled and he stumbled back into a sitting position, seeming unable to control his moves.

"I'm fine. I need ..." He flinched when she started unzipping his jacket and cursed under his breath, his face twisted in pain. He pushed her hand away to keep her from unzipping the jacket farther, but he was too weak.

"Cameron! You're not fine, dammit! Stop fighting me." She kept going. A gasp slipped through her lips. Blood covered his left side. Lots of blood. "Oh my God. This is bad."

She wanted to lift up his shirt, but her hands were

shaking too bad.

"Somebody help us! Call 911!" She heard the sirens, but he needed help now. More blood soaked one of his pants leg and he was so weak.

"I ... have to ... to get you out of here. Not safe," he struggled to say.

"Don't—"

"Need my ... phone." He tried digging into his front pocket, but she stopped him, her hand covering his.

"No, listen to me," he ground out. The pain must have been getting worse. His breathing became more ragged with every word, beads of sweat popping out on his forehead. "Need you to call Tree," he said of Malik. "Tell him, Cidal ... Boyz," he breathed, unable to stop his body from tilting to the right.

"Baby, please. Please don't talk. Here," she ripped off her coat, balling it up and dropping it on the ground, "lay down."

He didn't argue and did what she said, which only made her more worried. She slid the coat under his head. Tears filled her eyes.

"Don't cry. I ... I love you."

"I love you, too, but I need you to hold on." Hearing the sirens nearby, she stood and waved them over before dropping back down to Wiz.

He reached up to touch her face, but lowered his arm. "Tell Tree ... need Ghost."

"And I need you. I need you to hold on."

"If anything happens to me, Tree ... will ... keep you safe." His eyes drifted closed and his hand dropped to the ground.

"Cameron? Oh God no, Cameron!" she screamed. "Please! Please don't leave me! I need you. We need you. Our baby needs you!"

CHAPTER SEVENTEEN

Hours after being checked out in emergency, Olivia stared out the window in Natasha's office, looking at nothing in particular. Knowing how she felt about hospitals, Malik insisted she hang out in there until they got word on Wiz's condition. As Chief of Staff, Natasha had done everything she could to make the process easy on Olivia. What her friend couldn't do was guarantee that Wiz would make it through surgery. She also couldn't make the memories go away.

"He saved my life," Olivia mumbled more to herself than anyone else in the room.

"Of course he did." Malik strolled up to her, his arm going easily around her shoulder. She didn't know what she would have done without him or Natasha today. "You have to know by now that he would lay down his life for you."

"I know, but I don't want him to," she sobbed, bringing the crumbled tissue up to her face, trying not to shed anymore tears. It all felt like a bad nightmare and the fact that Wiz was still in surgery wasn't helping. Malik seemed so sure that he would be fine, but Olivia wasn't so sure. He had been so pale and had lost so much blood.

Flashbacks of the shooting trampled across her mind. It was as if she could still hear the edge in Wiz's voice, still feel the tenseness of his body when he yelled for her to get down. His skills, reflexes, level headedness, and the measures he took to keep her safe, gave her a whole new respect for his military training. Sure he had taken her to the gun range hundreds of times, but to see him in action felt like an out of body experience.

There was a moment she honestly thought they were going to die, but Wiz had saved them. Watching the paramedics load him into the ambulance was even more traumatic than the shooting. She was sure her heart had stopped when they couldn't get him to respond to anything they did.

Big, strong, and fearless, it was easy to forget that Wiz wasn't invincible. Seeing him on that gurney, not responding, and the paramedics working feverishly to help him, had been too much. She could barely remember calling Malik, the ride in the ambulance, or how chaos scurried around them when arriving at the hospital.

"Olivia, you need to eat," Natasha said when she walked into the office pulling Olivia out of her musing. Victoria and Travis strolled in next carrying enough food to feed a small army.

"We weren't sure what you felt like eating, but there's soup, sandwiches, and salad for you to choose from," Victoria said, placing the bags of food on the large round table in the corner of the room.

Travis held up a large duffle bag that Olivia recognized as Wiz's.

"Where would you like this?"

"By the sofa is fine," Olivia replied.

He and Victoria had gone to the house to gather a few items for her and Wiz. All they'd done for them in the last couple of hours reminded her that they were the family she thought she didn't have.

Olivia leaned against the wall between the windows. Her body felt as if it had been through the spin cycle of a washing machine. Watching as everyone helped unload the bags, she couldn't help but be overwhelmed with love for them.

She lowered her gaze. Thinking of family made her heart flutter. Soon her and Wiz's family would be larger. She still couldn't believe it. She was having a baby. Days ago, she had taken a home pregnancy test that came out positive, but it wasn't until after her doctor's appointment earlier in the day that she knew for sure.

She just wished she had told Wiz the moment she found out. If he didn't make it through … She shook her head to halt the thought. He had to pull through. He had to be okay.

"Come on, sit down and eat something." Malik held her elbow, walking her over to the table.

Natasha and Victoria sat on each side of her, pushing items closer to her while filling their own plates. Travis set several bottles of water in the middle of the table before snagging a seat at the table.

"I'm going downstairs for a minute. I'll be back shortly," Malik said to Natasha, kissing her on the cheek.

Conversation flowed easily and Olivia appreciated everyone's effort to take her mind off the situation. Unfortunately, it wasn't working. One minute she felt like crying and the next she wanted to do physical harm to the people who tried to kill them.

"Come on. It's getting late," Natasha said, her hand on Olivia's shoulder. "Why don't you stretch out on the sofa? One of us will wake you the moment we get word about Cameron."

Olivia glanced down at her half eaten food, barely able to stay awake.

"I think that's a good idea."

*

Wiz floated in and out of consciousness, unable to keep his eyes open for any period of time. Despite his effort to wake up, sleep pulled him back under into a peaceful bliss.

*

Hours later, Wiz struggled to open his eyes, feeling as if there was duct tape holding them down. An annoying beeping to his left and muted voices in the distance filled the space as everything started coming back to him.

Dark car. Tattooed hand. A gun. Olivia ... hospital.

Olivia.

His eyes popped opened and he bolted upright.

"Dammit," he said through gritted teeth, nausea rising to his throat and pain shooting through his body. He slammed his eyes shut and dropped back down to the bed, feeling as if someone had stabbed him in the side and was now shoving the knife in deeper and twisting it.

He cursed again, balling a fist full of the sheet in

his hands willing the pain to cease.

The door opened and Wiz open his eyes again, using the little energy he had to focus on the person who had just walked in.

"It's about damn time you woke up." Malik moved closer to the bed. "I was starting to think they'd screwed something up while you were in surgery."

"Where is she?" he asked, his voice scratchy. Is she—"

"She's okay." Malik pulled a chair closer to the bed and sat in it, leaning on the edge of the bed. "Olivia's upstairs in Tasha's office. She's been checked out, and though shaken, she's doing all right. Last time I checked, she was asleep."

Despite his foggy mind and the way his body was throbbing, relief flooded through his veins. "I have to see her."

"I know. She was down here earlier when you first came out of surgery. She met with the doctor. I have to say, man, based on how Ollie described the scene, you're one lucky brotha. You took a bullet in the left side of your abdomen that passed through some muscle, but no major organs."

"My leg?"

"A bullet grazed you, but you'll live."

Wiz sighed. They took heavy gunfire and he knew it could have been a lot worse. His only concern was that Olivia was okay.

"Go get her."

"In a minute. Let me catch up with stuff first." Malik sat back in his seat. "A nurse'll probably be back in here in a second to check on you. They've been coming in and out. And Sheldon was here earlier to ask you some questions. He got a statement from

Olivia, but said he'll stop by later this morning to talk to you.

Detective Sheldon Baker was a good friend of theirs who they could count on for help during times like this. He was definitely an ally to the agency.

"Olivia said that when you guys left the bakery, you saw a dark car with chrome wheels. What else?"

"Tattoo of a serpent on the guy's gun hand. Cidal Boyz."

"Damn. Anything else? Did you get a good look at the person?"

"Barely." Wiz closed his eyes, trying to relax and bear the burning pain in his side and the throb in his left leg. "Fair complexion, dark shades, and a dark skull cap." Flashes of the scene darted in and out of Wiz's mind. He reopened his eyes. "Everything happened so fast."

"I'm sure."

"Anything on Midnight?" Wiz asked, sure that whatever was going on, she knew something.

"She's vanished. We checked the motel again. Nothing. The cell number she gave Olivia, disconnected. It's like she's fallen off the face of the earth. I have Raeanna checking again to see if she can track her either via credit cards or by the car she's been driving around in."

"Okay."

Raeanna was good. If he couldn't do the behind the scenes work, she would be his first choice to pick up the slack.

"What time is it?" Wiz asked, feeling himself fading.

"One-thirty in the morning." Malik stood and stretched. "They tried kicking me out of here, but I guess there are certain perks to being engaged to the Chief of Staff."

Before Wiz could respond, a nurse waltzed in.

"Mr. Miller, glad to see you awake," she said calmly, a hand on his shoulder while she fiddled with one of the machines.

"How are you feeling?"

"A lot of pain. Nauseous."

"I can give you something for the nausea and increase the pain medication if—"

"No."

"Don't."

He and Malik spoke at the same time.

"O … kay." She looked from him to Malik. "Well, the doctor will stop by soon to check on you. If you need anything, just press the call button."

More pain meds was tempting considering how his body felt like one big, aching muscle, but he needed to be alert. More meds would just knock him out. He and Malik needed to figure out next steps. More importantly, Wiz needed to see Olivia.

"Go get Olivia," Wiz said to Malik the moment the nurse left the room. Not only did he want to see that she was all right, he needed to find out if he had heard her correctly. Was she pregnant?

*

Olivia released an anxious breath as she walked down the hospital hall, flanked by Malik and Travis. She felt bad that she was moving a little slow, her hipbone tender from when Wiz pushed her to the ground.

She stole a quick glance at Malik and then Travis. They had to be tired. The both of them had been overseeing security detail for her and Wiz since they arrived. They had barely taken a break. At least she had dozed off a couple of times. Granted her brief moments of sleep were restless, but they had helped.

"Okay, Ollie," Malik started as they neared Wiz's room. She didn't bother giving him a hard time about the nickname. As a matter of fact, she welcomed it today, needing some since of normal. "Either me, Travis, or Hank will be outside this door at all times. No roaming around without one of us. Understand?"

She nodded. She didn't know if she would ever feel comfortable roaming around anywhere alone again. Normally she wasn't so jumpy, but since arriving at the hospital, every sudden move around her had her jumping.

Malik nodded toward the door. "You can go on in."

"Thanks."

Olivia sucked in a deep breath then released it slowly before pushing the door open. Her heart thumped rapidly in her chest. She hadn't been to Wiz's room since earlier in the day, skittish about seeing him so pale and unmoving. The doctor said he'd make a full recovery, but she'd believe it when he opened those beautiful eyes and talked to her.

Walking farther into the room, she wrung her hands, trying to calm her erratic nerves. The beeping of the heart monitor was the only sound in the cool, semi-dark room. Olivia stopped near the foot of the bed, glad to see some of the color had returned to Wiz's face, but he was still. Too still.

She wasn't sure how long she stood there unmoving, thinking how she wanted her gentle giant back. He might recover physically, but how would he be mentally?

She startled, her hand moving to her chest, when his eyes popped opened. There was an immediate awareness in his gaze. She teared up, relieved to see those intense green eyes staring back at her.

"Hi." She moved slowly to the side of the bed, unsure of why she was still maintaining a distance. His gaze did a slow stroll down her body before returning to her face.

"Hey," he finally said.

Her throat tightened and her hand went to her mouth trying to hold back a sob. Her eyes blurred with tears. The magnitude of what they had gone through hours ago hit her harder now that she was standing next to him.

"Sweetie, don't cry." He slowly stretched his hand to her, pain showing on his face.

She grabbed hold of his hand, never wanting to let him go.

"The doctor said you're going to be okay." Her voice trembled despite trying to be strong. She swiped at a tear that slipped through and pasted on a wobbly smile. "I ... I." She wasn't sure what to say.

"Come here." He pulled on her hand. "Come up here."

She frowned. "I can't. The bed is too small, and you're in pain. I don't want to hurt you more. Besides, you need to get some rest."

"If you want me to get some rest, you need to climb up here with me. I need to hold you."

She folded her lower lip between her teeth and glanced at the door, Wiz still gripping her hand. He was a risk taker, she wasn't. What would the hospital staff say if they found her in his bed?

He tugged her hand again, regaining her attention.

"Come on."

Oh what the heck.

He held onto her as she climbed in on the right side of the bed. With his arm wrapped around her, she placed her head on his chest, careful not to touch his bandages. The stress from earlier immediately evaporated when she snuggled against him.

He placed a kiss on her forehead. "I needed to hold you."

"And I needed to touch you." She sighed.

His hand slid up and down her right side. Not intimately, but more in a soothing way. Less than twenty-four hours ago, they had literally been running for their lives. She tried not to think about how everything could have turned out, but she couldn't help it. She could have lost him. She could have lost the only man she ever loved.

She jerked slightly when his hand slid over her hip and he stiffened.

"You're hurt," he ground out. "Malik said you were okay." His words came out probably harsher than he meant them to.

"I am okay." She went back to rubbing his chest, hoping he'd calm down so the machine he was attached to could go back to the slow rhythmic beeping. "My hip is a little bruised. Nothing a long soak in some warm water can't fix."

"I'm so sorry. I never meant for you to get hurt. I reacted without—"

"Stop." She lifted slightly. "Cameron, you saved my life. A little bruise is nothing compared to what could have happened. Honey, you're my hero. Your quick thinking is why we're both still here."

He didn't say anything. She knew he was still

beating himself up for something so minor instead of realizing what could have happened.

She lowered her head again and her eyes drifted closed as peace settled around her. This was where she belonged, in his arms.

His love for her evident in the way he cradled her close.

"So we're having a baby," he said quietly.

Her eyes popped open and she leaned back to look at his face. "You heard me?"

"I did."

"Well ... that was my surprise, part of it at least. I had a nice romantic night planned for us and I was going to tell you the news once we got home."

"I guess I ruined the surprise, huh?"

A small smile touched her lips as she cupped his cheek, a two-day scruff growing on the lower part of his face.

"Surprise!" She put as much enthusiasm in her voice as she could muster, not sure how he felt about them having a baby.

He chuckled, but stopped and winced. "I guess laughing makes the pain worse."

"Cameron, me laying here with you probably wasn't a good idea." She started to raise up, prepared to climb off the bed, but he stopped her. "I really should let you get some rest so that you can heal."

"Stay here."

She studied him, his eyes barely open, but his gaze steady on her. He looked so tired and since he wasn't a complainer, he was probably in more pain than he was letting on.

"Okay, but just a little while." She settled back against him.

"Why didn't you tell me about the baby sooner?"

"I had just found out officially yesterday morning." She told him how Natasha had suggested that maybe her flu weeks ago wasn't just the flu, but Olivia had shot the idea down. She assumed she couldn't get pregnant again since they hadn't used protection since getting back together and she hadn't gotten pregnant. Her cycle had always been inconsistent so the possibility never came to mind.

It wasn't until a few days ago, when she was still feeling queasy weeks after having the flu, that she decided to take a home pregnancy test.

"I had made an appointment for yesterday with my doctor and Victoria took me."

"She didn't say anything when I called to check on you," he mumbled, his voice barely above a whisper.

"I swore her to secrecy."

He grunted. Olivia glanced up at him. His eyes were closed, but the arm he had around her remained firm and protective.

"Are you asleep?" she asked quietly.

"No. Tired, but not asleep. And no I don't want you to leave. I need you right here with me." He cracked his eyes open, meeting her gaze. "How far along are you?"

"Eight weeks."

"Wow … we're having a baby." He closed his eyes again. His hand that was originally on her hip moved to her flat stomach and a wistful sigh slipped through his lips.

Olivia lowered her eyes. She placed her hand on top of his, grateful their baby was okay considering what they had just gone through. Neither of them could handle another miscarry.

We can't lose this baby.

CHAPTER EIGHTEEN

Wiz woke with a start. He wasn't sure how long they'd been asleep, but probably not long considering it was still dark outside.

He remained still and listened. Someone other than them was in the room. He focused, his gaze slowly roaming around the space, which was larger than most hospital rooms. He froze when he saw a lone figure in the darkened corner.

"It's good to see your senses are still as sharp as usual." Quinn stepped into the low stream of light created by the wall sconce near the head of the bed.

"And I see you still move in and out of rooms like Casper the Friendly Ghost."

Quinn chuckled. "Yeah, but I'm not all that friendly."

His dark eyes twinkled and Wiz carefully lifted his left hand, greeting his longtime friend with a fist bump. He could always count on his brothers to be here for him, even when they lived out in the Pacific

Ocean somewhere. Bora Bora was where Quinn and Alandra called home now.

Quinn nodded toward Olivia who hadn't stirred. "My girl looks good." The moment Wiz woke earlier to find her standing at the foot of his bed, he could tell she was exhausted. Insisting she lay down with him wasn't just about him needing to hold her. They needed each other.

"She's good, all things considered. You're looking well. How's Alandra?"

He hadn't seen them in almost a year, though they kept in touch.

"She's amazing. Of course I brought her with me."

Wiz cracked a smile. "Of course." After all the mess that he and Alandra went through, Wiz was pretty sure Quinn rarely went anywhere without her. The fact that she was five months pregnant probably made him even more vigilante about keeping her close.

Wiz glanced down at Olivia. He not only had her to worry about, but now also their baby.

"Olivia's pregnant," Wiz said without preamble, liking how the words sounded as they rolled off his tongue.

Quinn cocked an eyebrow. "Seriously?"

Wiz nodded, finding it hard to keep the smile from his face.

"Congratulations, man. Malik didn't tell me that part. So how far along is she?"

"Eight weeks."

Wiz and Olivia had a lot to discuss. He wasn't sure how she wanted to handle telling their friends and family. But before they did anything, he needed to figure out why they were ambushed.

"I need your help in finding the bastards who attacked us yesterday."

"Cidal Boyz." Quinn rubbed the back of his neck. "So when I find them, then what?"

"Then I'll take it from there."

Quinn shook his head. "Nah, man. You can't take them on by yourself. We're not talking about some two-bit gang bangers. They're hard core and crazy organized. You don't just go after them. *We* can't just go after them."

Frustration rumbled in Wiz's gut, causing his muscles to tighten. The wound on his side felt as if someone had just punched him and the heart monitor went into a fit.

Wiz breathed in and out slowly, but seconds later, a nurse walked in.

Oh great.

The last thing he needed was for her to start fussing over him. Instead, she glanced from him to Olivia to Quinn and then back to him.

She moved farther into the room. "I totally understand the need to have your wife here, Mr. Miller, but it's against policy for her to—"

"If she goes, I go."

His comment was met with silence. Instead of responding, the nurse nodded and backed out of the room.

Olivia mumbled something, but didn't wake and burrowed closer to him.

Quinn said nothing. Probably because his stance would have been the same had it been him and Alandra.

"Malik told me this crazy shit started because of Midnight. For the record, this will be the last time we search for her." Quinn kept his voice low, but Wiz didn't miss the edge in his tone and the meaning behind his words.

Wiz nodded his understanding. He pushed down the guilt that was clawing at his conscious for not telling Olivia what happened ten years ago. But after the way they were attacked yesterday, Keisha would deserve whatever fate dealt her when this was all over. As far as he was concerned, this would be his last round with Keisha Abernathy.

*

Later in the evening, Wiz—propped against pillows in his hospital bed—listened as Quinn, Malik, and Raeanna discussed the latest developments in Operation Midnight part two. Malik insisted that this new search for Keisha ranked up there with one of their overseas missions.

Raeanna handed Wiz her laptop, the screen covered with snapshots of Keisha.

"Where did these come from?"

"While doing some more background checking on Keisha, I ... I also stumbled upon some chatter within the Cidal Boyz's organization."

"What?" Wiz, Quinn, and Malik said at once.

"Stumbled upon or hacked into?" Wiz knew her. She was good. Damn good. She might have stumbled, but he'd be willing to bet she knew exactly what she was doing.

"Rae, you're playing with fire. We don't want your digging around to start a damn war," Malik said.

"It won't, I was very careful." She glanced at Wiz and he knew for sure she intentionally dug into their system.

"So what did you find?" Quinn asked.

"Bishop wants Keisha found. He wants her returned alive. From what I can tell, whoever did the shooting, didn't act on his command. And the powers that be are still trying to figure out who was involved. It doesn't sound like anyone is admitting to the shooting."

"Bishop will find them," Quinn said dryly, running his hands over his dread locks that hung in a ponytail past his shoulders. Many years ago, his gang ties had brought him face-to-face with Bishop. According to Quinn, the guy was ruthless, but a frickin' genius when it came to business.

"Also, the media has been all over this and was at first saying that the shooting was some type of gang initiation, but I only heard that once. This morning they haven't said much about the incident. It might be because Victoria and the agency's PR department have convinced them not to release your names. But I'm sure she'll talk to you more about that."

Wiz nodded absently as he continued looking through the photos.

"Most of the pictures of Keisha were posted in the Boyz's system a few weeks ago, before she showed up in Chicago," Raeanna said. "The last four photos were more recent."

Wiz was pissed Keisha had intentionally made herself look like Olivia. These guys could easily go after Olivia thinking that she was Keisha. He hoped he was wrong about the direction his thoughts were taking him, but he knew his sister-in-law. He wouldn't put anything past her.

He scrolled down the page to the last few photos that Raeanna said were recent. His pulse cranked up as he studied each one. He had seen the outfits recently. He also recognized the backgrounds. Two of the pictures were taken near the university where Olivia worked and the other two were taken outside of … a bridal shop.

"What is it?" Quinn asked, approaching the bed. "Your heart rate just skyrocketed."

"The last four aren't Keisha. They're Olivia."

They all crowded around the laptop. Wiz pointed out the backgrounds and told them Olivia had recently worn those same outfits. For the most part, it looked like the same person, but Wiz was ninety-nine percent sure they were photos of Olivia.

"Which could mean they might not know they're twins," Malik said.

Damn. That means she might have intentionally led them to Olivia.

"I need Olivia back here." Wiz tried to remain calm, but the thought of her being a target was making that difficult.

"I'll find out their ETA," Malik said, his cell in hand as he stepped out of the room.

Wiz handed the laptop back to Raeanna. The more they learned the more afraid for Olivia's safety he became. Victoria and Hank had escorted her home to pack a couple of bags since they wouldn't be staying at the house until all of this was over. But no matter where they stayed, knowing this gang thought Olivia was Keisha scared Wiz.

"Do you need anything else from me right now, Wiz?" Raeanna asked.

"I just need you to keep digging and see what you can find on Keisha. We have to find her. Sooner than later. Also, can you finish going through the jewelry store's footage? I marked where I left off. I'm thinking we have at least another week's worth of footage to look through. Mark anything that looks strange, especially sections that include Clayton working alone in the back area of the store."

"Is Clayton the one you saw Keisha talking to on the video?" Quinn asked Wiz.

"Yeah, and I have a feeling they know each other."

"Actually, Wiz, Gary called this morning and said that he thinks he's ready to go to the police. Clayton didn't show up for his shift yesterday or this morning and he didn't call in."

Wiz flopped against the pillows. *This shit just keeps getting messier.*

"If what Wiz says is true about Clayton and Keisha knowing each other, it's pretty safe to say they're together." Quinn hadn't said much during the brief meeting, but each time he interjected a thought or asked a question, more and more of the puzzle came together.

Wiz lifted his head. "Raeanna, I'm going to have Victoria work with you. I want everything you can find on Clayton. His contact information is in the file we have on the jewelry store. I want a list of credit card transactions over the past month, all of his incoming and outgoing calls, where he's been the last few days—everything. Once I'm out of here, we'll lay out the information we've gathered on him and Keisha so far, and see if we can make any connections."

"Got it. We'll get on this right away. Feel better soon," she said before leaving.

Wiz and Quinn were the only ones left in the room. "What are you thinking?" Wiz asked.

"I'm thinking we have to find Midnight before

anything else happens. In the meantime, you and Olivia are all set to stay at the penthouse while you recover. Tyler will meet us there once you're released."

Quinn and Tyler owned one of the largest real estate development companies in the Midwest. A couple of years ago, they had purchase and renovated a building on Lake Shore Drive, turning the top-floor units into penthouses. Tyler kept one that they now used as guest housing. Since living out of the country, Quinn wasn't as active in the company and now was more of a silent partner.

"I appreciate you setting that up. I'm being released in the morning."

"Why don't you try to get some rest? I'm going to check on my wife and then start doing some digging of my own."

Wiz watched him leave the room. All of their lives were changing. Engagements, marriages, and now children. Their extended family was growing. The crap that everyone had gone through over the last couple of years was more than any of them bargained for, but they survived.

Now it was his and Olivia's turn.

CHAPTER NINETEEN

Olivia sat in the chair next to Wiz's hospital bed as Malik explained to her and Wiz how they would transport them to the penthouse.

Her gaze went to Quinn who was leaning against a wall, his huge arms folded across his chest. She hadn't seen him since they had dropped him and Alandra off at LAX to parts unknown a year ago. He was still as dangerously sexy as always, and according to Natasha, his presence in the hospital had all the nurses hanging out in the hallway near Wiz's door.

"Wiz, you and Olivia will ride with me and Quinn," Malik said. "Travis and Hank will be in the truck in front of us and we'll have another team taking up the rear."

"Is my computer equipment already at the penthouse or do we need to stop by the house first?" Wiz asked.

Olivia had been watching Wiz all morning. Some of his color was back, but he was still in a great deal of pain. She understood why he'd been weaning himself off the pain medication, but that didn't mean she thought it was a good idea. Like her, he was ready to put the whole mess with Keisha behind them. But unlike her, he was putting his health at risk, claiming he would never be able to rest easy as long as there was a threat against Olivia.

Wiz had told her his theory about Keisha's reason for being in Chicago. Her sister had done some underhanded, thoughtless things in the past, but nothing to this degree. Not once had Keisha mentioned being engaged. And diamonds? Why would she think she could get away with stealing diamonds of all things? But what Olivia had a hard time believing, was that her sister altered her style of dress in hopes of drawing the trouble away from herself and onto Olivia. Now that was unforgivable.

Wiz reminded Olivia that it was just a theory and that he hoped he was wrong, but Olivia knew better. Wiz was good at what he did and she would be willing to bet money that though it might've been a theory, he wasn't that far off.

"Ready?" Wiz asked Olivia when he climbed off the bed.

She nodded, but honestly, she wasn't. She wasn't ready to walk out of the hospital in broad daylight despite Malik's assurance that they would be safe.

The day before when Hank and Victoria had taken her to the house to gather some of her and Wiz's belongings, it had been at night. Somehow she felt a little safer under the cover of darkness.

"Let's rock and roll," Malik said.

They headed to an area for employees only, where the trucks were waiting to transport them. Olivia felt like royalty hurrying down the hall surrounded by big, strong men whose eyes were shielded by dark shades and who were all well over six feet tall. She didn't dare ask if this was a little overkill after what she and Wiz had experienced the other day. Instead, she appreciated the measures they were taking to keep them safe.

Wiz held tight to her hand, looking as if he were prepared to leap out of the wheelchair at any sign of threat.

No one was in the hall as the exit came in to view and Olivia wondered if Malik orchestrated that as well.

"Olivia, the moment the back door is opened, you're going to climb in first and then Wiz." She nodded her understanding.

Once they were at the exit, Malik's team jumped into action. No one spoke as they all moved in perfect sync, hustling her and practically carrying Wiz to the truck. Seconds later, they were on their way.

It wasn't until they were several blocks away from the hospital did Olivia breathe. Wiz squeezed her hand, encouraging her to move closer to him without saying a word. As a matter of fact, no one in the vehicle had spoken.

They had done a good job in keeping her in the loop, but Olivia couldn't help but wonder if something was happening that she didn't know about.

"You're shivering. Are you cold?" Wiz asked, his normally deep voice sounding strained.

She glanced at him. He had on a wool hat pulled low on his head that stopped just above his eyes. He wasn't looking too good and she was about to tell him that when he spoke again.

"Don't look so worried. I'm all right." His raspy voice contradicted his words. And the perspiration on his nose and above his top lip couldn't have been a good sign.

"You can keep telling yourself that if you want, but I'm not buying it. You're not well, Cameron. I can tell you're in pain. You should've stayed on the pain medication a little longer. As a matter of fact, you should have done as the doctor recommended and stayed at least another day in the hospital."

He didn't speak for the longest. He just caressed her cheek and stared into her eyes.

"Do you realize, we'll be married in two weeks and six days?"

"Really, Cameron? You're going to bring that up now when I'm worried to death about you?" She wanted to punch him. If for nothing more than to release some of the pent-up stress that had been building within her for the last few days.

The day before, her doctor had ordered an ultrasound. With her age and the fact that she had miscarried in the past, as well as the fall she took during the shooting, he wanted to make sure all was well with the baby. Arrangements were made and Wiz was able to be with her.

Olivia would never forget the expression on his face when they saw and heard their baby's heartbeat. She had experienced it before, with the baby they'd lost, but to experience it with him was something she wouldn't soon forget.

Though she and the baby were fine, the doctor did warn that she needed to get started immediately on prenatal vitamins, as well as eat more. She had to keep from rolling her eyes when he told her to try to keep her stress level down. That would probably be easy if she hadn't been shot at, her man hadn't almost lost his life, and she hadn't just found out her sister was a diamond thief. Who could stay stress free with all of that going on?

"Relax, sweetheart." Wiz broke into her thoughts and gently pulled her to him. She went willingly into his arms as his calmness slowly swirled around her. It was as if he sensed her anxiousness. Heck, it was probably written all over her face. After a few minutes, she settled in for the ride.

Thirty minutes later, Quinn escorted them to the apartment.

"You guys made it. Come on in," Tyler said when he and Dallas opened the door. They all exchanged hugs in the circular entryway.

The impressive space was larger than a normal foyer and showcased an impressive crystal chandelier, sparkling marbled floors, and two large bamboo palm trees. Olivia had always loved touring houses and watching home shows on television and couldn't wait to see the rest of the penthouse.

"I'm so glad you guys are okay," Dallas said taking their coats, keeping her arm around Olivia's shoulder.

"Thanks. Me too."

Olivia couldn't get over how Dallas always looked so pulled together. With her long, dark hair, flawless skin, and perfect body, she didn't look like a mother of twin boys who were almost two years old.

Dallas ushered them into the living room and just then, Alandra walked in carrying one of the twins and holding the hand of the other.

"Ma ma." The one whose hand Alandra was holding ran to Dallas.

Olivia's heart melted at the sight of them. She hadn't seen them in a while, and was surprised to see how big they had gotten. They were still the cutest little boys she'd ever seen. With their innocent eyes and head full of curly hair, they were the perfect combination of both Tyler and Dallas.

Oliva caught Wiz's gaze and they shared a smile. In a few months, they would be holding their little one. She had no idea how she was going to be able to wait another seven months for their child's arrival.

"Well, it's about time you guys got here." Alandra smiled and made a beeline to Olivia, hugging her with her free arm while the little guy she carried squirmed in her arms. "I'm so happy you both are okay."

"Thank you, me too," Olivia said against Alandra's head full of curls, appreciating her heart-felt hug. "It's so good to see you again."

Olivia stepped back and gave her a long look. "You don't look five months pregnant."

"Girl, I feel like I'm eight months pregnant. And congratulations, Q told me the exciting news!"

"That's right. Congratulations are in order," Dallas said, looking from Wiz to Olivia. "We're going to have to celebrate."

"Before you get carried away and start planning any celebrations, maybe we should let them get settled," Tyler chimed in.

"And why are you carrying him around?" Quinn asked Alandra, taking the little boy from her arms.

Alandra nudged him with her hip. "I'm pregnant, not fragile."

"I know, babe, but he's too heavy for you to be carrying." Quinn kissed her on the lips and the wistful smile Alandra gave him was so full of heat, it could have melted butter.

"Okay, so which is which?" Wiz asked of the twins.

Olivia shook the small hand of the one that Quinn was holding.

"Well, the little man who Dallas has is Evan, and this little one is Ethan," Quinn said of his godsons.

"He's the one who has a crush on Alandra," Dallas added. "Q, you're going to have to watch him. He hasn't let Alandra out of his sight since you left."

"That's because I told him to keep an eye on my woman. Ain't that right, man?"

Ethan grinned up at Quinn then shyly dropped his head to his godfather's shoulder.

"Are they talking yet?" Olivia asked.

Conversation flowed easily around the room and for a moment, Olivia had forgotten about their troubles. It felt good to be surrounded by friends.

A short while later, Olivia and Wiz lounged on the king size bed and stared out the huge windows that overlooked Lake Michigan. At the moment, it felt as if they were on a long overdue vacation.

"What's on your mind?" Wiz asked.

"I want our child so bad, but I'm afraid to get too excited about the baby. It's still early and anyth—"

"Stop. We're not doing this. We are going to have a healthy baby in a few months and I refuse to think otherwise."

"But—"

"But nothing, sweetheart." He placed his large hand on her belly. "This little one might not have been planned, but he or she is wanted and already loved. That's what we're going to focus on. All right?"

She nodded, knowing that he was right. Despite

what was going on in their lives, she had to stay positive. They had so much to look forward to in the coming months with their wedding and the baby. The only dark spot in their world right now was Keisha.

*

Two days later, Wiz and his team had gathered enough information on Clayton to know for certain that he and Keisha were working together. Up until a week ago, Clayton's phone records revealed numerous incoming and outgoing calls from her. He had since disconnected his phone and had moved out of his apartment.

Wiz sat in the comfortable chair near the window as Quinn, Malik, Victoria, and Raeanna talked at the table behind him. Tyler once used the spare room as an office when he and Dallas lived in the penthouse and left it as such once they moved out. The large space with a wall of windows accommodated Wiz and the team easily.

Wiz thought about the last two weeks and the conversations that he and Olivia had had regarding Keisha. There had to be something he was missing.

Using the facial recognition software that he had recently acquired, they had determined that Clayton was the person at the patio door that night Olivia thought she heard someone in the yard. Wiz would love to get his hands on the guy for scaring her. But right now, he wanted to get his hands on Clayton to get some answers about Keisha.

It was as if she and Clayton had vanished. No credit card transactions. No appearances around town. Nothing.

Malik leaned against the wall closest to Wiz. "I know you. Whenever you get quiet like this, especially in the middle of a brainstorming session, it means you have some ideas. So what gives?"

"Just trying to piece some of the parts together."

"Like?"

"Like whether or not Keisha was able to sell the diamonds. Or like why Clayton was at our house that night. And how do they know each other?"

"Well, I can answer the last question," Victoria said. "When Travis and I went to Clayton's apartment, we showed Keisha's photo to a couple of neighbors. The guy who lived two doors down mentioned that he used to see Keisha around years ago and thought that she and Clayton were an item. He said they used to get high together, but then Keisha disappeared and Clayton got clean."

"So now they're back together," Quinn said. "You know, Wiz, there was something you said at the hospital about Midnight trying to talk Olivia into going back to the house after they had brunch. What if she really did leave something there?"

Wiz rubbed his chin. "Yeah, I thought about that, but I would think that either Olivia or I would have seen something by now.

"Only if you were looking for it," Malik added. "And you know Keisha's sneaky ass. It's not like she would leave diamonds in plain view. After you left the party, it wasn't like she roamed around your house, but she did hang out in the family room and I also saw her in the kitchen."

"And when I cornered her, she was coming out of the first floor bathroom." Now that Wiz thought about it, she did seem a little skittish and it wasn't because of him.

"Looks like we need to make a trip to your

house," Quinn said.

"I agree." Wiz stood slowly, his side screaming in pain. Instead of the prescribed pain medication, he'd been taking ibuprofen which helped some. He rolled his shoulders to work out the kinks for sitting longer than he should have. "How about later, once it gets dark?"

"Works for me," Quinn replied. "I'm going to Tyler and Dallas's place to check on Alandra, but will head back in a few hours."

"You guys are on your own tonight. Tasha and I have a fundraiser to attend." Malik pushed away from the wall. "I'll make sure Travis is here before you leave and Hank is on call."

"And I'll be here. I'm helping Olivia go over the last items that need to be taken care of before the wedding," Victoria stated.

"Okay. Raeanna, why don't you take the rest of the day off? You've been putting in some long hours, which I appreciate," Wiz said.

"It's been a pleasure." She gathered her laptop and bag. "I've learned a lot these last few days. Just call if you need me to do anything else."

"Cameron?"

Wiz glanced over his shoulder to find Olivia standing in the doorway holding a cell phone with both hands to her chest.

"Hey, babe." When she didn't automatically walk in, he took a good look at her. The small hairs on his forearm stood at attention, foreboding lodged in his chest. "What's wrong?" He moved toward her.

"We need ... to talk." Her voice shook with every word and the ominous churning in his gut intensified. "Alone."

Wiz stood dumbfounded for a moment until she turned and walked away. He followed her to the bedroom they were using and closed the door.

"I received a text message ... from Keisha."

CHAPTER TWENTY

That uncomfortable gnawing in his gut amped up a notch when he leaned against the door and Olivia's back remained to him. She stood at the window, her arms folded around her midsection.

"What did the text say?"

She tossed the cell onto the bed. "Read it for yourself."

Wiz picked it up, steeling himself for what was to come.

Did your husband tell you he and his friends held me at gunpoint, threatening to kill me if I didn't leave town ten yrs ago? Call if you want details. Keisha.

Shit!

"Please tell me this isn't true. Tell me you didn't threaten to kill my sister." Her voice was low and he could tell she was battling to stay calm. "I'll believe whatever you tell me."

Oh damn.

He hesitated, debating on how to handle this conversation. Lying wasn't an option, especially since he had planned to tell her the truth someday anyway. How could he explain that night without it sounding as if threatening people was an everyday occurrence?

"Your silence speaks volumes. How could you? How could you consider killing her? Is this standard practice with you and your boys? Someone makes you mad and you shoot them?"

"Wait." That gnawing in his gut was quickly turning into irritation. "First of all, *no*, we don't go around popping everyone who gets in our way. Second, Keisha has given me more reasons than I can count to send her to an early grave. I know that's not what you want to hear, Olivia, but it's true."

"You guys held her at gunpoint and that's all right with you?" she asked, incredulous, pinning him with a cold, hard glare. "No way am I going to defend Keisha, but all of you are Navy SEALs who are twice her height and weight, yet you had to hold a gun on her." She shook her head and slowly paced the length of the room.

Wiz remained silent, letting her get it all out.

"The man I fell in love with would never do something like that. Threaten a woman's life? He would never consider taking a life just because the person pissed him off."

Wiz straightened, feeling a little uncomfortable in the direction the conversation was going.

"I can't … I just can't—"

"You can't what, Olivia?" Unease scraped up and down his spine. He already knew that if she ever found out about that night, she'd never forgive him, but …

She finally stopped moving and gave him her full attention as she gnawed on her lower lip. Wiz saw the conflict on her face, but he had no idea what she was thinking.

"You can't what?" he repeated.

"I can't do this right now. When I saw that text, I prayed Keisha was lying, but a part of me knew she was telling the truth. I just didn't want to believe that my man was capable of killing someone in cold blood."

"Don't keep saying that!" he snapped. "You still don't get it, do you, Olivia? No matter how I have tried to explain that night to you. You clearly will never understand the gut wrenching fear I felt on that plane from Germany, imagining the worse. I reacted the way any man in my position would have reacted."

Wiz took a deep breath, attempting to slow his racing heart. He was sick of trying to get her to comprehend just how much he despised her sister and with good reason.

"Because of your sister, I almost lost everything that night. We lost our unborn child, for God's sake and I almost lost you. Why? Because Keisha is a cold-hearted bitch who thinks of no one but herself. Who allows some asshole to drug their sister, their own flesh and blood, and then takes off and leave her to die? Who does that? Let me ask you, Olivia. How would you have responded if you were in my shoes? Mind you, I hadn't seen you months and had just returned from a horrific op. How would you have responded?"

At least she had the decency to look contrite, but she remained quiet. He didn't know how else to explain how that had been the worse night of his life.

It even trumped the other day when they were shot at.

"You're my everything," Wiz continued. "Knowing you were missing or maybe worse … I lost it, especially after we found you barely alive. I'll admit, I wanted her dead and I won't apologize for almost making that a reality. I wanted … and still want your sister out of our lives. I don't trust her and I never will."

"What stopped you from following through on your plans back then?"

"You. Despite you thinking that I'm some cold-blooded killer, I couldn't end her life because of my love for you."

She turned away from him, hugging herself once again.

"How do I know you haven't done something to Keisha now?" she asked.

Taken aback by the question, all Wiz could do was stare at her back.

"You don't."

He let the words hang out there for a while, angry that she thought that little of him.

"But I'm telling you I haven't done anything to your sister and I have no idea where she is."

Olivia's shoulders sagged and she plopped down on the bed, her face in her hands.

Still holding Olivia's phone, Wiz pulled out his own cell and texted Keisha's number to Raeanna with a message to trace the number.

Slipping his phone back into his pocket, he sat on the bed not missing the way Olivia stiffened. The cold shoulder he could handle. He just couldn't handle this mess coming between them, especially with a baby on the way.

"Why do you think Keisha suddenly decided to tell you about something that happened ten years ago? She's had plenty of opportunity. Why now?"

Olivia gave a slight shrug. "I don't know."

"So are you going to call her back, get her version of the story?"

Seconds ticked by before she said, "No."

Relief flooded through Wiz. He actually didn't care what Keisha had to say, he just wanted her to stay the hell away from Olivia.

He moved closer to her, but stopped when she pulled away.

"I know not to expect much from Keisha, but you?" she started quietly, "I expect so much more from you. I'll admit Keisha brings out the worse in most people, but I can't believe you would let her push you to the point of murder. That scares me to death, Cameron."

Wiz leaned forward to place his elbows on his knees, but stopped mid lean when his side protested. Placing his hand on the tight bandage wrapped around his midsection he remained still as he breathed through the pain.

"I'm human, Olivia. I'm not going to always make the best decisions or do the right thing. And when it comes to you and now my unborn child, there is nothing I won't do to ensure the safety of both of you. So hate me if you want." He stood slowly, his side throbbing. "Instead of expecting me to be some saint, which I'm not, try to remember that I'm human."

He left the room without looking back. More than ever, he needed to find Keisha and damn if he wasn't going to end this.

CHAPTER TWENTY-ONE

Wiz opened and slammed cabinet doors and drawers as he searched every inch of the kitchen. The more he thought about the conversation with Olivia, the more pissed he got. No, he didn't expect her to handle the news great, but he did expect her to understand his mental state at the time.

He wasn't sure what game Keisha was playing now. She disappeared and then sent the text to Olivia. *What the hell was that all about?* Raeanna had tried tracing the number, but either Keisha was using a burner phone or she had the cell off. They were no closer to finding her than they were days ago.

"Find anything yet?" Quinn strolled into the kitchen. "Or are you just slamming doors for the hell of it?"

Ignoring Quinn, Wiz bent to look in the cabinet that held the pots and pans and cursed under his breath. He'd been so riled up since leaving the penthouse that there were moments he forgot about his injuries. All it took was a move here or there and his body quickly reminded him that he was still not one hundred percent.

"Maybe if you calm the hell down, or better yet, sit down somewhere, then maybe you won't pull all of your stitches loose."

"I'm fine."

"I didn't ask if you were fine. I said sit your ass down."

Instead, Wiz leaned his back against the breakfast bar and stared out over the family room.

"Do you know what I keep thinking?"

"No, what?"

"If I had to do that night from ten years ago over again, knowing what I know now, I wouldn't have let Keisha off so easy. I would have stuck with my original plan. If that makes me a heartless monster, oh well."

Quinn stood across from him, his feet spread apart and his huge arms folded across his chest. "I'm not sure what you're expecting me to say. You know some of the shit I've done over the years. Do I have regrets? Hell yeah. But mostly I have learned to live with my decisions. What's done is done, Wiz. It's not like you can go back and change anything. All you can do is move forward and deal with the here and now."

It was mostly Olivia's reaction that bothered him. Since the day he met her, she made him want to be a better man. Disappointing her was not something he ever wanted to do.

"As for Olivia," Quinn started as if reading Wiz's mind, "the initial shock of what could have happened to her sister at your hands will wear off. I'm sure by now she understands what you were going through.

Her issue is probably more about not knowing that you were capable ... and willing to take a life, especially the life of her sister."

Wiz marinated on Quinn's words as silence fell between them. He hoped that he and Olivia could put this whole ordeal behind them and move on with their lives. Their wedding was in a few weeks and he definitely didn't want the hunt for Keisha and the diamonds to still be going on.

Having had enough of this pity party, Wiz pushed away from the counter. "Let's get back to work. Malik said that Keisha didn't leave this level. I'll check the first floor bathroom and you check the dining area and the closet in the front foyer."

"Will do."

Wiz rummaged through the cabinet under the bathroom sink and inside the toilet tank before moving to the linen closet. It was starting to look as if his theory about Keisha hiding something at their house was a wash.

He searched inside containers, dug behind toiletries, and even pulled items out of the closet, finding nothing. It wasn't until he lifted the last towel that he felt something bulky.

Bingo.

He opened the fluffy black towel and found a velvet bag like the one Keisha had on the video.

Wiz stepped out of the bathroom holding the loot in the air just as Quinn made his way into the hallway.

"Well, I'll be damn. You were right. Not that I'm surprised."

Quinn poured the diamonds into his hand, before shoving them back into the bag. "Why hide these here?" he asked

Wiz shook his head. "I don't know, but I'm sure she intended to come back for them."

"So how much do you think they're worth?"

"If I had to guess, I'd say about thirty thousand."

Quinn gave a long whistle. "I guess if you're going to steal something, might as well go big. I'm going to hit the head before we leave."

"Cool."

Wiz stuffed the jewels into the inside pocket of his jacket. Now he had to get them into the right hands so that he could get the gang off their backs and maybe even get Keisha out of her mess. He kept telling himself that anything he did to help her was for Olivia's benefit.

He strolled through the house, making sure lights were out and ended up in the kitchen. He sifted through the mail that had accumulated while they were away. He and Olivia liked the penthouse, but he was ready to return home, even if she did want to sell the house and purchase a different one together. All because he goofed and referred to the house as his.

Wiz picked up another envelope, but stopped when he heard noise behind the house. Slowly placing the letter back down on the counter, he pulled his gun from the back of his waistband.

He stood still. At first, he thought he was hearing things, but then furniture scraped across the wood deck out back.

Wiz slipped out of the house through the garage. He could use the back garage door that led to the yard, without being seen.

Stepping out into the brisk winter night, Wiz ignored the way the wind whipped across his face, sending a chill to his bones. He spotted a lone figure standing near the patio door with what looked to be a screwdriver in his hand. With his gun at his side, Wiz eased along the exterior of the house, careful to stay in the shadows.

The man was so focused on getting the patio door open, he hadn't heard Wiz's approach.

Wiz lifted his gun. "You really have a death wish trying to break into my house."

Startled, the guy dropped the screwdriver and quickly swung around, his elbow making contact with Wiz's wound.

"Sonofa—" Wiz's gun slipped from his hand. He grabbed his side, gritting his teeth against the breathtaking pain, like fire in his side and fell to his knees.

Damn.

The man tried to make a run for it, but Wiz grabbed him by the ankle and jerked him back, causing the intruder to lose his footing.

"Your ass ain't going nowhere," Wiz said through gritted teeth as he pulled the man down. Wiz jabbed him in the jaw with his fist and wrestled him to the deck. Catching the guy off guard gave Wiz a chance to retrieve his gun.

Wiz straddled him, his gun in the man's face. "Move again," he said before recognition settled in.

Clayton.

"What the hell are you doing here?"

"I … I …" Clayton's gaze froze over Wiz's shoulder. "Listen, I don't want any trouble."

"Looks like you're having all the fun," Quinn said from behind Wiz.

"Yeah, this type of fun I can do without out."

Quinn hauled the man to his feet.

"Clayton, you cannot be stupid enough to try and break into my home."

"I'm ... I'm sorry, just don't shoot me."

Wiz kept his gun trained on him. He had no intentions of shooting the guy, but Clayton didn't have to know that.

"I-I ..." Clayton stammered.

Quinn pushed him against the brick of the house. "You better start using some words other than I, otherwise you can talk to the cops."

"I-I needed to get something out of there."

"In my house?" Wiz yelled.

Clayton said nothing.

Wiz pulled out his cell phone. "I don't have time for this shit. Let CPD deal with him."

"Wait. Wait! No cops. Please."

"Sure, no cops, but you better start talking," Quinn said.

"I want to know what business you have in my house and where is Keisha?" Wiz asked.

Seconds ticked by while Clayton glared at Wiz, but then drop his shoulders. "Keisha came to me trying to unload some diamonds that her fiancé gave her. She said that if I helped her sell them, she would split the profit with me. But then someone started following her. She didn't think it was safe to keep them at her place and said that her sister would keep them for her."

Wiz cursed under his breath. That sister-in-law of his was a real piece of work.

"That still doesn't explain why you're trying to break into my house."

"We had to lay low for a few days and then Keisha said that her sister refused to give the diamonds back."

"Where is Keisha now?"

"I think they have her."

"They who?" Wiz asked.

"I don't know. I guess whoever was following her."

"Maybe you ought to start at the beginning." Quinn readjusted his hold on Clayton.

Clayton explained how Keisha had contacted him a few weeks ago saying that she had a proposition for him. Getting rid of the diamonds had been a little harder than they expected. Once they finally found a buyer, Keisha realized she was being followed.

"So how do you know they have her?" Wiz asked.

"They found out where we were staying. Last night, I was outside taking a smoke and these two cars with dark windows pulled up to the house. I saw them, but they didn't see me. Before I knew it, they were dragging Keisha out of the house."

"And what did you do?" Wiz asked. When Clayton diverted his gaze, Wiz shook his head. "Like a little punk, you did nothing."

"What was I going to do? There were four rough looking dudes, all tatted up. I …"

"You did nothing. Now you're here trying to break into my house."

Wiz lifted his cell phone and dialed 911.

"Hey, you said you weren't going to call the cops!"

"I didn't say that. He said he wouldn't call." Wiz nodded to Quinn who shrugged, looking as if he didn't have a care in the world.

"What are you going to do with the diamonds?"

"That's not something you should be worried about right now. What you need to be concerned about is what CPD is going to think about you stealing diamonds from a jewelry store."

"But ... I—"

"Save it for someone who cares. Right now I have more important things to take care of."

*

Sitting at the dining room table, Olivia pushed the pasta around on her plate, her mind everywhere but on eating. Wiz's question regarding why Keisha would pick now to say something rattled around in her head. She never knew why Keisha did half the things she did, which was why Olivia didn't understand why she had gotten so angry with Wiz earlier.

Had she been in his shoes all those years ago, she might have been tempted to do something crazy to Keisha, too. Even after the shooting only days ago, seeing Wiz lay lifeless in front of her, blood oozing from his body, was a scene she would never forget. A scene that made her want to kill someone.

"That pasta is probably more like paste considering how long you've been sitting here playing in it." Victoria, carrying a bowl of popcorn, pulled out a chair across from Olivia.

Olivia didn't think she would ever get used to seeing Victoria and Travis walking around with their gun holstered in plain sight. She might've felt a little more comfortable with having guns around, but she didn't want to stare at them all the time. It also reminded her that she was being babysat, because of Keisha.

"I guess I wasn't that hungry," she finally said to Victoria.

Natasha walked into the room and sat next to Victoria. "You have to eat, Olivia. That baby is counting on you to keep yourself healthy."

Olivia couldn't argue with her there, but how was she supposed to make herself eat when she wasn't hungry?

"I took the liberty of asking Malik to pick up a hamburger from your favorite restaurant on his way here," Natasha added.

Olivia smiled. She had mentioned having a taste for a burger earlier that day.

It was the small gestures like that which reminded Olivia that these people were indeed her family.

"I could definitely go for a hamburger. By the way, you look amazing." The royal blue gown made Natasha look like royalty.

"Tasha! Let's go," Malik called out from somewhere in the penthouse.

"Oh, so now he wants to rush me. He's the one who's late."

Malik stepped into the dining room and halted near the entrance.

"Mmm, hey beautiful." He grinned down at Natasha, pulling her close and kissing her on the mouth. "Sorry I'm late. I had to make a run for my little sister." He winked at Olivia and held up a grease-stained white paper bag, before setting it in front of her.

She hugged him. "Thanks, you're the best."

"I try." He glanced at his watch. "Okay, we have to get out of here. We missed cocktail hour. Now we only have ten minutes to get to the fundraiser before they serve dinner."

"You two have a good night." Olivia walked with them to the door, wanting to ask Malik if he had heard from Wiz. But instead kept her mouth closed.

All she had to do was pick up the phone and call him, something she should have done hours ago.

Malik opened the door, but Natasha pulled up short and hugged Olivia.

"Eat and try to get some rest. I'll call you tomorrow." She pulled away and pointed at Travis who was standing behind Olivia. "And you, do not let her talk you into finishing her burger like she did with the chicken the other day."

"Yes, mother," he cracked.

"Can we leave now?" Malik asked.

The moment they closed the door, Olivia grabbed her cell phone from the kitchen counter. She needed to apologize to Wiz.

"Oh, Travis, can you see if you can get the heat vent in the bedroom closed? Or at least partially closed? It feels like a sauna in there."

"Will do."

He left the room and Olivia called Wiz.

"Hey there," he answered on the second ring. "I was just thinking about you."

"And I've been thinking about you all evening. I owe you an apology."

"No you don't."

"Yeah, actually I do. I'm so sorry if I hurt you with some of the things I said. I guess I was just caught off guard with the news, but I get it. I—"

"Olivia, your burger is getting cold," Victoria called from the dining room.

"I'll be right there," Olivia hollered back. "Sorry about that," she said to Wiz.

"What were you doing?" he asked.

"I was getting ready to—" Someone pounded on the door. Olivia sighed. "I'll get it!"

"No!"

"Don't!"

Wiz yelled on the telephone and Victoria screamed from the other room.

Olivia stepped back just as a deafening crack sounded in the room and the door flew open.

She screamed and the cell phone slipped from her hand. Her heart raced as two men blasted into the room.

"Get down!" Victoria ran into the room.

It was as if Olivia was reliving the other night all over again. Gunshots rang out around her. Victoria shot one of the men, dressed in all black, and he crumbled to the ground.

Olivia ducked behind the large sofa. She covered her ears, trying to drown out the noise and closed her eyes.

This can't be happening.

More shots were fired from beside her, and thick arms circled her waist.

"No!" she screamed, her arms flailing as she kicked, trying to shake herself lose. It wasn't until Travis said, "It's me," that she stopped moving, but her heart felt as if it were going to beat out of her chest.

His large body covered hers as he practically carried her down the hallway toward the bedrooms.

Another shot echoed in the hall behind them and Travis cursed, dropping his arms from around her. It sounded as if more people were in the apartment.

"Run!" He turned and got off two rounds.

Olivia heard someone grunt, but didn't look back. She sprinted into the bedroom and slammed the door, locking it behind her. Struggling, she pushed a cushioned chair up against it.

More gun shots.

Someone was coming.

I need a weapon.

Her gaze darted around the room, as the knot in her gut tightened. No amount of self-defense classes could have prepared her for this moment. Her nerves were raw. She had no idea what to do in a situation like this.

She swiped at the tears streaming down her face and a silver candlestick holder sitting on the dresser caught her attention. She ran for it just as someone pushed against the door.

Oh God help me.

She quickly grabbed the holder and glanced around the room for something else. The stuffed chair she had slid it front of the door wouldn't keep whoever was trying to get in out for much longer.

Come on! Think, Olivia, think.

These guys knew she was in there, so hiding was out of the question. But she could put another layer of protection between her and her attackers. She hurried toward the attached bathroom, but the door shoved open.

A large, fair-skinned man—with an angry scar across his right jaw and dark beady eyes that could have cut right through her had they been a weapon—charged into the room. "Where are they? Where are the diamonds?"

"I don't know what … what you're talking about." She took several steps back as the man moved closer. "I … I don't know any … anything about any diamonds!"

A second man who was just as large and scary

looking stormed into the room. "Get her!"

"Stay away from me!" she screamed, holding the candleholder out in front of her like a shield. Her hands shook but all she had to do was hold them off until Wiz got there. She knew he would come for her.

"We have to grab her and get the hell out of here! This place is going to be crawling with cops in a minute," the same guy stated.

They rushed her at the same time and she swung the candleholder back and forth like a sword, as hard as she could. Anger charged through her body with every move.

The men cursed, ducked out of the way, but she made contact with one of them.

"Dammit!" Blood dripped from the side of the first man's head. "You bitch!"

He yanked her wrist with such force, the candleholder slipped from her hand, and pain shot to her shoulder. She kept swinging with her free hand. With her balled fist, she jabbed him in the neck, then clawed at his face and stomped on his foot hoping he would loosen his hold.

They both grabbed her arms. "Let's go!"

She dug in her heels, grateful she was wearing running shoes. "I'm not going anywhere with you!" She pulled, jerked, and kicked to free herself from their grasp. No doubt they thought she was crazy, but no way was she going to let them take her from the apartment.

"That's it!" The biggest of the two released her, brought his arm back, and let it rip across her cheek.

Searing pain shot through her face and an explosion went off in her head. She fell to her knees. Stars danced in front of her eyes as she willed herself to get up.

"That's what we should have done in the first damn place."

"Whatever. Let's just get the hell out of here."

One of them lifted her from the floor. She couldn't move, couldn't speak, and couldn't stop the room from spinning. She had no fight left. Her face stung. Her head throbbed. Tears and pain blurred her eyes as darkness descended upon her.

CHAPTER TWENTY-TWO

"Sheldon's there. He'll meet us outside to get us in," Quinn said, taking the next corner on two wheels.

Wiz said nothing. He could barely breathe. He slammed his eyes shut and gripped the sides of his head, unable to quiet Olivia's screams and the gun shots from looping through his mind.

His voice was hoarse from hollering her name, as if that could save her from whatever hell had broken out in the apartment.

When her phone went dead, Wiz had called 911. He not only feared for Olivia's life, but not hearing from Travis and Victoria by now wasn't a good sign.

Quinn slowed when they were a half a block away from the penthouse. Unable to get closer due to the number of cop cars, EMT vehicles, and other emergency trucks, they both leapt out of the SUV and ran the rest of the way.

Spotting Sheldon near the entrance, Wiz shoved his way through the crowd, Quinn right behind him.

Sheldon held his palms out right when he saw Wiz. "I'm sorry, man ... she's not here."

Dizzy with fear, Wiz staggered, but remained upright thanks to Quinn's hold on his shoulder. Wiz didn't know whether to be glad she wasn't there laying in a pool of her own blood or be scared that some assholes had her and might be doing God knows what to her.

"The paramedics just loaded up Vicky and that kid that works for you guys." Sheldon's words broke into Wiz's thoughts.

Travis.

"How were they?" Quinn asked as they stepped into the elevator.

Sheldon shook his head. "Not sure. Vicky took a couple of rounds. I think one to the shoulder and one to the neck. Travis was shot in the back. I called Malik and Stan. They're on their way to the hospital."

Dammit.

Wiz leaned against the back wall, his fists clasped tightly at his sides, trying to keep it together. Sheldon filled them in on as many details as CPD had so far, which wasn't much.

"We missed the intruders by seconds. Witnesses say they charged out of a service entrance, shooting two women on the side of the building before speeding away in a dark sedan."

These guys had to have had some inside help, Wiz thought. Either that or they somehow obtained access to the code or a key card in order to have gotten into that part of the building.

This was all like a bad dream and it scared Wiz to death of what he might find once they saw the scene.

"Also, the medical examiner just arrived. There are

two vics in the apartment. Neither look like your guys though."

Sheldon lifted the yellow caution tape blocking the entrance. Wiz and Quinn followed him underneath. The place was crawling with emergency personnel. Broken glass, bullet casings, and furniture littered the place.

Wiz's pulse pounded in his ears as they roamed through the apartment, taking in the small tents with numbers on the floor that marked evidence. They viewed the two bodies, confirming they weren't any of the agency's security specialists. One had a tattoo identifying him as a member of the Cidal Boyz.

"So are you ready to tell me what's going on?" Sheldon asked Wiz as they stepped out of the way of the medical examiner who had just bagged a body. "Somehow I think you know more than what you told me when I questioned you at the hospital."

Wiz shook his head. "Not much more." He basically repeated what he had already told Sheldon about how he thought the Cidal Boyz were behind the attacks. He would eventually tell him about the diamonds, but not yet. He needed the jewels as leverage to get Olivia back. Besides, the less he shared, the better chance the cops wouldn't get in his way.

When Sheldon was pulled away, Wiz walked back to the bedroom that he and Olivia were using. The room had been tossed. Someone had clearly been looking for something.

Standing in the doorway, his gaze traveled around the whole room and landed on a candlestick holder laying on the floor. His heart stuttered when he saw blood near it on the off-white carpet.

A surge of fear shot through him.

She has to be all right.

He rubbed his chest and bent forward, his hands on his knees. Their baby had to be all right. Wiz wasn't sure what he would do if anything happened to either of them.

A large hand gripped his shoulder and squeezed.

"We'll find her. Let's go." Quinn led him out of the apartment and it was as if Wiz could finally breathe.

Once they were out of earshot of everyone, he said, "This ends tonight."

*

"I brought you some company, Keisha. Maybe now we'll get some answers."

Olivia glared at her sister, whose battered face stood out like a neon sign against a black tarp. She sat in a wood chair across the room, her hands tied behind her back, and her feet bound to the chair.

"Come on! Keep moving," Olivia's abductor, Frankie, said. She had learned their names on the short ride. And thanks to being blindfolded until a few moments ago, she had no idea where they were.

Frankie jerked on her arm, pulling her toward the only other chair in the room. Her hands were bound behind her back as well and her head hurt so bad, it felt as if someone had taken a bat to it multiple times.

She said nothing to Keisha. Her main concern now was keeping her and her baby safe until Wiz found them, which she knew he would. In the meantime, she would do as they say and try to keep warm. Wearing only a fleece jogging suit and a long sleeved T-shirt underneath, the layers did nothing to ward off the chill in the room.

Frankie untied her hands and pushed her down into the chair.

Thank goodness. She rubbed her hands together to warm them up, trying to ignore the pain in her right wrist.

"Oh no you don't." Frankie jerked her arms behind her back and retied her hands. "We know what you're capable of."

The second man, JT, waltzed into the room. Based on how he bossed Frankie around, it was safe to say he was the man in charge.

"Make sure you secure her feet, too. We don't want a repeat of earlier." He stood in the middle of the floor and looked from her to Keisha. "Now one of you better start talking."

Though he made it sound like either of them could respond, he stepped in front of Olivia.

"Well?"

She gulped. "I told you. I don't know anything about your diamonds."

"Wrong answer." He backhanded her across the face and her head jerked back. A blast of pain shot through every inch of her face and tears swelled in her eyes.

Licking her lips, the metallic taste of blood on her tongue only increased the fury raging through her body. Her face stung like she had been burned with a soldering iron, but she refused to let one tear drop fall.

"I'm just going to keep slapping you until you remember where those diamonds are."

She braced herself when he drew his hand back again, slapping her other cheek.

"Stop!" Keisha yelled. "Please … leave her alone.

I'll tell you. Just leave her alone."

"Where are the diamonds?" he asked Olivia again as if Keisha hadn't spoken.

She shook her head and this time tears did slip through. "I swear, I don't know." When he drew his hand back again, she quickly said, "But I know who might. My husband. Call my husband."

She gave him Wiz's telephone number, praying that she hadn't just made things worse. If nothing else, maybe Wiz would find her quicker.

Once they were locked in the room, she turned her attention to her sister. "What have you done?" Olivia ground out, her voice shaking with rage.

"I'm ... I'm sorry," Keisha cried. Olivia couldn't remember the last time she saw her sister shed a tear, not even at their parent's funeral. "I'm so sorry."

"Why would you send them after me?"

"I didn't mean for this to get so out of hand. I'm so sorry."

"Stop saying that! I already know how sorry you are! I can't believe you did this to me. Dragged me into your mess, almost got me and my husband killed and for what, Keisha?"

"They were going to kill me. I figured by now, Cameron probably knew about the diamonds and I knew that after the shooting ..."

Olivia's body stiffened. The way she was feeling right now, she could probably break through the ropes holding her hands and feet and put an end to her sister's useless life herself.

"I figured he would have so many security people on you that no one would be able to touch you. So I texted you. I thought you'd call me back and I—"

"Stop!" Olivia screamed, her head hurting even

more. "I never thought I could hate another human being, but there's a first for everything. I have sacrificed so much, including my marriage, because of you. I can't do it anymore. I will *not* do it anymore. You are like a terminal disease, Keisha. You worm your way into people's lives and taint every aspect of their world, making them suffer, lose money, or die."

Olivia shook her head, tears flowing faster as her heart broke into tiny pieces.

"I will not let you ruin the rest of my life. Starting right now, you are dead to me. You are no longer my sister and I want you to stay the hell away from me and my family." Her thoughts went to Victoria, Travis, and everyone else who had put their lives at risk because of her.

"Olivia, I—"

"I'm done, Keisha. I'm done with you. And if anything happens to my family, Cameron will be the least of your problems! I have gone to battle for you more times than I can count, I lost my baby because of you, and my husband was almost killed because of you! I'm done!"

Keisha nodded slowly, tears streaming down her face, her body slumped in the chair.

"I really am sorry ... for everything."

For the first time in their adult life, Olivia believed her. Too bad it was too late.

"I pray to God that I'll be able to forgive you *again* one day, but it won't be today."

CHAPTER TWENTY-THREE

Wiz stopped pacing when Quinn walked back into the office rubbing his head. After leaving the penthouse, they went straight to Supreme. Thanks to the watch Wiz had given Olivia for her birthday, he was able to track her to an abandoned industrial park on the south side of Chicago. But Quinn insisted that rushing in and going Rambo wasn't the way to handle the situation with this group.

"So? Did you get a hold of Bishop?" Wiz asked.

"Yeah. Here's the thing."

"No. Don't give me no *here's the thing* shit. We called him out of courtesy. When his *Boyz* open fired on Olivia and me, I listened to you and didn't start a damn war. But now, all bets are off. They have my wife, dammit!"

"You need to calm the hell down!"

Wiz glared at him as if he had lost his mind. "Would you be calm if this was Alandra? Would you be calm knowing that some assholes, capable of doing

God knows what, had her?"

"Listen."

"No you listen. I don't give a fuck who this Bishop guy is or what his people are capable of. All I know is when I get my hands on the punks who took Olivia, they will regret the day they ever involved us in this shit."

He snatched his jacket off the back of a chair, pocketed his cell phone, and grabbed the keys to the company's Chevy Suburban truck. He had already loaded it with enough fire power to take out a small village.

"I'm going to get my wife. You coming?"

Quinn chuckled when he climbed into the driver's seat of the truck. "You've changed, man. You used to be the voice of reason, the person who kept Malik and me from going half-cocked. What happened?"

Wiz wasn't sure. The last few weeks, he hadn't felt like himself and now that Olivia was in danger he was a man who was willing to do anything to get her back. Anything.

"The easy answer is that I had to deal with you and Malik for so many years. I guess you guys finally rubbed off on me and apparently not in a good way. I will say this, though. I have a whole new respect for both of you. I am feeling the anger and torment you two must have felt when your women were in danger. This shit right now feels like a damn nightmare that I can't wake up from."

"Been there. And you know as well as I know that we need a plan before we go after these guys."

Wiz nodded.

"Now if you're ready to listen for a minute, I'll tell you how my conversation with Bishop went."

Wanting to make sure they hadn't moved Olivia, Wiz double checked the app he used to identify her location.

"Go ahead, but talk and drive. Head south toward Englewood. I sent Hank ahead of us to get the lay of the land."

"All right. So it seems these four guys that stormed the apartment were trying to work their way up the ranks here in Chicago. They thought that if they brought in the diamonds and Midnight, they could make a name for themselves with Bishop."

"So they're making a name for themselves by first trying to kill me and Olivia, and now kidnapping."

Quinn shrugged. "Supposedly, no one knew Midnight had a twin and Bishop wants her back alive and unharmed. He said you can do whatever you want to these guys, but don't kill them."

"I can't guarantee that won't happen. Anything else?"

"He wants a courtesy call when we're … done. We leave the guys, Midnight, and the diamonds, and he'll take it from there."

"Fine. Whatever."

For the first fifteen minutes of the trip, they rode in silence, which was fine with Wiz. All he could think about at the moment was seeing Olivia and wanting this to be over. They should be taking care of the last minute details of their upcoming wedding. Instead he was out in the middle of the night praying that his wife and unborn child's life would be spared.

Wiz glanced at the app on his phone. "Turn left at the next light. Assuming she's still wearing her watch, they're holding her at an abandoned factory."

"They have to know by now that Olivia doesn't

know anything about the diamonds."

That's what Wiz was afraid of. Considering the mess left back at the penthouse, these guys were stopping at nothing to find those jewels.

His cell phone rang and an unfamiliar number showed on the screen. Any other time he would let it go to voicemail.

"Yeah."

"I have something I'm sure you want."

Wiz straightened in his seat. "Yeah you do."

"She's all yours once I get those diamonds."

"What diamonds?" Wiz asked.

"Motherfucker, don't play with me! If you ever want to see this bitch alive, I suggest you find those diamonds."

"And you won't get a damn thing from me until I talk to her."

"No."

"Then we have nothing else to discuss. Find your own damn diamonds."

"Wait ... hold on."

Wiz blew out a breath. His heart pounded double time, feeling as if it were going to leap out of his chest at any moment. So many emotions rattled around inside of him as he waited for her to answer.

"Cameron." Olivia's shaky voice came through the phone line. If he hadn't have been sitting he would have collapsed to the floor as relief flooded his body.

"Are you all right?"

She hesitated. Wiz heard the man he was just talking to yell at her to speak up.

"We're fine. There's two of them and we—"

"*Aarrgghh!*"

Wiz jerked and he squeezed the phone in his hand

when Olivia cried out.

Wiz's blood turned to ice. "Olivia! Olivia!" He pounded on the dashboard, his teeth clenched in an effort to stay put.

"Now you heard her. Find the diamonds."

"I'm going to kill you! So help me when I—"

"You have an hour. No cops, otherwise she's dead. I'll call you back."

Wiz glanced at the screen.

"Dammit!" Maybe it was good the guy hung up because what Wiz was about to say to the punk might have made things worse for Olivia.

"What happened?" Quinn asked.

We're okay.

Wiz wasn't sure if she was talking about her and the baby or her and Midnight. All he knew was that he couldn't lose his family.

"She said she's okay and that there were two guys. Then the asshole hit her or did something to her and she screamed."

"Did the guy say anything else?"

"He said we had an hour to get the diamonds. Then he'll call back." But by then, Wiz would have whooped the man's ass and Olivia would be safe.

Wiz pressed redial. He doubted they would answer, but he tried anyway.

No answer.

"So it sounds like Clayton was right about them having Keisha, since they didn't mention her," Quinn said.

"Maybe. Or they could just be planning to keep the diamonds and the hell with Keisha."

Wiz slammed his hand against the door in frustration. He needed this to be over, but first he had to get his mind straight. Otherwise, going in there unfocused could get them all killed.

Quinn slowed when the industrial park came into view and stopped the truck in the shadows under a tree.

Wiz scrubbed his hands down his face and peered out the window of the dilapidated building. The more he glanced around the area, the madder he got. It was killing him that he had to sit and wait despite knowing that it was safer this way.

There were three abandoned buildings on the property and from where they sat, he couldn't see any vehicles or movement. A small amount of light from the two street lamps nearby illuminated a portion of the parking lot and part of two of the buildings. The other one sat in complete darkness.

Wiz's phone rang again.

Hank.

"Yeah." Wiz put the phone on speaker.

"Okay, so I'm at the back of the property. I already made my rounds. My guess is that she's either in the largest building or the one story that's north of it. In the front, you won't be able to tell that they're attached, but they appear to be in the back."

"Have you seen any movement? Can you see through the windows?" Wiz asked.

"No movement. But there are two windows in the back of the one story that might have some type of lighting. I'm not positive because the windows are painted and on the other building they're boarded up. There are four doors, but I think it's safe to say that our best option is to go through the one on the south side of the four-story building. There's a dark four-door sedan with tinted windows parked near it and someone is a smoker."

"How can you tell?" Quinn asked.

"Fresh cigarette butts are littering the ground in that area."

Wiz glanced at the building. "Q, pull up to that mound of dirt." That would give them a better view of the door but kept them out of sight.

"How many cigarette butts are near the door? Are we talking one or two, or enough to fill a pack or two?" Quinn asked.

"We're talking enough to guess that someone is a pack a day smoker or more than one person smokes."

"All right. Since there are only two guys, let's give the smoker a few minutes and see if he shows. When he does, we'll be ready for him," Wiz said.

"Oh, one more thing," Hank said. "Stan called from the hospital with an update. He said Vicky is out of surgery. A bullet grazed her neck, and during the shootout, she fell on a glass table, catching some shards in her back. She also has a concussion."

"What about Travis?" Wiz asked.

"He's still in surgery. He took a few slugs in the back."

Quinn cursed under his breath and shook his head.

Frustration grated on Wiz's nerves. Granted they all knew the risks that came with the job, but when one of them got hurt, they all hurt.

"Thanks for keeping us in the loop, man." Quinn grabbed his gloves and hat from the center console. "Ready to do this?"

"Definitely." Wiz patted the front of his jacket, ensuring the jewels were still in his pocket.

"This looks like it's going to be too easy," Quinn grumbled and climbed out of the truck. He fastened a second weapon to his thigh.

"I hope so. I can use a little easy after my last few weeks."

They all checked their earpieces. Quinn and Wiz would go in together, while Hank kept watch.

Wiz had popped a couple of ibuprofen before leaving the agency, hoping the pain in his side and leg would subside. So far the meds were working.

They hurried across the parking lot. Quinn stopped near the car that looked like the vehicle the shooters used days ago and shined his flashlight into the windows.

He shook his head at Wiz who had flattened his body against the building.

"Hold up, guys. We have company," Hank said into Wiz's ear.

So much for easy.

"An SUV just pulled up to the north door of the one story building. Two guys getting out and going in."

"Great. Now it's getting interesting," Quinn said.

They maintained their positions and didn't have to wait long. A big man that was about Wiz's height and weight, wearing all black, strolled outside. With his size twelves, he slid a brick closer and stuck it in the doorway. A sliver of light shone through the door, but not enough for them to be seen.

Adrenaline pumped through Wiz's veins as he eased along the side of the building for the perfect opportunity to strike.

When the man turned, he cupped his hand around his cigarette to block the slight breeze as he lit it. Wiz inched closer. It wasn't until the guy took a couple of puffs did Wiz moved in.

He clubbed him in the back of the head with the butt of his gun, making sure not to hit him hard enough to knock him out, but hard enough to take him to his knees. Then Wiz kicked him in the side, knocking him over. With the toe of his boot, he smashed the lit cigarette that fell to the ground.

"Where's my wife?"

"I don't know who you're talking about."

Wiz cocked his gun and shoved it in the man's face. He agreed to try and honor Bishop's request, but right now, he couldn't make any promises.

Quinn eased from the shadows and the man's gaze jockeyed between him and Wiz.

"I said, where's my wife?"

"She ... she's in the other building." He pointed his thumb over his shoulder.

When Quinn cleared his throat, catching the man's attention, Wiz clocked him in the temple with his gun, knocking him out cold.

Wiz texted Hank.

Gotta package for you to wrap.

*

Olivia's heart almost stopped when two other men, dressed in black, walked in. What shocked her was that Amanda's brother, Corin, was one of them. She prayed he would ignore her, or just glare at her from across the room like he'd done in the past. She didn't want anything to do with him. No attention. No conversation.

No such luck.

He slowly approached her, but stopped when he noticed Keisha in the corner.

Olivia glanced at her sister, who hadn't said a word to her since their argument and was now dozing in her chair. Olivia didn't know how she could sleep when the room was freezing despite the space heater hooked up to the generator.

"I can't believe that all this time there were two of them. Which is which?" Corin asked.

"That's the sister." T.C. pointed to Olivia.

Corin moved toward her and she bunched her shoulders and slouched in her chair as if that could make her invisible.

"I thought you looked familiar the first time I saw you," he said. He started to say more, but T.C. spoke.

"We made contact. Her old man knows where the diamonds are. He's got forty-minutes."

Corin turned away from Olivia and she released the breath she hadn't realized she was holding. She would never be able to look at Amanda the same, now that she knew her brother had something to do with the attacks.

"That's good. Maybe we should head to the meeting place," the third guy's words cut into Olivia's thoughts.

"Nah, we got time." T.C. stuffed his hands in his pocket and rocked on his heels as if he didn't have a care in the world.

"So what about the sister? What you gon' do with her once you get the diamonds?" the third guy asked.

T.C. leaned against the dingy wall where plaster was peeling and folded his arms, crossing his legs at the ankle.

"We'll take care of her and her old man once we get Bishop's diamonds."

A chill crawled up Olivia's spine. They had to know that she could hear them, but what could she do?

Her gaze went to her sister who was now looking back at her. Did she finally understand that her selfishness might get them all killed? Sure, she said she was sorry, but for Oliva, it just wasn't enough.

Olivia lowered her eyes, and took a deep breath, releasing it slowly. She prayed Wiz had a plan, especially if these guys were planning to kill them.

"I heard Bishop is heading to Chicago," Corin said.

T.C. nodded and grinned. "Yeah, get ready to move up the ladder, Boyz. I got in contact with him earlier and told him that we'll have his items by midnight."

"What'd he say?" Corin asked.

"He said he'll see us at midnight."

"That's cool. By the way, where's Frankie?" Corin asked.

T.C. looked at his cell. "He should have been back by now. His ass is out there smoking again."

"I need a smoke, too. I'll be back," the third guy said.

"Hold up. I'll go with you." Corin glanced at Olivia, and goosebumps crawled up her arms at the creepy grin he gave her.

A short while later, Olivia jerked when a loud commotion broke out somewhere in the building.

"What the ..." T.C. hurried out of the room.

Grunts and punches echoed through the building and Olivia couldn't believe they were fighting each other. She thought gang members were like brothers. Why would they be fighting?

Unless ...

Her gaze met Keisha's and Olivia couldn't help the slow smile that crept onto her face.

Cameron.

"I was wondering when he was going to come for you." Keisha lowered her gaze and sighed. "Olivia, I really am sorry for everything and I swear you will never hear from me—"

They both jumped in their seats when two gunshots thundered in the distance and a wave of panic scurried through Olivia's body. She believed in Wiz's skills, but he was still recovering and—

"Where is she?" he yelled. Loud footsteps sounded through the building, doors banged against walls, and seconds later, he appeared. He stomped into the room like a bull storming into an arena.

A cry of relief slipped through Olivia's lips and all she could do was stare at him. She had never been so happy to see her man as she was at that moment.

When Wiz spotted her across the sparsely furnished room, he stopped in his tracks and his expression quickly changed. The love radiating in his eyes brought tears to hers and she couldn't hold back the sob clogging her throat.

He slowly approached her and she knew the exact moment he noticed her bruised face and busted lip. She had no idea what she looked like. But if the sudden crimson tint to his skin and the way his jaw tightened was any indication, her bruises were bad. Very bad.

"Who did this to you?" he growled. He hadn't even bothered to untie her hands and ankles. Anger bounced off of him in waves, leaving her speechless.

Just then, Quinn appeared and shoved T.C. into the room.

"I know we can work something out. All we wanted to do was return the diamonds to their owner," T.C. pleaded, his palms held out in front of him.

Wiz looked from T.C. to Olivia and back again. Before she could stop him, he made a beeline for T.C. Wiz grabbed him by the neck and slammed him against the peeling wall, ignoring the way the guy swung at him, missing every time.

"You put your hands on my wife!" He punched T.C. in the face so hard Olivia could have sworn she heard bones crack.

Quinn strolled to her, his reaction similar to Wiz's when he got closer. At first, he didn't speak, as if reining in his own temper.

"Let's get you untied." He held on to her when he undid her ankles. "Can you stand?"

"I think so," she said absently, her attention on Wiz. "Quinn, you have to stop him! Cameron's going to pull out all of his stitches."

Quinn shook out of his jacket and wrapped it around her shoulders. "He'll be fine. Besides, he needs to do this. He's been through a lot these past few weeks."

Olivia frowned at him, but then straightened her face. Quinn knew this side of her husband a lot better than she did. Whatever Wiz needed to do to make peace with the recent events, she wouldn't stop him.

Wiz used T.C. as a human punching bag. Even when T.C. slid to the floor, blood streaming from multiple cuts, Wiz didn't let up. It wasn't until he started stomping and kicking T.C. that Quinn intervened.

"All right. That's enough."

Wiz didn't stop as if he hadn't heard Quinn.

"Cameron, please." Olivia inched closer. "Please,

baby. Let's get out of here."

That's when she remembered Keisha. With all of the commotion, Olivia had forgotten about her. She knew it was going to be hard to leave without her sister, but this was something Olivia had to do.

"C'mere." Wiz pulled Olivia into his arms, holding her tight. "God, sweetheart. I was so worried. I love you so damn much." His voice, muffled in her hair, held so much anguish it tore at her insides. How could she end up in a similar position as before, knowing he would be beside himself with concern? If only she had listened to him sooner about her sister. If this experience didn't teach her anything else, it taught her to never let anything or anyone come between them.

"Are you all right?" He kissed her lips and placed his hand on her belly. "Are you both all right?" His words were strained and concern covered his face.

She nodded and held him tight until he winced, reminding her of his wounded side. "I knew you would find me. I just knew you would find me."

He gently cupped her face. "Always. You know I can't live without you." He lowered his mouth, placing a soft kiss against her bruised lips, careful not to put any pressure on them. Her whole face hurt, but his sweetness helped take her mind off the pain.

This was the second time that they'd been in this type of position and she hoped to God they would never have to endure anything like this again. Unlike before, at least she would be able to walk out on her own and their baby was safe.

Wiz glanced at Keisha. He and Quinn had yet to say anything to her. Why would they? It was because of her that they had to risk their lives because of her nonsense.

Wiz stepped away from Olivia, reached inside his jacket pocket, and pulled out a velvet pouch. He dropped it into Keisha's lap.

"Your diamonds. I hope they're worth the shit you put us through." He wrapped his arm around Olivia and guided her to the door. "Q, make the call."

EPILOGUE

Two weeks, six days later
Wedding Day

Olivia's heart was about to burst with the love she had for the man standing before her. And he was so handsome. His black tuxedo fit perfectly over his muscular frame, and he looked as if he had just stepped off the cover of GQ magazine.

She couldn't wait to be Wiz's wife. During her short walk down the aisle, she had alternated between smiling and crying. Overwhelmed with all that she and Wiz had been through lately, there were moments that she couldn't believe that this day had finally arrived.

"The couple has written their own vows," the minister said and nodded for Olivia to start.

Olivia took a deep breath in and released it slowly in an effort to still her nervousness.

"Cameron, I was a lonely soul when we first met.

Yet over the years, you have filled a void in my life with your love. With your patience. With your understanding, and … and did I mention patience?"

Everyone laughed and Wiz smiled, his green eyes watching her intently. He squeezed her hand as she fought back the tears threatening to fall.

"Thank you for choosing me to share your life with. There are not enough words in the world that can express how happy you make me. You have brought so much joy and laughter into my life. You're my real life hero, making all of my dreams come true. You are the perfect example of what a man should be. I love the way you take care of me, the way you watch over me, and most importantly, the way you love me.

"I am so excited to spend the rest of my life with you and raising our baby in a loving home. I will always be loyal to you. I will support you in sickness and in health, through good and bad times. I promise to love you, cherish you, and respect you from this day forward. And I make this vow to you in front of God, our family, and our friends."

"Cameron," the minister prompted.

"Olivia, twenty-two years, one month, two weeks, and six days ago," he grinned and she laughed, "when you moved into the neighborhood, you became the most beautiful woman in the world to me and you became my best friend. Since then, you continue to amaze me with your tolerance, your selflessness, and your loving spirit. You inspire me to be a better person, a better man. Today, you are so much more than my best friend and the woman I love. You're my heart. I am looking forward to starting my life over with you.

"Olivia Shanta Miller, I promise to be a faithful,

loving husband. I will cherish you, respect you, and *I will protect you* until the day I take my last breath. I pledge my life to you in front of God, our family, and our friends."

He wiped the tears streaming down her cheeks as the minister continued with the ceremony. Olivia thought the first time she had married Wiz that it had been the happiest day of her life, but she was wrong. This day, standing in front of their friends and family, after the harrowing last few weeks, was definitely the best day of her life.

Minutes later, after the exchange of rings and a prayer, the minister said, "You may now kiss the bride."

"I've wanted to do this since the moment you walked down the aisle," Wiz whispered before covering her mouth with his. She melted into him when his arm circled her waist and he pulled her closer. Gripping his thick biceps, excitement soared through Olivia's body as she savored the feel of his lips against hers and their tongues mated. His love for her came through loud and clear, and joy bubbled in her stomach. They had finally done it. They were officially husband and wife.

They didn't pull apart until cheers sounded throughout the small chapel.

"Ladies and gentlemen, I present Mr. and Mrs. Cameron Miller."

Olivia glanced around the room feeling so blessed. Wiz's family had arrived in town earlier in the week and almost all of their friends were in attendance. As everyone greeted them, she thought about her sister. As promised, so far, Keisha hadn't contacted her. Olivia wondered if she was even still in the city. Wiz had told her about the events leading up to the rescue, and how the leader of the Cidal Boyz wanted Keisha returned along with the diamonds. Olivia had made peace with how things ended and would keep her sister in her prayers. Keisha would never be a part their lives again, and for the first time, Olivia was okay with that.

*

"Congratulations again, man. You finally made an honest woman out of Ollie." Malik tapped his glass against Wiz's beer bottle.

Wiz chuckled at the ongoing joke. For the last few years, Malik had asked him every chance he got, when was he going to make an honest woman out of Olivia and marry her again.

Wiz glanced across the banquet room. She was beautiful. When she walked down the aisle in that sexy, long flowing gown, he almost swallowed his tongue. Never had he seen her glow and look as lovely as she was today. He continued to study her as she laughed at something one of their guests said. Nothing brought him more peace than to see her happy.

Now that the delicious sit down dinner and dessert had been consumed, he and Olivia were floating around greeting their guest. The fifty people they had invited, except for Travis, were in attendance. Wiz would admit the celebration wasn't the same without his young buddy. Home recuperating, Travis was still in a great deal of pain after the shoulder and back surgery. Though the three bullets that hit him hadn't punctured an artery, they damaged some soft tissue and cartilage as well as nicked a bone. Wiz knew that could have been Olivia had Travis not put himself between her and the shooter.

Wiz shook his head, trying to free the sudden thought. He returned his attention to Malik.

"I'm glad Vicky was able to make it," Wiz said to Malik when he saw her sitting at the table with her date and Raeanna.

"Yeah, me too. She's making a good recovery and planning to return to work in a week."

"That's good."

She was still suffering from headaches and back pain, but to look at her, she seemed like her old self. She had even removed the bandage from her neck where a bullet had grazed her.

Olivia still struggled with guilt that the two were shot while guarding her. Victoria had told her more than once that she was fine and didn't blame her. The reassurance helped, but it was Travis who seemed to get through to her after she visited him in the hospital. He had assured her that none of what had happened was her fault and that it was all part of the job. Travis, the smooth talking lady's man, had her blushing and laughing by the time the conversation was over.

The last two weeks had been rough. After his numerous interviews with police detectives, Wiz was more than ready to go on his honeymoon. He, Malik, and Quinn had weaved a believable story and the cops bought it. What surprised Wiz was Olivia's willingness to go along with the tall tale. He was so proud of the way she had handled everything, including Keisha's betrayal. He knew the decision to walk away from her sister wasn't an easy one.

The day after leaving Keisha behind, there had been a news report that four members of the Cidal

Boyz gang had been found dead, a bullet to each of their heads. The media claimed another gang had gunned down the victims. According to Quinn's sources, it had been Bishop's work. When he found Keisha beaten, supposedly the gang leader went ballistic. Maybe Keisha had been telling the truth about her and Bishop being in love.

I guess there really is somebody for everyone.

"I'm sure you know how lucky you are," Hunter said, cutting into Wiz's thoughts as he joined him and Malik. "That's a hell of a woman you have."

"I agree, but I remember you saying the same thing to Malik about Tasha a few months ago."

Hunter laughed. "What can I say? You guys have some amazing women in your lives."

Hunter had once been engaged until his fiancée married his stepbrother two years earlier. Since then, he floated in and out of meaningless relationships, vowing to never give his heart to another woman.

"Did you tell Wiz the latest about the NBA's commissioner's claims?" Malik asked. Wiz knew Hunter was having some issues with the media railroading him about his gambling, but it sounded like something else was going on.

"Malik, we're here to celebrate. Why'd you even have to bring that up?" Hunter and Malik argued back and forth.

"That's my cue," Wiz cut in. "I'm going to let you two hash this out. But, Hunter, you know where to find me if you need me for anything." They shared a one-arm hug and Wiz excused himself to go in search of his wife.

He spotted her talking with Quinn, Alandra, Tyler, and Dallas.

"Well here's the man of the hour," Quinn said when Wiz approached. "I was just telling Olivia that I'm surprised you let her out of your sight."

Wiz wrapped his arm around her waist and smiled down at her. "She was never out of my sight. I figured I'd let her spend a little time with everyone since I'll have her all to myself for the next two weeks."

"We're so happy for you both," Dallas said, and Alandra cosigned the sentiment. The women exchanged hugs while Wiz pulled Quinn and Tyler off to the side.

"I know you guys said you would take care of the damages to the penthouse, but we're willing to—"

"Don't worry about it. Our men have already made the repairs. Considering how instrumental you were in helping me and Dallas with the stalker and the Ponzi scheme mess, this is the least we can do," Tyler said.

"And you already know where I stand on taking any money from you," Quinn added. "We're brothers for life. There will be no money exchanged between us."

The times that he had helped each of them was something he wanted to do. He never thought he would be in a similar situation to where he would need to call on them for support. They had truly come through for him.

"Well, just know that I appreciate the way you all helped me and Olivia. I'll never forget it."

They talked for a few minutes longer before Tyler and Dallas said their good-byes, needing to get back to their sons.

"What time does your flight leave in the

morning?" Quinn asked Wiz.

"Six. How long are you planning to be in town?" Except for dealing with the situation with Keisha, they hadn't had a chance to really hang out the way they used to.

"We're thinking about sticking around at least until after the baby is born."

"Really?"

"Yeah. Alandra said she would feel more comfortable giving birth on American soil, and you know I'm not about to argue with a pregnant woman."

"I heard that!" Alandra laughed and looped her arm through Quinn's. "Instead of you talking about me behind my back, why don't you dance with me?"

"I think I can handle that." Quinn took her hand and led her to the small dance floor.

Wiz's gaze met Olivia's. "Hey, my beautiful wife. You doing okay?"

"I'm better than okay." She slipped her arms around his neck and pulled him down for a kiss. He would never get tired of the sweetness of her lips.

"Today you made me the happiest man in the world," he mumbled against her mouth before lifting his head.

Her lips tilted into that smile he loved so much.

"I'm glad to hear that because I have something to tell you that I hope will make you even happier."

His eyebrow lifted. "Okay, but I don't know what you could possibly say that would make me feel better than I do right now."

"We're having twins."

Wiz's mouth fell open. He knew she'd had another ultrasound after being checked out at the hospital again for her bruises and dehydration, but she never said anything about twins.

"I know I should have told you sooner, but I had planned to include the news in my wedding vows. This morning I changed my mind because ... well, because I want to keep this little surprise to ourselves for a while."

Wiz still stood stunned. Their little family would double in size in a few months and words escaped him.

"Are you mad?"

"Are you kidding?" He cupped her face within his hands, emotion clogging his throat as he stared into her worried eyes. "Sweetheart, I ... I'm crazy happy! I'm almost tempted to hop onto one of these tables and scream it to the rafters that I'm going to be a father, twice." He lowered his voice when a few heads turned in their direction. "This is truly the best day of my life. What more could I ever ask for? You are officially my wife and I get to spend the rest of my life with you raising our children."

She grinned. "I know, right? Today feels like a beautiful dream, but it's actually our reality. I'm so excited I feel as if I'm going to burst."

He touched his forehead to hers. "I feel the same way. A love like ours doesn't come around often."

"I know. And I will never take your love for granted again."

Wiz kissed her with everything he had in him. He had no doubt that their love for each other would only get stronger with time.

"What do you think about us sneaking out of here?" Wiz asked.

"I'd say I love the way you think."

*****

*If you enjoyed this book by Sharon C. Cooper,
please consider leaving a review on any online book site,
review site, or social media outlet.*

ABOUT THE AUTHOR

Award-winning and bestselling author, Sharon C. Cooper, spent 10 years as a sheet metal worker. And while enjoying that unique line of work, she attended college in the evening and obtained her B.A. in Business Management with an emphasis in Communication. Sharon is a romance-a-holic - loving anything that involves romance with a happily-ever-after, whether in books, movies or real life. She writes contemporary romance, as well as romantic suspense and enjoys rainy days, carpet picnics, and peanut butter and jelly sandwiches. When Sharon is not writing or working, she's hanging out with her amazing husband, doing volunteer work or reading a good book (a romance of course). To read more about Sharon and her novels, visit www.sharoncooper.net

Other Titles by Sharon C. Cooper:

Jenkins Family Series (Contemporary Romance)
Best Woman for the Job (Short Story Prequel)
Still the Best Woman for the Job (book 1)
All You'll Ever Need (book 2)
Tempting the Artist (book 3)
Negotiating for Love – (book 4) – *Coming Soon*
Seducing the Boss Lady – (book 5) – *Coming Soon*

Reunited Series (Romantic Suspense)
Blue Roses (book 1)
Secret Rendezvous (Prequel)
Rendezvous with Danger (book 2)
Truth or Consequences (book 3)
Operation Midnight (book 4)

Stand Alones
Something New ("Edgy" Sweet Romance)
Legal Seduction (Harlequin Kimani)
Sin City Temptation (Harlequin Kimani)
A Dose of Passion (Harlequin Kimani)
Model Attraction (Harlequin) – *Coming April 2016*